Our Late Member

Many of Mr. Raymond's finest novels have appeared in a sequence which he has called 'A London Gallery'. This story is part of that sequence, a story which begins in 1942 when London was the capital of the free and fighting world and ends when Europe is at peace again. It is the story of Rodney Merriwell, Member of Parliament, his wife and his twin sons, Everard and Stanley. Rodney Merriwell had first won his seat as a Liberal in 1918 and his constituency of Ridgeway, north of Hampstead and Highgate, had returned him with a comfortable majority in all the five general elections between 1918 and 1942. 'Ridgeway Returns Roddy' has for long been a campaign slogan.

Now the German army occupies the coasts of Denmark, the Netherlands and France. Rodney's wife, Grace, is showing her mettle as a member of the W.V.S. among the bomb-blasted homes of North London; Everard is a bomber pilot—a skipper with the enviable reputation of always getting his crew safely home; Stanley is a still uncommissioned gunner in an anti-aircraft battery stationed amongst the orchards of Kent. The whole position of Stanley is wrapped in mystery. Rodney, the Member for Ridgeway, is proud of London fighting for her life, and, as a back-bencher, proud of playing his minor part in Britain's Parliament in these terrible yet stirring times.

Through his eyes we watch the years unreel; suffer with him and Grace the tragedies of the war: see Rodney at the great moment of his career in his beloved House of Commons, and, finally, his personal struggle for survival as the shocks and agonies take their toll. Through him Mr. Raymond shows us yet another facet of the city he loves, another inimitable portrait to grace his 'London Gallery'.

BOOKS BY ERNEST RAYMOND

NOVELS

A London Gallery *comprising:*

We, the Accused	*Was There Love Once?*
The Marsh	*The Corporal of the Guard*
Gentle Greaves	*A Song of the Tide*
The Witness of Canon Welcome	*The Chalice and the Sword*
A Chorus Ending	*To the Wood No More*
The Kilburn Tale	*The Lord of Wensley*
Child of Norman's End	*The Old June Weather*
For Them That Trespass	*The City and the Dream*

A Georgian Love Story

Other Novels

The Bethany Road	*Mary Leith*
The Mountain Farm	*Morris in the Dance*
The Tree of Heaven	*The Old Tree Blossomed*
One of Our Brethren	*Don John's Mountain Home*
Late in the Day	*The Five Sons of Le Faber*
Mr Olim	*The Last to Rest*
The Chatelaine	*Newtimber Lane*
The Visit of Brother Ives	*The Miracle of Brean*
The Quiet Shore	*Rossenal*
The Nameless Places	*Damascus Gate*
Tell England	*Wanderlight*
A Family that Was	*Daphne Bruno I*
A Jesting Army	*Daphne Bruno II*

BIOGRAPHIES, ETC.

The Story of My Days (Autobiography I)
Please You, Draw Near (Autobiography II)
Good Morning, Good People (Autobiography III)
Paris, City of Enchantment
Two Gentlemen of Rome (The Story of Keats and Shelley)
In the Steps of St. Francis
In the Steps of the Brontës

ESSAYS, ETC.

Through Literature to Life
The Shout of the King
Back to Humanity (with Patrick Raymond)

PLAYS

The Berg
The Multabello Road

WEST RIDING COUNTY LIBRARY

This book must be returned by the last date entered above.

An extension of loan may be arranged on request if the book is not in demand.

Readers should make the fullest use of the County Library service, asking for any books and information they need.

OUR LATE MEMBER

A NOVEL

by

ERNEST RAYMOND

CASSELL · LONDON

CASSELL & COMPANY LTD
35 RED LION SQUARE, LONDON WC1 4SJ
Sydney, Auckland
Toronto, Johannesburg

First published 1972

I.S.B.N. 0 304 93873 4

Printed in Great Britain by
Cox & Wyman Ltd
London, Fakenham and Reading
F. 1071

for

ELIZABETH LLEWELLYN

and all her family

with love

Contents

1

London, '42

Two people, a man and a woman, emerging from the north
flank of London's Northern Heights, came by way of Hampstead Lane on to the ridge of the Heights, which runs for half a
mile along the Spaniards Road, looking eastward at the vast
spread of London in the misty Thames Valley below. Nowhere
else is there such a prospect of our vast and undisciplined city
because the ridge, for all its half-mile, runs level with the top of
St. Paul's distant dome. The walking of these two was of a
lively fashion, although neither was young and neither was
slim. The man, Mr. Rodney Merriwell, M.P., was in his middle
fifties; Grace Merriwell, his wife, was two years older than he;
and both had gathered weight in their time; the man only a
little, the woman (in her view) far too much. Neither was long-
limbed for such lively walking, Mr. Merriwell being but two
inches taller than his wife, and she having no great height. Nor
was either a figure of much distinction, though Mr. Merriwell,
walking hatless, displayed a head of fine, waving, silky hair,
prematurely white; hair in which (one would have guessed) he
took pride.

They had already walked a long two miles from their home
in his constituency—and steep miles at that—for this constituency lay low on the north side of the ridge; the wrong side,
some would say, especially if they live in Highgate or Hampstead, which two villages, ancient and proud, slope southward
and downward into the great well of London. The constituency's name is an odd one because, while lying well below the
ridge, it is called Ridgeway, the old name (once upon a time
and long ago, North Ridgeway) having implied, one supposes,
little more than 'the way to the Ridge'.

The long steep walk had been forced on them because Mr.

Merriwell's ration of petrol, allowed to him as an M.P., was all too small.

Rodney and Grace came to a familiar point on the ridge where there was a gap between the oaks and hornbeams, the birches, hawthorns and hazels that climbed the sandy slope and fringed the summit. This break in the trees allowed a vista, over gorse and broom, of almost the whole of London from Brentford and Hounslow to the parts around Greenwich. There, sovereign over all the steeples and towers, rising higher than all, a grey wraith in the mists, was Paul's dome. And there, to the west of it, grey phantoms too in the river haze, rose all the towers of Westminster. There, under Mr. Merriwell's eyes, was the Palace of Westminster, scene for twenty-four years now of his dutiful and happy but undistinguished labours. This vast panorama of a London unending was made the more remarkable in these days by the barrage balloons aloft on their leashes all round it and in the midst of it. They might look like silvery airborne porpoises but really they were playing the part of guardian angels for a capital city. Aptly enough, a westerly wind had swung all their blunt grey noses towards the east, whence the threat might come.

For this was '42, with the German enemy occupying the coasts of Denmark, Netherlands and France. And no fleet of a hundred German planes could dive-bomb or fly low amid those taut cables that sang so gently in the wind.

'42, and this was why Grace's stocky and plump figure was in the uniform of the W.V.S., 'Women's Voluntary Service': a grey-green coat and skirt with a red jumper and a grey-green felt hat.

Mr. Merriwell did not speak at once, and then he spoke two words only. '*Ici Londres*.' And again because he was pleased with the words '*Ici Londres*'.

Two proud words, and his heart was swelling behind them.

He had to vent his emotion. 'Mrs. M.,' he began, 'are you realizing properly that down there, in a dozen different uniforms, all very picturesque, there are the soldiers and sailors and airmen of a dozen different nations, because our old London is now their sole capital. The capital of all the Free and

Fighting World. Czechs, Dutch, Polish, French, Norwegians, Danes. Can she ever have known such days in all her two thousand years of history? No, there's been nothing to equal this since the days of Boadicea.' Then he became lyrical about all the ragged and fanged ruins among her hideous Victorian streets where the bombs of the Blitz had fallen. 'Honourable scars' he called them, such as were not to be found in Paris, which had refused to submit to such treatment. He could never pass, he said, the wild rosebay willow herb, now grown tall in them, their yellow ragwort, and the pink starlets of their ragged robins, without a leap of pride in them. 'London chose to "take it". My God, I wouldn't have lived at any other time. I thank God we weren't born too soon to live to see this.'

'I'm not as pleased with it all as you are. I——'

'Why not? Why not?' It disappointed him to have his enthusiasm discounted.

'I could cheerfully have avoided seeing it all. I can see it's all very dramatic and exciting, but——'

'But *what?*' An unwelcoming 'what?'

'Everard . . . Stan . . .' There was fear in her voice when she spoke these two names—and more than fear when she mentioned Stan: a bewilderment then, and a sadness.

Everard and Stanley were their twin sons; true twins, twenty-one years old and both much taller than their father; both dark and each a copy of the other in face and figure, though in these days they wore different uniforms, Everard the blue of the R.A.F. sergeant and Stanley the khaki of a humble gunner in an anti-aircraft battery.

Rodney felt ashamed that in his exulting appreciation of this vision of London at war he had forgotten, as it were, Everard and Stanley. He was proud of his twin sons, both so much taller than he. ('It's only one's children,' he would say, 'who please one by beating one.') And he could feel fear for them, like Grace, but a temperament incurably sanguine helped him always to rest on a hope that somehow good things would happen for him, for Grace, and for them. He knew these sanguine dreams to be irrational, but there they always were. In amends he now sought comforting words for Grace.

3

'Everard has survived nearly fifty raids, and that means he'll soon have completed two tours and be rested for a while. Given some ground job, more or less safe.'

'Yes, Everard's been lucky, but how long can he go on being lucky,' she demanded, not ready for comfort. 'You know what Everard is. The more risky a thing is, the more he looks on it as a lark and insists on having what he calls a "bash" at it.'

'Not so much now that he's skipper of a plane and responsible for his crew and determined to get them home.'

'But they're probably all as wild as he is.'

'Don't you believe it. At the back of their minds they all want to get home. And his C.O. told me they swear by Everard just because they say he always gets 'em back.'

'And how do *I* ever know that he's safely back? How can I know any night that my son's still alive?'

'That'll be over soon. When he's rested.'

'If he consents to be rested. If he doesn't insist on volunteering for some new and horrible raid. It's Everard who keeps me always afraid. I've no great fear for Stan—unless the Germans come.'

'They won't come now. It's we who'll go to them.'

'Then I imagine Stan's as safe as we are. As safe as any of us except for a bomb. They may bomb his battery, I suppose'— Stanley's anti-aircraft battery was among the orchards of Kent —'but he'll do nothing rash like Everard. Not now that he's changed so.' Very different this note in her voice when she spoke of Stan from that when she mentioned Everard; it was a note of love, but of disappointed love. 'Oh dear . . .' she sighed; 'I wish this awful change hadn't come over him.'

'Yes, I can't see anything happening to Stan,' he agreed. 'Stan'll do nothing to get himself killed. Nothing in his present mood. Heaven knows what has worked such a change—and how can any of us know what it's all about, if we never hear a word from him? It's more than a year, isn't it, since he honoured us with a letter. I can't understand it. Once he was as lively and dashing and fearless as Everard. Once there was nothing to choose between them. They did everything together. It was for the fun of it that Everard went into the Air Force and

4

Stan into the gunners. And that was only two years ago. But now—now they might not be brothers at all. Still less twins. One is almost everything a parent could wish, but the other——'

'Why are you always for Everard and down on Stanley?' she interrupted, without reason, but with a steady will for argument.

'Now please don't start a row, darling. Me down on Stanley? Never. Never. It's only that he's become a total mystery to me. There've been times when Stan has seemed to mean more to me than Everard. I've never known so complete a change in anyone.' Then, fearing again that these words would distress her, he added, 'Something's upset him of which we know nothing. That's all. There's nothing basically wrong with our Stan, I'm sure. Your Stan's all right,' he comforted her after a pause; and didn't believe his words.

2

Our Late Member

Rodney Merriwell, our late member, first won his seat as
Liberal member for our extremely odd constituency in the
famous—or infamous—'Coupon Election' of 1918. Not that he
won it for Liberalism; it had been a Liberal seat long before he
was chosen as our new candidate. I think we rejoiced in being
a constituency so extremely odd, a pocket of 'pure Liberalism',
as we called it, or 'true Liberalism', among Tory and Labour
seats all around it as far as eye or imagination could reach. This
traditional oddness was a force in keeping us unique; it is
always gratifying to be unique. At all costs let us save our
uniqueness. We were pleased with the young Mr. Merriwell
when he was chosen. He was then only about twenty-nine years
old; he had played cricket for Middlesex, our county, and once
even for the Gentlemen against the Players. It was typical of
him, perhaps, that in these matches he had played creditably
and reliably but with no newsworthy distinction; but they were
a notable help for him in his election campaign. We are a
sporting nation.

He came to us well stocked with money, for his father was
the wealthy Sir Peter Merriwell, chairman and dominant
shareholder in Pierce, Merriwell and Co. Ltd., Produce Mer-
chants. Sir Peter was a hot Conservative and it is likely that he
got his title for a heavy contribution to his party's funds when it
was serving in the wartime Coalition under Lloyd George.
Thus young Rodney's politics, brought down from Oxford,
were the extreme opposite of his father's, but Sir Peter was
proud of his only son (had the boy not got his blue for cricket
and played for the Gentlemen?) and he did not hesitate to give
him all the money he might need to live in comfort as a Liberal
M.P., even though all such radicals would probably ruin the
country. Rodney had no difficulty in winning the seat for 'pure

Liberalism'; he survived the election as one of the lonely twenty-seven independent Liberals who had refused to be any part of Lloyd George's post-war Coalition or to have any truck with his 'coupons'. Of course he had no difficulty. Tories might come and go, Socialists might come and go, all around us, but Ridgeway stayed Liberal. Pure Liberal. From 1918 to 1942 when Rodney was walking along the ridge looking down upon London, there had been five general elections, in all of which he had held the seat with thousands of votes to spare. By now he was a member greatly liked—even loved by the women since his hair went beautifully white and wavy—a wonderful coiffure. He was now a set habit for Ridgeway. So much so that in the recent elections the slogan on posters, in windows, and on car-stickers was no more than 'Ridgeway Returns Roddy'. Which invariably Ridgeway did.

If this nickname, 'Roddy', revealed a constituency's affection for its member, Rodney by now loved his constituency, much as a captain loves his ship and all his crew. He might be no outstanding success in the House, a mere back-bencher whose voice was seldom heard, but when he did rise, nervously, to speak, he preached the true gospel both nervously and fearlessly. But he was no easy speaker; when he decided that he must be heard as a matter of duty to his constituents the wretched speech laid waste long hours and days before it, while he rehearsed and rehearsed it pacing his study or lying in bed or walking round the garden or driving the five miles from Ridgeway to Westminster to deliver it. Once it was delivered with no disastrous breakdown, and safely behind him, there was joy in his heart and he repeated it to himself all the way home. If by ill-chance—or was it good fortune?—the Speaker did not call him, he always said that the speech must not be wasted, and he delivered it instead to Grace. What else was Grace for?

However inadequate as a speaker in the House there was no member in all the country who tended and nursed his constituency more affectionately than he. His talents blossomed far more bravely among individuals in streets and houses and pubs and clubs than among more gifted and illustrious politicians in

7

an awe-inspiring House. He really loved us, the people of Ridgeway, just because we were his constituents. With any and every one of us he had to express his good-will by a joke—often a joke of a simple pattern, but at least a joke. It was said of him that he had his own tankard in every pub and wasn't sure how far this contravened the Registration of the People acts. Many of his jokes, whether good or poor, ran as legends through our streets. The story that one of his speeches in the House had been a humiliating mess 'because, half way through, he couldn't remember how it went on, or indeed what it was about', and another story, told to us by himself, that he was so nervous and tied up all the way through a beastly speech that he kept calling the Leader of the Opposition the Prime Minister while the House roared—such cheerful records of failure only served to endear him to us and to add to the sum of his votes. Somehow, not in the course of seeking votes, but simply by way of his natural gaiety and good-will he managed to communicate to the people that he delighted in them, and there was the end of it: Ridgeway returned Roddy.

Such popularity as he enjoyed in the House sprang in part from this easy friendliness in Smoking Room, Lobbies, or Committee Rooms and in part from the many jokes in the Chamber about his old-time Liberalism. The wittiest member in the Chamber was generally held to be the Welshman, Embrys Morgan: he was a Socialist of the far Left but liked by all because of his wit which he expressed in an idiom and a vernacular that brought all the hills and valleys of Wales into Westminster. Some other wit had dubbed him, after the pattern of 'Morgan the milk' or 'Morgan the post' as 'Morgan the humour'. And 'Morgan the humour' was seldom happier than when exercising the humour on the Member for Ridgeway, calling him in rich but amiable tones, 'Our Little Liber-al' or 'The last of the Incorruptibles whom it is pleasant to have in our midst, but who with his nineteenth century Liberalism is really nowadays no more than an object of historical and architectural interest'. Or he referred to him as 'Our ancient monument commemorating for us, as is only right, old far-off forgotten things and battles long ago'. Why, when there were

8

twenty-six other 'pure Liberals' in the House, he aimed these gleeful shafts only at our member I don't know. But it seemed that Rodney with his vivid white hair above a youngish face and his welcoming tickled smile had a special charm for him. Once 'Morgan the humour' went so far as to speak of the honourable member's uncorrupt body which like that of one or two saints in history did not see corruption. The House enjoyed the jokes, and to that extent rejoiced in Roddy, because it is human nature to feel a fondness for those one teases and ridicules.

'Rodney has a rather simple sense of fun,' Grace would say to us; and this on the whole was a true enough picture of him. Over the years we learned how he liked to address her as 'Mrs. M.' or 'Mrs. Merriwell' or 'Mrs. Roddy'. Inevitably he called her 'Grace Darling' at times, but after he had read and delighted in Bunyan's famous book she became 'Grace Abounding', and this, to be sure, was no bad picture of her. She was 'Grace Abounding' for him when in some argument or in self-justification she 'went on and on and on. And on.' Or when she took his words out of his mouth, confident that she could tell his anecdote or state his true opinion more accurately than he could; this was a habit of hers that chafed him far too frequently. 'Who was telling this story, Grace darling, you or I?' She was 'Grace Abounding' when she spent hours—and hours —dressing for a social visit. Fully dressed himself and pacing the hallway with umbrella or walking stick, he would say 'Every married man spends twenty-five per-cent of his life waiting for his wife but I suppose it's all right when she's worth waiting for. Let us then so bear ourselves'—here remembering his Prime Minister—'that if this lasts a thousand years it will still be one of my finest hours'. She was 'Grace Abounding' when she stood gossiping at her house door, or outside a shop, or at the telephone, time having apparently ceased to exist. 'Is Grace still abounding?' he might ask of Everard if he was at home and his mother on the telephone; and if Everard agreed that she was, then Rodney would sigh, 'And they say that a woman's work is never done. How can it be if she's gossiping most of the time?' Grace was certainly abounding when she

B

wrote all day those endless letters to her throng of friends, and spelled the words in twenty different ways. He used the name more in admiration when, as a W.V.S. organizer, she was hurrying with tea or blankets to the Rescue workers after bombs had fallen, or drumming up the mobile canteens to a street of ruins, and cooking hot meals in one of them for those whose kitchens were dead, or supervising with a dozen other women her chain of day or residential nurseries for the children of mothers at work or away. Grace abounded splendidly then. Once it had occurred to him that this excellent title of John Bunyan's, 'Grace Abounding' might be applied with some felicity to her increasing girth, but naturally this was a little thought that he kept to himself. A pity, because it was a good variation, but it would have been coldly received; and in any case he had no use for jokes that wounded.

He never minded repeating old jokes to her again and again, justifying them with the confident (but debatable) statement, 'East and west, old jokes are best'. He enjoyed such minor idiocies as giving affectionate names to his possessions such as 'Georgie' for his travelling clock, and 'James and John' for his bedroom slippers, and 'Edgar Allan' for the vessel in his bedside commode; also in deliberately mispronouncing words and talking of the Oneth of June or the Tooth of July, or spoonerizing the names of famous firms so that one became 'Sparks and Menser' and another Messrs. 'Ullen and Anwin'. The Roman Catholic publishing house of 'Burns, Oates and Washbourne, Ltd.' became 'Urns, Boats and Washbourne, Ltd.' 'Chatto and Windus' became 'Whatto and Shindus'. Mispronounced, the counties followed suit; they became Hurts and Burks and Durby. Such idiocies were, I think, a mild defiance of all regulations and conformities imposed upon a free people. Within the narrow compass of his home he liked to be a little local Lord of Misrule.

Grace knew well enough why he said '*Ici Londres*', looking down upon wartime London.

Ici Londres. If an incident stirred him deeply he would speak of it to Grace again and again—and again and again—and often the telling of it drove him to the edge of shameful tears, so that his voice broke and he had difficulty in completing the tale properly. And it was only the day before their walk to the ridge that he had spoken for perhaps the fourth time of his recent performance in a tiny studio of the B.B.C., when a very famous Frenchman, using a strange name, had opened the programme for listeners in France with the two thrilling words, *Ici Londres*, and then introduced him as 'a distinguished member of England's parliament and a great lover of your country'.

'Yes, Mrs. Merriwell, "*Ici Londres*" he said—as you might say, "Here is London undefeated. Never surrendering. Fighting on to the end. And here in London are all the governments in exile, undefeated too, and fighting on *jusqu'au bout*. Here, *mesdames et messieurs*, is your government. *Ici La France Libre*." Yes, Grace my beloved, "distinguished" he called your husband, which was a hell of a lie, but the rest was true enough: "a great lover of your country". *Mais oui. Mais* ever so greatly *oui*.'

'And I suspect you did your stuff for him splendidly.'

'I did, Mrs. M. I did very nicely what *la bibici* wanted, and in pretty good French too, but all the time I knew that, fundamentally, I was a cheat and a fraud. Give me a script before me which the audience can't see, and for once I'm at ease. I know how to make it sound like spontaneous oratory, but that's only because I've worked on this wholly impromptu speech for days and nights till I've got it off by heart. But if, as in the House, everyone can see that I've got a manuscript, or copious notes, they can see also that any show of spontaneity is just a damned bad act. I know it, and that's why I've been a flop in the House for twenty-four years.'

'You're not a flop. Ridgeway wouldn't return you every time if you were a flop. There are other things besides spontaneous oratory.'

'Well, thank God for that, and thank God for *la bibici* which puts the French programme in their tiniest studio where there are only one or two Frenchmen to see your script. My excellent introducer after his *Ici Londres*, said "*Baissez vos postes, s'il y a lieu*"—in other words "Lower your sets lest there's an enemy listening". And when he closed it, he said "*Ceci termine notre programme français. Bon soir, Mesdames. Bon soir, Mesdemoiselles. Bon soir, Messieurs.*" It was those demoiselles that really got me. I felt an especial tenderness for them. And when, immediately after these words, the B.B.C. burst into the Marseillaise I wept.'

'I'm pretty sure I should have wept too. Abundantly.'

'Oh yes, you would. But *you're* allowed to weep; I'm not. In the afternoon they'd given a programme which they call their *quart d'heure des petits enfants de France.* And this programme, which contains no politics but only stories and plays and rhymes for children ends with the words'—but here Rodney felt the customary charge of tears in his throat and had to halt while he conquered a gulp before speaking the words—'it ends with the words, *Voici termine votre quart d'heure de jeudi après-midi. Au revoir chers petits enfants de France. Au revoir'*—whereat his voice really did break so that he could tell Grace no more. He had to leave the story where it stood.

3

The Sirens Again

On that summer night of '42 darkness did not fall till long after the true sunset hour because of the 'double summer-time' which had been ordained for these years of war. But at length the last of the light was drained out of the visible world, and an ultimate darkness lay upon London: the ultimate darkness of the blackout. Whenever this pitch-darkness shut them indoors behind their black-out curtains Grace's thoughts flew to Everard—and possibly flew with him, because it was after nightfall that the plane which he captained might be over Germany amid the anti-aircraft shells and the searchlights seeking for him. Rodney, with his inveterate optimism about himself and his family, and with his pleasure in drama and excitement, but not without some doubt and even shame, enjoyed the black-outs. This night before bolting his front door he switched off the lights in his hall and, opening the door looked out at the black nothingness which was his Quentin Street in Ridgeway. The black nothingness was empty of human sounds; no footsteps; no voices. All the neighbourhood seemed to him as empty and silent as in that first dark before the great words came, 'Let there be light.' Oh, but surely it was drama, great drama, that the old orange glow in the sky which used to reflect like a boundless halo the world's greatest city was now but a black velvet pall under a night of cloud. And in the same way he was exhilarated—yes, rather shamefully exhilarated—when, soon after he'd returned to Grace in their breakfast room an air-raid siren loosed its undulating wail. At first it was only a moaning in the distance, but very quickly it multiplied into many and much louder whines, and then, almost at once, it was a great chorus of howlings round and about his home. And one could hear the planes.

After nearly three years of war they could always distinguish the hum and throb of German planes from the long low roar of the British. But nowadays, having experienced and survived the nightly Blitz of September to November 1940—seventy nights of it—neither of them went down to the gas-proof shelter which they had laboriously formed in their wine cellar under the instructions of their local air-raid wardens during the last days before the war began. For two years and more the cellar of this old Victorian home had been in sole possession of their fast diminishing wines.

Yes, surely it was wrong to be exhilarated by these howlings with their promise of disaster for many—and worse still to be pleasurably excited when in the far distance they heard the crump of a bomb; then one nearer and louder; and then one so close that the walls of the room in which he stood with Grace trembled, its hanging lamps swung, and even its floor-boards vibrated. Exhilarated by disaster! All wrong; but there it was, and one could not deny it. Drama in its first moments outweighed both fear for oneself and thoughts for others. The guns! The great guns of London, far, near, and all around, roaring their indignation at the insolence of this visit! He opened a tiny slit between his black-out curtains to see their wrath exploding in the sky; and to see their comrades, the searchlights, which had come to instant life, sweeping their long fingers above the blackened world to find the invaders. Did they find one, they converged on it and held the poor illuminated insect in their merciless grasp while the guns hounded it. Great the excitement, surely.

Not so with Grace. Grace, as the nearer bomb shook their room like a local earth-tremor, screamed and rushed into his embrace; but this too was pleasant; it was pleasant to think of oneself as a rock of consolation and support, waiting there for her. He patted her on the back as he clasped her tight and assured her that the danger would soon be passed.

'But they sound overhead,' she insisted. 'They sound right overhead.'

'They always do if they're anywhere near. But they're probably getting far away now.'

14

'There's more than one. I can hear more than one.'

'Of course you can. I can hear plenty. They come not in single spies but in battalions. Don't worry; they'll soon be far away.'

And with this promise he released her from his embrace and went to the black-out curtains to peep again at the sky.

'Don't *do* that,' she ordered. 'Put out the light first. Put out the light.'

'You're right, darling. You always are. But it was only a very tiny slit. However, we'll be good.' And he switched off all lights in the room, which allowed him to open the black-out curtains wider and see more of this drama.

'Come away from the window. Blast may blow it in.'

He did not at once obey her. That neighbouring bomb must have been pretty close because they had heard the shards of splintered window-glass clanging on to the pavement.

'I'd say that bomb fell in Silverdale Street.'

'Yes,' said Grace in a tone very different from that of her scream. The woman who had screamed and rushed for masculine comfort was not the true Grace. Or not the whole of her. Far from the whole of her. After the crash of that near-by bomb with its noise of windows shattered and scattered, and as she heard the bells of fire engines claiming their free passage through the black-out, she suddenly became the W.V.S. organiser. 'I must go,' she said.

'Must you go at once?'

'Of course.'

'Let 'em get a little further away first.'

'No, I must go at once. The wardens'll expect me. They're always pleased to see me. They like to have me there.'

'Well, I suppose you'll be all right now. The stinkers have passed and missed us, I fancy—unless they're circling overhead.'

'Yes,' she agreed impatiently, looking round for her torch.

'Or unless they're coming in waves, as they did in the Blitz. They may, darling.'

'I can't help that. If the wardens can get there right away, I can.' She saw the torch, ever ready on the sideboard, picked it up, and dimmed it, according to orders, with its two hoods of tissue paper. 'You wait here.'

'Not on your life. I'm coming with you. Dammit, they're my constituents, aren't they?'

'No, you wait here. I want you here. I must have somebody here. I'll send someone to tell you exactly where it is, and I shall want you to ring up Dorothy and Alice and tell them to come with their torches. I shall want them to guide any homeless people to the Rest Centre and some children perhaps to the nursery, and to settle them all properly there. If it's a big incident, get Sally and Win. The Rescue teams may be glad of Win as a doctor. We'll see. I may send you a message to rustle up a canteen. I'd like one standing by. The Rescue workers like their tea, so do any poor dears they dig out. And I'll tell the Incident Officer that if any gas main or electricity cables are burst you're on the telephone and can get Control or whoever is needed.'

'Thank you.' He grinned in satirical gratitude for this very minor job.

'Not at all. These are your constituents, aren't they, and a demand for immediate assistance'll come splendidly from you. And we might need a mobile first aid post.'

'All right, my dear.' He laid an encouraging hand on her back. 'I'll stay here and hold the fort. You go. You're a wonderful girl, sweetheart. But do take care. No standing up if there's a whistle of a bomb. Down on your face on the pavement.'

'You bet. We all do that, wardens and all—except perhaps the Incident Officer who may think it's his duty to remain upright. You take care of yourself too. They may come back.'

'And look, dearest, if some of the homeless are no more than shaken bring them back here, or send them back by one of your underlings. I've still got some brandy left and I'll have it ready for them. I'll give them real stiffeners as we did in the Blitz, and to hell with the Representation of the People acts, whether they apply or not. A strong brandy mixed with a little bribery and corruption will do them no harm. Go and do what you have to do, Grace my pet—not forgetting "Grace Darling". I'll do what I'm told. I'll be the orderly room corporal here.'

4

The Secret Everard

Everard in the pilot's seat of his Wellington bomber was speeding the aircraft home. 'Let's get the hell out of here,' he had said to Nick Spenlow, his second pilot in the collapsible seat at his side, and to Jack Mackson, his bomb-aimer in the couch under his feet. Jack had just said, carelessly enough, 'Bombs away', and the ship had leapt at the words. Everard's heart had leapt too when he saw what the bombs were doing down there. The target was hit. The target was got. 'Okay, Jacamac. We seem to have done our job like one o'clock. Never better. By God, never so good. So for Jees' sake let us beat it. Who's for home?' The roar of his twin engines with their noses facing homeward seemed to answer him, 'We, by God.'

Pleased with his night's work, he said cheerfully, 'Not a bloke hit, and the flak was bloody enough. Now I'm damned well going to keep my reputation of getting all home alive.'

'You certainly have the luck, skip,' said Nick.

Everard would have liked to add, 'And some skill, too, I hope,' but he only thought it and tried to say modestly, 'Don't know where the luck comes from, but I seem to be the opposite of a Jonah. You haven't had to throw me out yet and save the ship. Not so far, at any rate.'

The crew said nothing to this, but perhaps the engines roared their endorsement.

Everard's fame as one of those who always got home had become a superstition in the squadron. 'Comic,' they said, 'but no vessel seems to crash or ditch if old Merriwell's skippering it.' And others explained, 'The Devil's on his side, you see,' to which many would retort, 'Never mind who's on his side. Wish I was in his crew. I've never been particularly anxious to drown or to fry.'

Everard had nearly completed his second tour of operations,

each of which was thirty raids and then a rest; and unlike far too many he had returned to Base from all. His ship had been winged more than once, but himself only twice: once in the shoulder by shrapnel; once in the thigh by a machine gun bullet. And now as he got his Wimpey (pet name for a Wellington) through high cloud and away from the Messerschmitts he shouted 'That was quite a party, all said and done. Our biggest success, what have you? Biggest ever. And you'll agree that it calls for one hell of a party—two parties, in fact, one when we get back, and the real show tonight.'

They agreed, Nick, and Jacky too as he clambered from his bomb-aimer's couch, and Rory Longden, the wireless operator from his rack of equipment behind the skipper, and Tim Betts, the tail gunner, and Chiefy Betterson, the navigator, from his table in the midst. 'You're bloody well right, skipper,' they said, or similar words.

'Yepp,' Everard agreed. 'It's a case for getting plastered tonight.'

And Rory affirmed, as if after careful meditation, 'Yes, I certainly think it's a case for a blind. I'm convinced it is.'

'Well, should it be at the old Red Cow or in the Mess?' asked Everard.

'Mess every time,' Jacky insisted from somewhere along the catwalk. 'Then maybe we'll get some of the waafs in for a dance.'

So they flew home at ten thousand feet, agreeing that it had been one hell of a party because the bombs from their ship, J for Johnnie, and from Chris Brewer's L for Love-a-duck, had torn in one blessed, intoxicating, unlikely moment of successful precision bombing a wide gap, a glorious gap, two spans down and their neighbouring piers wrecked, in the high viaduct over the Unterfeld Valley in the Ruhr. This, if anything ever did, demanded a celebration, a jubilee, a blind, even though they had seen bomber after bomber, crewed by their messmates of a few hours before go spiralling down to earth trailing its slip-stream of flame. Flame that, on the crash, turned into billows of black smoke with an orange glow at its heart. They had seen Collie Webb's P for Pussy fall to earth in fragments, most of the fragments ablaze. They had seen G George dive nose-first and for the most part aflame from nose to tail, but with its tail-gunner firing his last defiance at the Me 109 which had pounced like a firefly on to its back out of the clouds. They had seen their leader's starboard wing tank catch alight and heard his voice on the R.T., 'Hallo, B Butter, you okay so far?'

'B Butter to Leader. All okay so far. Receiving you loud and clear.'

'Fine, Ritchie. Stand by to take over if I go down.'

'Okay, Leader. Understood. Can you make it?'

'Doing our best, old cock. But get cracking yourself. We . . .' but they heard no more from Jimmie Taylor, one of the best and most popular of leaders.

They heard only B Butter asking, 'Are you hearing me, Leader?'

No answer.

In all they had seen nine ships lost and they knew—so far as they allowed themselves to think—that nine crews had been cremated alive. Eight crews out of seventeen were all that would return home. And that was to say that Everard had lost at least fifty of his friends—'good chaps, all of 'em'—in one midnight hour. A few might have baled out to the safety of a prison camp, but this was improbable because they had dived and were flying low at the target when hit. Fifty friends lost in a moment of time but this was commonplace enough in Bomber Command, and meanwhile their own J for Johnnie, along with L for Love-a-duck, had wheeled into an ever accelerating dive out of cloud, levelled out over the target, and smashed it precisely as planned. The loss of its bombs after tossing J for Johnnie like a ball into the air, had lightened it so that, in Everard's words 'it seemed ten years younger', and now at a speed of two hundred and forty miles an hour they were tearing home in the safety of thick cloud. Soon the cloud thinned out and died away at their high level so that its roof below them lay at little more than three thousand feet, and they were flying through a clear summer night under multitudinous stars. Then all cloud was gone and they were over the Netherlands and could drop low, for the Netherlands seemed asleep.

'Only ten minutes to the drink now, sir,' said Chiefy Betterson, the navigator, which was to say that in ten minutes they would be over the sea with the dawn coming up behind them. 'Sir' to his captain, though he was one rank senior to Everard; 'Sir', while it was an operation and Sergeant Merriwell captain of the ship.

'Hurray, Nav. Good for you,' said Everard and exalted by the triumph behind them, he tried, though masked, to lead them in song:

> 'Ops in a Wimpey, Ops in a Wimpey
> Who'll come on Ops in a Wimpey with me'

but he got support only from his second pilot at his side. The others could not hear him above the engines' roar, and Chiefy as a flight sergeant, much older than any of them, was not given to song.

But even if his intended chorus through the intercom was a failure he was not going to be beaten—or not at once—and he went on singing the song to himself:

> 'And we'll sing as we swing and prang her on the hangar
> Who'll come on Ops in a Wimpey with me?

'Variation, please; any one who's interested:

> 'She's got old-fashioned engines
> All tied up with strings,
> It's a wonder she was ever airborne.
> Still she's quite safe and sound
> When she's safe on the ground,
> And there's something that makes her divine—'

But the ensuing and last couplet he changed into one of his own, joyously composed on the spur of the moment and in memory of a viaduct paralysed:

> 'For the Huns in the Ruhr have learned to adore
> This old-fashioned Wimpey of mine.

'Thank you, all.'

His song having lacked support he dropped into safety of mere talk through the intercom. 'But thank God we'll be getting our Lancasters soon. Four engines, dear lads, and we shall be able to limp home on three of them or two of them or even one and a half. We'll get home all right with them. Still I shall always adore this old-fashioned mother of mine.'

Now they were over England and the sun was bright over the horizon, so for the fun of it he flew low so that the shadow of J for Johnnie might race for home before him, over fields and hedgerows, cattle and trees.

Silence now, and Everard's thoughts became very different from anything his crew would suspect. Very different from the musical gaiety to which he had just treated them. Some of the thoughts were such as he would never disclose to a crew who liked to call him 'Sergeant Merrihell'.

As on a hundred other airfields of Fighter and Bomber Commands in these touch-and-go years of the war the Group Captain on Everard's station allowed a liberty of behaviour to the aircrews unimaginable in Navy or Army and capable of horrifying both. This not only because these boys were young and death was their likely lot, so let them have some riotous times while life was still simmering high within them; not only because at this moment their country's freedom lay in their hands as they went off to play their double-or-quits with death; but also because it seemed one of nature's laws that the more irregular and mischievous their behaviour on the airfields, the finer the behaviour in the air. Thus it came about that in all the wars of Britain's long history it is probable that never had so many blind eyes been turned on so much disorderly conduct or undoubted indiscipline as in the first forties of this century on the airfields of Fighter and Bomber Commands.

And never was there a better customer than Sergeant Merriwell for any indisciplined behaviour that was lying around free of charge. On the outbreak of war he had deserted his college, Univ., Oxford, after only one year to join the R.A.F. and *fly*. Where was such adventure to be found as up in the air above or among the clouds? Seeing it always as a chance for new adventure he had volunteered for aircrew and been accepted. Some months, all too many, of Deferred Service, and they summoned him for training. He reported at a Recruits

Centre and with no small pleasure saw himself in Air Force blue, the wear that just then was most honoured in the country and best pleased the girls. From the Recruiting Depôt to a Training Centre, and here they put him with the other rookies through some unexpected Battle Training: rifle drills, parade drills, route marches and mock battles over the heaths, when often he was crawling on his belly with a Lewis gun. What on earth (and literally on earth) had this to do with fighting in the air? What had it to do with the skies? Had the R.A.F. got him wrong? But after some months of these irrelevancies he found himself flying at last.

This was the real investiture when for the first time he was wearing helmet, harness, goggles, Mae West, and oxygen mask. Only for training flights at first, but, still, these flights were high above the world, above an ocean of cloud, perhaps, and in the sun. Some months of this, and at last they posted him to a squadron of Bomber Command. And to Operations. He was operational. That had been a year ago, and on this early morning, as they chased their plane's shadow over the fields of England, returning to their airfield at Coulton-Harvey, he allowed himself to fall into thoughts that he could never speak aloud. In the Air Force it was not acceptable to talk patriotism or anything that smelt of idealism, and, least of all to mention what the Prime Minister had said about the young airmen who, in their prowess and mettle, were transcending the knights of old—one kept quiet about it or, if one mentioned it, one made fun of it. Irreverence and some cynicism and plenty of self-mockery were the religion of the messes. Everard conformed to it, but this morning, in the flush of dawn over England, as he looked down upon her hedgerows and woodlands and swelling hills he was glorying, just as his father had done not long since, in—but not a word to the others—in the mighty task she had accepted with a mad, incredible confidence that she could and would sustain it. There she lay, green and simple and domestic, so small an island lying off Festung Europa, but none the less Liberty's last battleship—at least until the great American armadas came. Yes, surely it was good—no matter what the issue—to be a part of her in this moment. In his present mood,

23

flying over England, he was inescapably his father's son and could have said with pride—but only to himself—'*Ici l'Angleterre.*'

Funny to think that in spite of his mock-boast, 'I always come home' the odds were that soon he would have done with England for ever. Never to see her again. One did not speak of this—or only with grim jestings, but old Squadron Leader Death travelled with every aircrew, ready to take command when his hour came. Some clever statistician had worked out that every young airman after twenty-five trips must expect to die. Then Everard with his fifty trips had cheated old Death twenty-five times, and the odds stood at twenty-five to one that, unless he was grounded, the day must be near when he would come home no more. Some of the trips of course were hardly raids at all, but merely pieces of cake; all the same, no one could deny that so far he had beaten the old bastard with points to spare.

This led him to another thought best kept to himself. It was a new troubling doubt. Adventure was good; excitement was good; flying through tracer, yellow, red, and green, could be joy even though salted with fear; sometimes weaving at speed through the Ack-Ack could be almost pure fun because spiced with less fear, so seldom could it get you then—it was only enemy fighters that came and spoiled the fun by whipping up the fear again. Yes, excitement and fun but—what about the people, probably like the people of England down there; some of them children in bed, perhaps, or babies in cots. War was war, and he and his fellows had only done what they'd been obliged to do; and what had been done to them by the enemy; this was war—but—but he would be happier if it had been only soldiers or Ack-Ack gunners they had killed. Was it a fair argument to say that because the enemy had slaughtered civilians in their thousands, it was right for him to do it too? Only of late had this thought really troubled him, and it brought him to a new reflection: this year of crowded life, lived shoulder-to-shoulder with death, had probably matured him more than ten years of peace would have done; to that extent he was probably wiser (in secret) at twenty-one than he would have been at thirty-two in days of peace when one's death was an almost unimaginable thing, out of sight and far away; and was it not a pity that such early enlightenment should be dowsed by death in a matter of weeks or days?

Good lord, what would Nick and Jack and Chiefy and Tim say to these cocky thoughts if he spoke them aloud? Better to forget all such musing and let the roar of the engines deafen one's mind to it; better to begin singing to oneself again, 'Who'll come on Ops in a Wimpey with me? She's got old-fashioned engines, all tied up with—' and anyhow there was his airfield with its Nissen huts and hangars and control tower, and his faithful ground crew who'd probably been waiting for him in hope and wonder and doubt since long before sunrise. Plainly he was the first of the survivors to appear, and his self-love could but delight in this support for the airfield's superstition that Merriwell always got home.

§

Jeanie Lynn, eighteen and one of the lowliest of the waafs, lay sleepless in her undistinguished bed. Five o'clock in the morning now. Perhaps during the night she had dozed once or twice, but it didn't seem like that; it seemed that she had tossed awake from that midnight hour when she had seen the squadron take off. More than all the other craft she had watched J for Johnnie; watched it till it had gone into the clouded darkness and she could see it no more. Perhaps she would never see it any more: so many were never heard of again. And it was five o'clock now, with summer daylight in the room; they should be back soon—those who would come back. 'Oh God, let Everard come back, please . . . please.' If only he came back he would riot and make whoopee for a while with the others, but just as soon as he could, or just as soon as she had finished her shift on the switchboard, he would escape from the rowdy frivolities to come and find her. He would come into her embrace; there would be passionate kissing; and when they had wandered together out of the sight of all others, his arm around her shoulders and drawing her against him, hers about his waist and responding with a like pressure, they would find

c   25 their favourite bed among the tall summer grasses of the heath country, where he, with a wild and gasping excitement, would extract and wring his joy from her.

Sometimes when there were no ops that night he did not come to her at all though she longed for him; he went off with friends to drink the hours away in the Red Cow; but always after a night raid he came. Came in secret to her as soon as might be, and took her as if, more than all the drinking in the world, she with her young body could give him the healing he needed; the release and peace he had earned; the one lovely, exquisite reward after the stabbing fears and racing doubts of a raid.

And never in her life of eighteen years had she known a joy like this use of her for his reward and comfort. It carried a joy far above any physical ecstasy he sometimes raised in her; indeed often, so impassioned was his craving, her pleasure reached no climax, but her joy in *his* transports was little impaired by this failure. What mattered above all was the satisfying of his hunger and his love. Many of the other waafs had a 'crush' on him, but it was she whom he had chosen and, after his choice, given never a glance at any other.

Always he came and looked for her; but for how long? She believed enough in his love to be sure he would come for her till—till that terrible night, that all too likely night, when he did not return. Five o'clock; all thought of sleep was impossible now because they might be returning at any moment. Listen: was she not hearing the drone of a plane coming in to land? She leapt from her bed and ran to the barrack window from which the airfield was just visible. Her heart pulsed quickly when she saw that a ground crew was waiting there as if a plane was coming in. And it was *his* ground crew—yes, yes, she believed she could recognize his men. The drone of the plane was a full-throated roar now as the splendid ship, that huge grey bird, swept in a graceful circuit to land easily. Yes, she could see, or persuade herself she saw, the letters and figures on the fuselage that denoted his Wimpey. 'Oh God, thank you, thank you . . . Oh God, I do thank you.'

Jeanie Lynn, daughter of a Cornish lay-preacher, and a

chapel-going girl at home, had lapsed from all church services now, but who could be other than religious in moments like this and either cry to God or pour forth thanks to him? Yes—yes—that was Rory Longden coming down the ladder—she was sure of it—and Chiefy Betterson after him. Thanks be to God.

Then, even as she saw Everard come down unhurt and alive, taller than the others, dragging off his helmet and showing his dark hair; even as at last she saw him with never such an uprush of thanks—'Oh, God . . . God . . . Oh, thank you, thank you'—her eyes were drawn to a surprising fact. Not half-past five, and there on the field, unmistakably, was the Queen Bee herself, their senior officer come down from her distinguished chamber somewhere in the Officers' Mess. Flight Officer Maud Gretton, perhaps thirty years old, was unsuitably small for her high position. With her brown hair set boyishly close to her head, she always looked small among tall and striding airmen. This morning on the field she appeared to be wearing only a long coat over her pyjamas. Why was she there, watching and waiting? A happy and soothing idea struck Jeanie as she stared from her window. Could it not be that the Queen Bee herself was in love with one of the officers who'd been among the raiders? Was there perhaps a love affair between her and, say, a flight-lieutenant skippering one of the planes or perhaps some other commissioned officer in a ship like Everard's captained by a sergeant? And did she, endowed with her own private room instead of the tall summer grasses . . . did she know the same ecstasies when her man came home and took her? Was she craving them now, down there on the field?

Whether or not this was the hidden truth she suddenly, after talking to some of the ground crews waiting, did a thing even more extraordinary. She left the field and came towards the very barrack holding Jeanie's dormitory; Jeanie heard her feet on the stairs; and here she was, opening quietly the door of this small room and asking in a low voice, 'Anyone awake?'

One or two lifted their heads and answered, 'Yes, ma'am.'

Jeanie from her window answered, 'Yes, ma'am.'

Either the Queen Bee observed Jeanie at the window for the

first time, or she pretended to do so. She swung her dark eyes towards this girl at a window.

'Well, I thought you'd all like to know that J Johnnie's safely home. And there are several others coming home. Ritchie Drewitt's just behind Sergeant Merriwell, and Flight-Lieutenant Milton behind him. Several others are homing: S Soapy and G Garbo. All are safe and unhurt in J Johnnie and in the others, so far as we know.'

The few girls awake said, 'Thank you, ma'am'; and Jeanie was one of these.

The Queen Bee turned her eyes again to Jeanie and said laughingly, 'I suggest you'd be better in bed now, Lynn. I know it's all very exciting but get what rest you can.'

And in that moment Jeanie knew why she had come. She had come because she was well aware—she who was reputed to know everything—that one of her girls, the youngest and newest, was in love with the skipper of this ship just home; that night after night, if he was away on a raid, the girl was waiting in anxiety for his return, mostly in silence but sometimes feigning the normal gaiety; and that there could be no harm in coming into a room where this girl slept and mentioning her lover's name among several others carelessly and, as it were, ignorantly. No doubt this sight of Lynn standing alone at a window and gazing out had made her pleased with this visit and justified it. She went away, quietly shutting the door.

This was the moment too when Jeanie, to her delight, suspected that the Queen Bee allowed herself a special feeling for Airwoman Lynn, the youngest in her small hive, and a sympathetic but secret interest in her love-affair.

Jeanie got back into bed with all the happiness that comes with the end of a dread; into bed but with no desire for sleep now, because her heart was swelling, her breaths shortening, and her loins quickening, as she dwelt upon what would be, when Everard came and took her away.

Was the Queen Bee perhaps now back in her bed, her heart shaking and inflating with an expectation no less?

§

Four of the surviving craft were home: Drewitt, Taylor, Flower, Merriwell. Four more were believed to be safe and back soon. So to the eggs and bacon, and after that, the party around the bar. And let it rip. Nothing could alter the fact that two of their eighteen kites had made their target good and proper. Remember that moment—in all his flying career never such a moment, thought Everard—when by the light of a flare he and his crew saw two spans of the Unterfeld viaduct smashed and agape like a broken jaw. Pints all round; and same again. Forget the cost in young happy lives; nine planes lost; forget it; nearly sixty friends of last night missing; many of them dead. Every success had its price, sometimes cheap enough, and sometimes damned dear; and this was to be the celebration of an amazing success. This was to be a festival, not a wake. Everard drank pint upon pint with the others till he was roaring at their jokes, and after a time roaring most heartily at his own; he yelled a greeting to other crews as they came in; and allowed entry to none of the doubts and worries that had been his as they came home through the dawn. He joined as loudly as any, and louder than some, in a chorus which nowadays filled the mess at any party, though it was little suited to their neighbouring village, the tiny and friendly Coulton-Harvey. But what did that matter. This admirable song had been carried to them from other airfields in larger towns like an infection through the air.

> This bloody town's a bloody cuss,
> No bloody trains, no bloody bus,
> And no one cares for bloody us—
>   Bloody Coulton-Harvey.

> The bloody roads are bloody bad,
> The bloody folk are bloody mad,
> They make the brightest bloody sad—
>   Bloody Coulton-Harvey.

> Everything's so bloody dear,
> A bloody bob for bloody beer
> And is it good? No bloody fear,
>   Bloody Coulton-Harvey.

In the middle of the next verse just as Everard was in full voice with:

> No bloody sport, no bloody games,
> No bloody fun, no bloody dames—

the Squadron Commander's clerk, an old relic of the First War, and coming up fifty, touched his elbow and said, 'Wingco wants you, Sarge.'

'Wotcha? . . . Wotter . . . hell, mate? Have a drink.'

'No, ta, Sarge. Wing Commander said I was to bring you at once.'

'Hell, no; not now. This is a party.'

The old boy shrugged. 'Dunno anything about that. He wants you at once.'

'At once? At bloody once? *No.* Talk sense. I'm enjoying myself.'

'That's me message.'

Everard expressed his opinion of the message with one word, a synonym for homosexuality. To this he added his view that the squadron's commander was illegitimate. But in truth he was not sorry to be called away. Not all this dutiful drinking and singing and dancing could compete with a mounting lust in his heart, so he went cheerfully with the old clerk, asking only, 'What's it all about, Jack? Am I in the doghouse for something, or could there be some joy in it for me?'

'I dunno,' was all the answer he got. 'He ain't told me nothing.'

He demanded where was the illegitimate now.

'In the Briefing Room jest at present.'

'I see. What's he there for?'

'I dunno.'

'You don't know much, Jack, do you?'

'Only that he wants you to come at once.'

'Yes, you've made that clear already.'

The Briefing Room, large and bare was empty except for the Squadron Commander, who was seated at the table on a dais, turning over a sheaf of papers with a contemplative air. He

looked up for one second at Everard, then down again at his
papers, turning over two more.

'Oh, good morning, Merriwell.'

'Good morning, sir.'

'Good show last night.'

'Wizard, sir. We did the trick this time. Probably an acci-
dent, but no mistake about it.'

'Good . . . very good . . . but one doesn't like the losses.'

'No, sir. The flak was bad. And the M.E.s a nuisance.'

'Nine out of eighteen good crews lost is pretty steep. Fifty-
odd chaps. Could any of them have jumped safely?'

'Doubt it, sir. One or two might have done. But most of us
were fairly low.'

'Well, *you* seem to have had your usual luck. I sent for you
to tell you that your commission has come through.'

Some joy in the heart at this. All promotion was sweet, but
promotion to commissioned rank had a flavour of its own. Yet
all that Everard said was 'Oh, good. Thank you, sir.'

'Yes, the Station Commander and I both put in good words
for you. Though I had no doubt about it when you applied.
Congratulations. It could hardly have come at a more suitable
moment, after your achievement last night.'

'That was luck, sir.'

'Not altogether. Well, this means a week's leave for you, so
that you can get your uniform. Your old man lives in London,
doesn't he?'

'North London, sir. Ridgeway.'

'He's sort of member for it, isn't he?'

'Kind of, sir,' Everard agreed with a smile.

'Good. Well, all London's the same to me. I should get your
kit at the Army and Navy Stores. You'll make quite a happy
landing there. It's a respectable place.'

'You mean I go to-day, sir?'

'Naturally. You're a pilot officer now, and we don't want
you captured over Germany as anything else. They'll give you
a better deal as an officer.'

'I see, sir.'

'So take off now and steer a straight course for London and

the A. and N. I imagine your parents'll be glad to see you. Or do they prefer you out of their sight?'

'I don't think so, sir.'

'Well, that's fine. You'll be able to mess with them. So farewell for the present. Get the list for your kit.'

Everard did not return to the party, which was still chorusing and dancing before the bar. He hurried away in search of Jeanie. He was on leave, and she, he believed, must be free. After all, she had been on duty at her switchboard till late last night and Shirley Lucas, her senior, who had taught her to operate the panel, must have told her to 'scram' for this morning and afternoon. He hurried to her barracks and at its door, as a waaf emerged, he asked her with a pretence of ease, almost of indifference, 'Jeanie Lynn anywhere about?'

Oh yes, she was in the mess, the girl said.

'Well, double back and yank her out, Beautiful. D'you mind? I only want her for one moment. Tell her Sergeant Merriwell wants a word with her.'

Listen to the lies, he thought. One moment. Only one word. Then he remembered. 'No. Say Pilot Officer Merriwell wants half a word with her.'

The girl's eyes opened wide and shot to the sergeant's stripes on his sleeve. 'Is it really "Pilot Officer" . . . sir?'

'My child, it is. And thanks for the "sir". Shouldn't you spring smartly to attention? It's been P.O. for at least an hour. What about a salute? My first ever.'

'Oh, good, sir. Congrats, sir.' And she pretended to salute.

'Thank you, darling. Now cut out all that boloney and bring me Aircraftwoman Lynn. It was this that I wanted to tell her. No more. So jump to it.'

'Okay, sir.' And she went quickly back, carrying her small burden of lies.

Jeanie came running out to him. That her figure was slight and her face childish, and that both looked the more seductive for her quasi-masculine uniform; that unlike most of her fellow waafs she was shy and socially ill-at-ease rather than a good 'mixer'; and further that, as a one-time chapel-going girl, she was no easy giver of herself to a lover, and yet would now give herself to him with a desire and a passion that equalled his own—these lifted the desire in him, in heart and body, till it was like that which had troubled and shaken her in her bed a few hours before. The contrast between shyness and fervour, between timidity and a capacity for wild desire, made of her the sweetest pleasure he'd ever known in the possession and rough mastery of a woman.

'Is it true, darling?' she asked. 'Is it true that you're an officer?'

'Yes, but damn the old commission. What's more important is, are you free for an hour? For I'm a P.O. on leave, dammit, and I want to enjoy myself. I'm on orders to go off to London, but that's going to wait for a little. That's going to wait my pleasure.'

'Yes, I'm free.' It was said modestly, even shyly, but he was not deceived; he knew that she knew what was before her, and that she was ready for it, alight for it, aching for it, as he was. Indeed the shyness was overturned for a moment by a small significant smile, quickly withdrawn behind a steady mouth though it was transferred, perhaps, to the blue eyes above. Jeanie's eyes were the one beauty in her round childish face. Though her hair had lost its childish fairness the eyes, large and well-spaced, were still a deep blue.

'You're free. Then come away. Come away.'

'Yes, but look: with you being an officer, won't it mean that we shan't be able any more . . . won't it make a difference? Oh, don't say it will.'

'Don't you believe it, my heart's delight. This isn't the Army. Come along, and I'll show you exactly the difference it'll make. Come now. Can you come now?'

'Yes. Yes.'

'As you are? You look adorable. I dream of Jeanie with the light brown hair.'

'I could come. For a little.'

For a 'little'! As if she thought of it as a 'little', but the necessary shyness had to be resumed, and they walked away in apparent innocence, properly apart, but when they were out of sight of all—and this was not soon, for the airfield was large and its buildings many, but at last its perimeter track and hard-standings were well behind them—when they were among hedgerows and trees, he gathered up her hand, his own hand trembling and hers trembling a little too; and led her into the empty heath country, where, away from all beaten tracks, they knew of many a covert in this late summer time amid the withering willow-herb and the high seeding grasses.

5

Pilot Officer Everard, Gunner Stanley

It was seven in the evening when a shameless knock hammered on the door, and the bell sounded through the house with apparently no likelihood of stopping. It went on ringing like a burglar alarm or a bell gone mad. Grace knew instantly who it was that knocked. No one else would disturb a whole street with so graceless a knock or use a hall-door bell as an instrument of high comedy. If only it could be Stan, she thought, as she hurried to the door; in the old days it could well have been; but not now; not now. She loved them both equally; what else with twins?—but it was Stan now who was the ache in her heart. True, one lived always with the dread that Everard would be killed, but there was no new mystery about him; he remained a merry and affectionate son, writing all too seldom, of course, but gay and impish letters when he did write, and always he came happily to his home in the first hours of his leave. But Stanley! Of late he'd ceased to write at all, though of old he had been a more considerate, frequent and loving writer than Everard; and not once in more than a year had he spent a leave at home. Oh, Stanley, what is it? What has happened to change you? Still, if this uncivilized knock could only be Everard's, it was lovely to think of him there behind the door. Yes, she could see a tall silhouette behind the leaded glass panes of their old Victorian door. And here was this disgraceful, unneighbourly knock again. Really, Everard, there are neighbours to think of. To knock like that! But she rejoiced in him for it.

Heart beating irregularly, she pulled open the door. Everard grinning.

'Pilot Officer Merriwell,' he announced.

'*Darling—what?*'

'Pilot Officer Merriwell. Hallo, Mum.'

'You mean . . .?'

'Good to see you. Dad at home?'

'No, he's at the House. But—'

'Conscientious man; and damn it.'

'But "Pilot Officer" did you—'

He halted all questions by taking her shoulders and kissing her on both cheeks, left and right and left again. 'Yes. P.O. Merriwell. Came through this morning. Week's leave to get my kit with some small advice from you and the old man, if you're interested.'

'Oh, but how marvellous.'

'The Wing-co more or less ordered me to get it at the Army and Navy Stores. Said it was a fairly respectable place. Well, Dad won't be on his Ops tomorrow afternoon, Friday, and the A. and N.'s almost next door to his Hot Aerodrome so he can come too and, after duty done, we must have a celebration. A good one. A blind.'

'Yes, yes; but Dad'll want to do that at the club.'

'And that'll be all right by me. One can't really put the boat out on a sergeant's pay. Heard anything from Stan?'

'Not a word. The boy's a mystery.'

'D'you mean to say he doesn't write?' Everard asked this, as if he were the best of correspondents instead of one of the worst.

'Good heavens, no. Never any news.'

Everard stared at her, unable to think of any comforting words; then shrugged. 'Funny that he remains only a gunner after two years. I should have thought he'd been at least a bombardier. But don't worry. That's probably because far too few get killed in an Ack-Ack battery based in England, so everybody has to stay put in their current rank.'

'I wish I could believe that. But I don't.'

'What do you believe then?'

'I don't know. I think he turned sour and remote about something more than a year ago. What it was I can't imagine. But come in, darling. Oh, it'll be lovely to have you for a whole week.' She led him towards the drawing-room. 'What difference will this make, your being an officer?'

'Not much. A change of mess. I guess I shall still skipper Johnnie and have the same marvellous crew.'

Her heart fell. 'But don't you finish your tour soon?'

'Nine more trips, and then I should be due for a rest. But I'm damned if I'll stay on the ground for six months teaching other blokes to fly. What's the good of a brand-new pilot officer who only pilots a desk or a table or a chair?'

Silent, Grace looked at him as he said this. How long, how long? Nine more trips. It was possible she was looking at him for the last time. A week of leave, and then . . . never again? She had read in that evening's paper, now lying on the occasional table beside her, of last night's raid, with its familiar close: 'Some of our aircraft are missing.'

'Were you in that raid last night?'

'I was. But actually it was a raid early this morning.'

'What was it like?'

'A wizard show. Absolutely wizard. Target shot to blazes. Bowled middle stump. And since one may shoot a line to one's mum, if to no one else, it was my J Johnnie and Chris's Love-a-duck that put the target where we wanted it. Did you read that the viaduct was wrecked and they'll have a hell of a job getting it back into service again? Did the papers say who done it?'

'No. No names were mentioned.' Not a word had he said about missing aircraft. 'Were there many aircraft . . . lost?'

'I really don't know, Mum. Some were, but I don't know how many. I'd hardly got back when I was sent home to you and Dad.'

'Were many killed?'

'I suppose some bought it.'

She said no more, and for a while they sat together in the drawing room. Strange and sad, she thought, but, loving each other, neither could find much to say. She dredged up unexciting remarks, and he did the same. This uncomfortable session was broken by another knock on the door; but a reasonable one. And only a touch on the bell.

'Who the hell's that?' Everard asked irritably.

'Well, at least it's someone who knows how to knock respectably,' said Grace, as she rose.

'No, darling, I'll go and see. Probably it's one of your Voluntary Women come for an interminable chatter which you'll thoroughly enjoy and encourage just when I wanted you to myself.'

Everard walked to the front door, and Grace, no less curious than the next woman, went as far as the drawing-room door to peer round it and learn who the visitor was; and, if it was no one she knew, to hear what passed between Everard and a stranger. Before Everard got to the door, she had time to see, once again, that the silhouette behind the door's glass panes was that of a man unusually tall. Stan? Oh, could it be Stan at last . . .?

Everard at first didn't open the door wide enough for her to see who it was, but she heard—not Stan's voice—a stranger's, and from Everard a surprised, questioning, 'Oh, yes? Good Lord!'

More words from the stranger, and then Everard's friendly 'Oh, come in. Of course come in. My father's not here but my mother is.'

He opened the door wide to admit the visitor, and Grace saw with surprise that for the second time within an hour someone in uniform had come and knocked on their door. But this tall man was in a smart police-blue uniform, and she smiled as she thought how much neater this dark blue uniform was than the loose air-force battle dress which had come earlier. To judge from the two silver stars on his shoulder, and the gloves in one hand he must be an inspector at the least. This was interesting, even exciting. There was always something dramatic about a policeman at your door. This policeman seemed young for his rank, for he had a fresh skin, a fair soft moustache (which looked odd in a policeman) and a figure as spare as it was tall. A figure beautifully made for that uniform, she thought.

He was saying something inaudible, but Everard's further 'Good lord!' was very audible. And interesting, even alarming.

'Come and see my mother and tell us all,' he was saying. 'When Father'll be back I don't know. He's our member as you may know.'

'Do I not?' laughed the officer and quoted, '"Ridgeway Returns Roddy". We all know that.'

Grace retreated quickly from her observation post and seated herself properly on the settee by the fireplace, as if she were one who had never dreamed of moving from it.

Everard brought the officer into the room, saying, 'Mother, this is—but I don't know your name, sir . . . Chief Inspector . . .' he added, preferring to flatter than to devalue.

'Oh no, sir. *Inspector* Garrett.' And he touched the two stars, his well-trained eyes having probably seen Everard's swing towards them. 'Merely "Inspector". Three for a chief inspector. Good evening, madam.'

'I'll leave the Inspector to tell you his news, Mother. Prepare yourself for something very strange.'

All arranged themselves about the room for the Inspector's explanation.

'I only want to know, madam, whether your son, whose name I have here—' he looked at a notebook— 'is Gunner Merriwell, 4887631 of 917 Heavy Anti-Aircraft Battery stationed at Claverton, Kent—whether he's come on leave to you within the last few weeks.'

'No, Inspector. We've seen nothing of him for many weeks. Why do you ask?'

'Well . . .' The Inspector gave a shrug, as if to say, 'There's a lot of this sort of thing going on.' 'He's been absent without leave for a good many days now. And his battery has asked the police to help find him. That is all.'

Grace's heart was now trembling, but she tried to speak naturally. 'He's certainly not been here. Nor has he written to my son. This is my son,' and proudly she gave him his new rank, 'Pilot Officer Merriwell.'

The Inspector slipped a glance at the sergeant's stripes on Everard's uniform and doubtless drew the right conclusion.

Grace, trying to hide her dismay, pursued, 'You've heard nothing from Stan, have you, Everard?'

'Heavens, no; but who ever writes to a brother?'

'So I'm afraid we're not much help, Inspector. If we do hear anything, we'll certainly tell you.' But would she? Would she

39

not hide any knowledge that would get Stan into trouble? What was this but polite talk?

'Thank you, madam. If you'll just tell one of us at the local police station. The Kent County Constabulary have got in touch with us to see if we can help. That is all.'

Grace, trying to smile, asked, 'Is it a serious offence, Inspector? Will he get into trouble? What will happen when you or they find him?'

'We don't know. If we were to find him—' he avoided the word 'arrest'—'all that we would have to do would be to hand him over to the military.'

'And what would they do?'

'That's their affair. There could be a court-martial or his C.O. might let him off quite leniently. I shouldn't worry about a court-martial, madam. You can't very well have court-martials for sixteen thousand men who are absent without leave at present.' He smiled at the idea of it. 'Since the war began nearly sixty-five thousand men have gone "awol"—'

'"Awol" is "absent without leave", Mother,' Everard explained.

'Yes.' The Inspector nodded; 'and if your son's usually a good soldier they might even turn a blind eye to it, but—but I'm afraid not in this case. He's been away too long and—er— he's done this before.'

'He *has*?'

'Yes, he went on leave some time in April and remained absent for quite a while, but he came back of his own free will, and they dealt with him lightly then.'

'He didn't come here in April,' said Grace sadly, 'and I simply don't know if he's been a good soldier. It doesn't sound like it. What do you say, Everard?'

'I'd say he could have been a splendid soldier once, when we joined the forces together. But he should have joined the Air Force like me. He's always been a bit of an independent rebel, and he could have done almost all the rebelling he wanted in an aircrew. He chose wrong when he chose the Army.'

A key turned in the hall door. For a second Grace had the thought, at once pleasant and alarmed, that it might be Stan himself, who usually had a latch-key with him. But if so, what about the policeman here? What would happen now? But no—the door shut, and some objects were laid upon the hall table. It was Rodney unexpectedly home from the House.

'This will be my husband, Inspector. You can talk to him.'

Rodney entered. 'Good evening, Grace beloved. I trust I'm a welcome surprise—' but then he saw the two uniformed figures seated in the room. 'Lord save us! Everard! Where've you sprung from? And Inspector Garrett. Whom have you come to arrest, Inspector? Me? If so, I'll come quietly. It's a fair cop.'

The Inspector adopted the same laughing manner. 'No, we've nothing against you . . . so far, sir. There's nothing been found out yet.'

'Thank God for that. Well, it can't be Grace. She carefully commits no crimes against the criminal law; only against her husband's. It must be Everard. Come along, Ev. Game's up. I'll go bail for you. Unless it's a crime so serious that bail's not allowed. Murder perhaps.'

Grace intervened. 'You mustn't mind him, Inspector. He has his own ideas of humour. He must have his jokes whether they're good or bad.'

'They vary,' Rodney told the Inspector.

Meanwhile Everard assured them, 'The only crime I've committed today was to smash up a rather beautiful viaduct in the Ruhr.'

'Well . . . well . . . And I meant to be a delightful surprise for Grace. There's no chance of a division tonight, so I came home without a word.'

Grace was in no mood for this levity. 'The Inspector's come about Stan.' At once Rodney's face ceased to be a jester's; the facetiousness in his eyes yielded place to anxiety. 'Tell him all, Inspector.'

The Inspector retold his story while Rodney sat uncomfortably on the brink of the nearest chair.

Silence from all followed the end of the story. Then Rodney spoke. 'And of course my wife has told you we've seen nothing of him and heard nothing from him for over a year. You say he's done this before? Deserted?'

'Once before, sir. But "deserted" is too hard a word. Absence without leave is not desertion.'

'None the less the punishment can be stern in wartime?'

'Sometimes, sir.'

'He's on active service. Is it death for desertion?'

Grace loosed a small scream, and Rodney whose chair was near hers laid a consoling hand on one of hers. There could be no greater contrast, she thought, between the jester of seconds ago and this new, competent, clear-minded and resolutely objective speaker.

'There's not much of that sort of thing now, sir,' the Inspector comforted them. 'Not as there was in the First War. But if they choose to call it desertion, that's a court-martial for certain. Even then, if he was ready to confess to desertion, they'd talk him into pleading "Not Guilty", so that everything could be said in his favour.'

'And if it comes to a court-martial we could help him by instructing counsel and so on?'

'Most certainly, sir.'

'Well, you don't have to tell me, Inspector, that if we come to know anything, we'll have to help you, or we'd be liable to a conviction for aiding an absentee. That's so, isn't it?'

'More or less, sir. The best thing you could do, if he comes home, or you hear from him, would be to persuade him to surrender, so that he could be delivered at once into military custody without—' the Inspector tactfully dropped his eyes to the carpet—'without having to come before a magistrate's court. That would avoid all publicity.'

'Thank you for that reminder, Inspector. I can only promise you we'll do our duty whatever the consequences—'

('Will *I*? I don't know,' thought Grace. 'My son's more to me than any law.')

'One word from him, and his mother and I will beg him to surrender. But if we hear nothing, I imagine you're sure to find him in the end?'

'I think so, sir.'

'And if you do, you'll tell us, of course?'

'Of course, sir.'

The Inspector rose, declined a drink, and let Rodney escort him to the door, while Grace and Everard sat in silence.

Rodney, returning, said, 'It's good to have Everard here. No one knows Stan as well as he does. If only we could get in touch with him, I believe Everard would be the most likely to help. Stan always had such an affection for Ev.'

'Once, Dad, yes. Not now.'

'But you used to do everything together.'

'Once upon a time.'

'But he can't have lost all the common interests you and he had as boys together. You were inseparable.'

'Not without some truly imperial rows. But on the whole, yes.'

'He was a mass of affection at one time,' Grace put in. 'There must be a mass of good in him still, wherever he's got, whatever he's doing.'

'Of course there is,' said Rodney. 'And if only we could get him back on to the lines that are right for him—which probably means, if only we could get him out of the army . . .'

'But how ever could we do that?'

'I don't know . . . I don't know . . . A doctor, perhaps . . .'

'But physically there's nothing wrong with him,' Grace asserted indignantly. 'Nothing at all. He's always been in perfect health like Everard.'

'I didn't mean physically. Some sort of mental plea, perhaps . . .'

'There's nothing wrong with him mentally,' she insisted no less angrily.

'Oh, yes, there is. Which of us isn't a bit daft?' Obviously Rodney had decided that it would be better to speak cheerfully again. 'But we don't have the misfortune to be in the Army. There are places where it's no great handicap to be reasonably mad. The House is one.'

'And the R.A.F.' Everard took up his father's point. 'I'm sure I'm a little mad, but it doesn't matter in the Raf. If you've a touch of the rebel and the outcast in you, you can satisfy it

43

splendidly at 20,000 feet with the clouds all below you and the sun shining on you alone, or a million stars existing for you alone, and no sight of a damn-silly world anywhere. I fancy there's a vent for all sorts of neuroses in flying through tracer or diving and waltzing through curtains of flak. Dodging among the searchlights too—till your tail-gunner snuffs 'em out, which always seems to me a trifle unfair. And shooting down a Junker 88—that ought to heal up a lot. You may sweat with fear sometimes but it's Life. I can see no joy for poor old Stan in a regimental orderly room which was the last job they put him to. The funny thing is that the biggest spice of all is when it's all over and you know that their defences and their searchlights are all behind you, and you can do a few crazy turns for the joy of it which proves to you that however mad the world is, you're more than ready to go on living.'

'Oh, don't talk about these things,' Grace pleaded. 'Don't talk about them. I don't want to hear them.'

'But there they all are. And they're all part of the job. And I'm only telling you what's fine about them.'

Rodney, understanding his son, said thoughtfully, 'I suppose you mean that Stan would have been better fighting in Egypt than stuck in an Ack-Ack battery in Kent. Though there ought to be innumerable chances of fighting the enemy over Kent.'

'Not if they've made you a clerk in the orderly room. Time to walk out then. The sort of abysmally silly thing the Army would do. A dreary monotonous job in an office is the last place for a properly restless and rebellious type, such as our Stan has always been.'

'I *know*, I *know* what I'm going to do!' Rodney spoke as one on whom a light had just fallen. 'There's some sense in what Everard says, Grace. I'm going to talk it all over with Monty while we've got Everard here. I'll ring up Monty now.'

6

Monty Wiseman

Rodney counted Monty Weizmann one of his two best friends.
Dr. Gabriel Montefiore Weizmann, disliking his first name
because it suggested an attractive girl or, even more inaptly, an
archangel, begged his friends, if they loved him, to remember
his second name and call him Monty. Rodney did better than
this: having no German or Yiddish or whatever was the source
of 'Weizmann', and never certain how to pronounce it, he
adapted it to 'Wiseman', maintaining that this exactly defined
Monty, 'my mentor and most excellent witch-doctor. Monty
who had lived next door for the twenty years they'd occupied
their present large Victorian home, was only a third-generation
descendant of Jews who had fled from Russian pogroms in the
late nineties. Born in Britain, he had distinguished himself at
school and university, adding to his M.A. an M.D., an Sc.D.,
and a doctorate of psychological medicine; and he now prac-
tised solely as a psychiatrist in expensive Wigmore Street
chambers. Rodney always declared that, like many highly
civilized Jews, he had a 'velvet charm' towards all, whether
patients, friends or warm opponents; and if also, like many
second or third-generation Jews, he had contrived to amass
'lashings of money', he was more than generous, he was lavish,
in the disposing of it. Severely intellectual, he acceded to no
religion, styling himself, if sounded on the question, 'an unbelieving Jew', but since he went much of the way with the
psychoanalysts who based their practice on determinism, this
ensured that his attitude to all attained the utmost of Christian
pity; indeed, as he would say, 'if you believe that a man's
actions are largely determined for him, how can you be other
than all-pitying?'

He liked to live, wine, and dine richly, and, so far as it
was possible, he pursued this course in wartime, paying his

wine merchant enormous prices for 'under the counter' whiskies, brandies, wines and liqueurs. Rodney, while loving him, would often discuss with Grace how Monty's scruples differed from those of a Gentile: he seemed to find nothing wrong, if he was ready to pay the prices, in dealing with the 'under the counter' market, which he called the 'grey market' or 'twilight market', as distinct from the 'black market'. There was certainly some point between the grey and the black, between the dusk of the day and the darkness of night, which he would not overstep, but Rodney could never determine where this frontier lay.

A further point in which his Jewish temperament differed from the Anglo-Saxon seemed to be this: he had built himself a large, costly and massively secure shelter in his basement and slept in it regularly with his wife; whereas Rodney and Grace after the first few days of the war had never slept anywhere but in their usual second-floor bedroom.

An active Socialist, Monty had been a prominent supporter of the Republicans in the Spanish Civil War—so much so that, to his pride and pleasure, he learned that his name was on the Germans' list of 'anti-fascists' for whom they proposed an immediate liquidation on their arrival in Britain. Though delighted with this distinction, and even hanging in his consulting room a framed page from the list which included among the W's 'G. M. Weizmann', he yet had no desire for liquidation if it could be avoided. And when, after the fall of France in 1940 he believed—wholly unlike Rodney, unlike Everard, unlike Stanley (in those happier days for him) and partly unlike Grace who didn't know what to believe, but continued to organize her W.V.S. as thoroughly as if nothing new had happened—when he could but believe that Britain would admit defeat and sue for peace, he was on the point of transferring himself and his family to California so as to put all of an ocean and a continent between him and the Antisemites raging in Germany. But when, to his astonishment, Britain showed no intention of surrendering but rather declared her resolve to fight on alone; and when he learned that the King himself was practising with a revolver in Buckingham Palace so that, if it had to be, he could die fighting, Monty thought that the whole spirit was as magnificent as (in all probability) it was mad, and he cancelled all his Californian plans, so as to stay and support a country which he loved for its tolerance and for its welcome for all the outcasts and persecuted of the world. 'My God, if she's going to fight, I'll fight.' This proud statement he sometimes modified into 'My wife, Jessica, is one of Grace's heroic women and my daughters Ruthy and Maxy are joining the R.A.F. and brother Davy is in the Home Guard, so I reckon I'm doing my bit;' but, in fact, he supported Britain's lonely fight in every way open to him, just as he had supported the Republicans in Spain. This was a change of front not ignoble, Rodney thought, because he knew that Monty still supposed that Britain must be beaten in the end, and accordingly kept a couple of lethal pills for himself and Jessica to be used on the day the Germans arrived. As a doctor he had no difficulty in acquiring these pills, and he kept a further supply for any Jewish friends who might wish, when the hour came, to share this meal with him.

§

On an evening after Everard's return, he sat in his study with Rodney, Grace and Everard, Rodney having appealed to him as 'the one friend from whom they had no secrets'. He sat there, a short figure no taller than Rodney with plentiful black hair, a face unmistakably Hebraic and dark eyes brilliant with intelligence, laughter, and an affectionate, even eager, solicitude for the troubles of friends.

Jessica was not present; he had advised her to have occupations elsewhere.

'You want the truth from me, dear Rodney and Grace. And Everard too. Doesn't Everard look a gent in that new uniform? Congratulations, Ev. May I tell you all what I've been thinking for some time about Stanley?'

'That and nothing else,' said Rodney. 'You know how we trust you.'

'All right. Then let me say first that his trouble is more prevalent than most people realize. And I fear that the Army'll be the last people to know anything about it. And that as long as they're busy with the war, they'll have little time to know anything about it.'

'Exactly what I said. More or less,' Everard reminded them.

Grace intervened. 'But there was nothing wrong with him in the old days as a boy or a young man. He and Everard were two happy boys together. Both of them always well and always lively.'

'True enough, Grace dear. Often boisterously lively, as youths should be. But all that tallies with what I'm suspecting. The thing of which I'm speaking usually appears in boyhood, but it can strike late.'

Grace was hardly heeding Monty. 'And like Everard,' she went on, 'he got a good exhibition to Oxford, and, like him, they both joined up when war was declared. Always they used to do everything together.'

'All of which fits my picture, Grace. You say it was only two years ago during the alarms of 1940 that he began to withdraw into a kind of self-isolation and to be moody and depressed.'

'Not because he was afraid,' Grace hastened to declare. 'He's always been as fearless as Everard.'

'Which isn't saying much,' Everard murmured. 'Not over Essen and the Ruhr. Not over Unterfeld last Thursday.'

Rodney said, 'We knew it was nothing to do with the war. We just thought of it as exhaustion and a nervous breakdown.'

'A nervous breakdown it is, but a very true one, not the imaginary thing we all like to think we're suffering from. The patient turns inward and gives all his emotions to himself, abandoning interest in the realities around him. He lives with day-dreams in which all his unattained ambitions are gloriously fulfilled——'

'But that's me,' Rodney interrupted. 'That's me to the life. I'm not a case, am I? I don't walk out and disappear—however much Grace might wish I would.'

'Don't be idiotic,' said Grace.

'Of course there's a touch of this in us all, but most of us are the captains on our bridges and manage to steer our ships through troubling waters. But what happens when the Captain comes down from his bridge and locks himself up in his cabin alone?'

'And that's what you think Stanley has done?' It was Rodney who spoke.

Monty softened his answer. 'Yes. But I don't think it's his fault.'

'But isn't it strange, Monty, that two twin brothers should be so different?'

'I don't think they're so different. They were both boys who showed high ability at school and college—if Everard will allow me to say this——'

'I certainly will, sir; and thank you.'

'—and this kind of dislocation of the personality—Stanley's trouble, as I see it—often appears in young people of exceptional intelligence. But Everard's job in the R.A.F. happens to fit him well, while Stanley's doesn't fit him at all.'

'Isn't that just what I said, Mum,' Everard demanded. 'After the war I'll be a psychiatrist.'

Rodney interrupted, 'But the first symptoms of a tendency to "desert" showed themselves before the war started. In his third term at Oxford he began to cut lectures and neglect all work and shut himself up alone. There was some trace of the old Stanley when he walked out of Oxford and joined up with Everard——'

'But not a trace the first time he came on leave,' Grace hastily interjected. 'He was like some strange new creature then.'

'How?' Monty asked.

'So silent. So shut in. So uninterested in any of us. Even in Everard.'

Monty nodded. 'Exactly. And the shame of it is that all the time he looks big and strong—as Everard does—so people just dub his aloofness and his slacking as no more than laziness and loafing and bad manners. They know nothing about it. People with this peculiar mental disturbance get precious little sympathy.'

'Certainly none in the Army,' said Everard.

'And all too little in the eyes of the Law. Desertion is desertion and a crime, and there's an end of it. How can they see in a fine, strapping, normal-looking lad what may be at work within him. They only ridicule us who provide excuses for such behaviour. You've got to be physically ill to get the sympathy. I can see what happened in his battery. They detected a new carelessness and incompetence and bungling in him, and some bright M.O. decided he was only fit for clerical work and best kept away from the guns.'

'Whereupon he walked out,' said Everard.

A general silence, till Rodney asked, 'But, Monty, what can be done for the boy? What can *we* do?'

Monty thought for a while, twisting the glass with its generous tot of grey-market whisky. 'A recovery in time is possible,' he foretold at last. 'But only if there's infinitely patient treatment and drugs are properly administered. I can't see him getting any such treatment in the Army. It'll be just "medicine and duty" there. They don't easily listen to anybody like me. They laugh at us psychiatrists calling us "trick-cyclists", which was never a good pun and is now an abominably tedious one.'

'I know, I know,' Rodney agreed; 'I've heard the P.M. himself in the Smoking Room say, "I suggest we restrict as much as possible the work of these gentlemen"—that means you, Monty— "because they're capable of doing an immense amount of harm with their activities which so easily degenerate into charlatanry".'

'Yes, Rod, that's the view of all too many. Our P.M. is often the voice of the people. And I must say I've not much faith in a mental hospital for lads with the trouble I see in Stanley.'

'And anyhow he'd desert,' Everard put in.

'For sure. No, the best place for him would probably be with his family if they could be infinitely patient. It wouldn't be easy, but it's the only thing.'

'His home is waiting for him,' said Grace.

And Rodney endorsed, 'We're here to help him at whatever cost. But, Monty, there are psychiatrists in the Army, aren't there? Some of high rank. Couldn't you get in touch with one of them?'

Monty laughed satirically. 'Oh yes, there are psychiatrists

serving as consultants in all the services, with the rank of brigadiers and commodores and air-commodores. Some may be good enough, but all too soon most of them, in my view, take the colour of their messes and call Stanley's trouble mere malingering. But perhaps I'm unfair to them. There's always been a notable *odium theologicum* among us psychiatrists; we're just as much split into schisms and sects as the churches are, each with its own prophet, its Luther or Calvin or Wesley, and some with its own sacred books like the holy writ of Freud or Jung. In Everard's R.A.F. things are probably better. I believe they listen to psychiatrists there. I'll do what I can, Rodney, where I can. But you'll have to give me time. To get anything done in peace time is difficult enough; in war time and in the Army it'll probably take months and months. The Army's mills grind slowly, and I doubt if they'll ever grind small enough to find Stanley's trouble. But we'll hope, dear Grace; we'll hope. I'll do all I can.'

So Monty talked with them, but not once had he given to Stanley's trouble the harsh-sounding and unnecessarily frightening name, *dementia precox*, a blend of psychoses, appearing sometimes in youth, which in his secret view defined it.

7

Among the Orchards

It was a Thursday, some weeks later, and about ten in the morning when a tall young man in khaki battledress was walking along a hedge-bound lane between apple orchards in Kent. Except for the unkempt hair and the blue, unshaven chin it would have been difficult for a stranger to distinguish Gunner Merriwell from his brother, the pilot officer. His height was the same, his dark hair the same, his features the same. Only the life in his eyes was different; it seemed to be dulled into a total self-preoccupation and a total misanthropy. Everard's air-force battle-dress when he returned home was slack enough, but this khaki battle-dress of Stanley's was so crumpled, disarrayed and stained that one might have supposed him to have been lately crouching in some muddy trench or crawling along some sodden battlefield.

Today he had nothing of Everard's quick and lively walk; Stanley's walk between the hedges was furtive and apprehensive as he came from this narrow lane to the corner of Pine Wood Road. Here he stopped abruptly because he could see, three hundred yards away, the Pine Wood gun-site. He waited here guiltily with his eyes on the gun-site gates. It was Tess's 'day-out'. He was waiting there for Tess—Private Christie of the A.T.S. Should anyone but Tess come out of the gates and walk towards him he had his cover at hand. Beside him was the gateway into the well-timbered garden of a small mansion, whose family had left it empty because of the bombing in these eastern areas of Kent. Strangely they had gone to London for greater safety; the Blitz on London was now two years in the past, and the judge, his wife and daughter decided they would be safer in his Temple chambers than in these fields so near a gun-site. The house stood blinded and empty in its timbered garden. So, if any undesired person—say a soldier from the gun-site—appeared in the road, Stanley could dodge through the gateway and be screened by the mansion or by the bole of some huge forest tree.

No need for such evasion so far. Pine Wood Road stayed empty. He waited and waited by that garden gate, growing more and more impatient. He beat a foot, he beat his fingers on the gate-post. He muttered to himself and cursed.

In this long maddening wait his mind wandered over the last weeks since he'd absented himself from his Battery 917 in Claverton Fields. The battery was only eight miles from where he now waited, so he stood in danger of discovery. At first after deserting from the camp he had sought to hide himself in the swarming jungle of London, for he had plenty of money in his pocket, his father being generous to his sons, but since he had no ration book the money had drained quickly away into the tills of cheap eating-houses and the coffers of dubious hotels. So he had come back to this dangerous area for two reasons: one, because he knew that in these autumn weeks he could earn money as a fruit-picker in the orchards; the other because he longed, longed, for Tess's body and caresses, she being the only creature in the world for whom he felt affection or desire. There was no more dangerous step he could have taken, but like his brother he had an appetite for risks and challenges, and now, unlike his brother, he had a sense of hostility and defiance towards all men.

About the money there was no difficulty at all; it might be only ten shillings a day, but this was his for the taking from any farmer, since the fruit had to be gathered; and the workers were few in these wartime days. A farmer asked no questions; an applicant in khaki might be a Home Guard, a soldier lent by the Army for the fruit harvest, or even—but why ask questions?—one of the many soldiers 'on the loose'. In the last two weeks Stanley had fruit-picked at Duncan Holt Farm, at Wash Green Farm, and at 'Whitfields', working four or five days at each, and then leaving one for another because he had taken a dislike to the farmer, to some of his fellow-workers, or to them all.

But a wage of only ten shillings a day meant that he must

53

make a free bed for himself wherever possible: among the hay-stacks on fine nights, and when the rain was falling, in a distant and disused shed on Farmer Wakeman's meadow. He needed all his money for meals in the cafés, and for an occasional visit to a cinema or restaurant with Tess. A girl expected such things.

Tess was an orderly in the officers' mess at Pine Wood Camp, and he had got to know her during the three months when he was attached to the site. She was twenty, a brunette with brilliant brown eyes and a long-legged, graceful figure so that she was only a few inches shorter than he. This was a girl of far more formidable character than Jeanie Lynn who was his brother's choice and comfort. And of late, as this new over-whelming moodiness had withdrawn him more and more from his fellows she had become more and more his single refuge and occasional spring of pleasure. The daughter of a grocer in South London, she had been proud to have for her 'boy-friend' the son of an M.P., even though he was only a private like her-self, and it was not long before she was ready to lay herself down for him wherever a solitude might be found. This possession and enjoyment of Tess in empty orchard or garden had been a brief and fugitive healing, like a drug, from the strange and bitter apathy that now enveloped him.

At last—there she was: standing in the road outside the camp's gateway; standing there in her khaki uniform which was as spruce as his was dishevelled and dirtied—but an unexpected thing happened. She looked up the road, saw him as he walked towards her, and immediately turned away to walk in the opposite direction—to walk fast as if to escape him. He ran and came abreast of her.

'Here! What the hell? Tess, what're you doing? You saw me.'

No response at first. She walked straight on, as quickly as before, or quicker.

'Tess, what's the matter? What's happened?'

'I've told Bombardier Crabtree all about you, and he said it wasn't safe for me to be carrying on with you any more. He said it might get me into trouble.'

'But why the devil did you say anything to him? You swore you'd say nothing to anyone. And, anyhow, what the hell's he got to do with us?'

'He's a friend, and I had to ask someone. I was getting worried about meeting you.'

'Good God, if you've been and told him, he may report me. Have you thought of that?'

'He won't do that because he says it'd involve me in trouble.'

'He's as fond of you as all that, is he?' Stanley could walk as fast as she. He kept pace with her, almost as if he must do this or lose her. 'Is he all that mixed up with you?'

'He's my friend.'

'And how much does that mean? This is something new to me. How much? How much?' Of a sudden he knew that he was suffering a heart-pain beyond anything he'd known before. So sudden was the attack, so complete the fear of losing his only comfort and drug, that it felt like some ultimate pain in the heart. 'Tess, how much? How much?'

'It's nothing new. He's been my friend for a long time.'

'Then why have you never mentioned him to me before?'

'Why should I?'

'Listen, young woman. I know what "friend" can sometimes mean. Does it . . .' he could hardly force himself to ask it . . . 'Does it mean he's been your lover same as I have?'

'I'm not going to answer that question.'

'Oh, yes, you are.' He seized her arm with a fierce quivering grip, arresting her walk and his. He forced her to halt and stand still. He grasped the other arm and held her in front of him. Her refusal to answer had surely been the answer Yes. 'Have you let him?'

She tried to drag herself away, but his two gripping hands were like two vices of steel and clawed. 'You don't go, Private Tess Christie, till you tell me every damn thing.'

Fear of him stood in her eyes. 'Well, if you must know, yes, I have.' And she repeated defiantly, 'I have.'

At these words his hands fell from her, their power strained away by a sick and helpless despair. The only words that came from him were simple. 'I never knew this . . . I thought you were mine only.'

Some part of his brain told him it was absurd that these should seem to him like words from a death-bed, but such they seemed. Only now did he know how dependent his sick heart had been on the comfort of her body and her apparent love which at times had been so fierce and impassioned in its response.

Freed from his grasp, she began to walk on and away from him, but he instantly caught up with her and was walking at her side. 'I can't believe that this has been going on while we have been lovers together. I thought you loved me. You always acted as if you did. You always seemed full of love.'

'I did like you a lot and I was sorry for you because you seemed unhappy. I could see that you were often suffering and hoped I could help you a bit.'

'Oh, it was only pity, was it?' He scoffed at her, 'It seemed a good deal more than that at times. God in his mercy, and I was mad enough to come back here because I thought your love was real! But all the time you'd just been playing about with me. I suppose I've only just learnt what a whore is. Are you just playing about with him?'

'Weren't *you* playing about with me?' she demanded furiously.

'Yes, if you like; but with you only. You may not believe it but there was no one else. No one else in the world I cared for.'

Now, in spite of his deliberately violent insult something of affection and pity crept into her words. 'There are plenty of other girls, Stan. You can find someone nicer than me.'

'But I didn't want any other. This means you're never going to see me again, I suppose?'

'Yes. Yes, it does. I'm afraid it does. You see, Dicky's talking about marrying me, and he really means it, I think. But he insists that for all our sakes I must give up meeting you.'

'I might have married you.'

'Oh no, you wouldn't. Your parents wouldn't have allowed that.'

'I pay no attention to them. I go my own way.'

'Well, there's nothing we can do about it. Dicky says you can go to prison for aiding an absentee and I could never have got away with the story that I didn't know you were a deserter.'

'Oh, yes, everything that Dick says is now God's truth for you. And what's he but a twopenny-halfpenny barrack room lawyer?'

'No, don't be silly, Stan. Whether he's right or wrong, you must see I'm not going to risk prison for anyone.'

They were now approaching the end of Pine Wood Road where it ran into the main highway. And as they drew near the corner a bus came into view and stopped at the bus-stop, a few passengers alighting from it. Tess rushed towards it as a means of escape from him, and he called after her, 'Where are you going? Tess, where are you going?'

'Into Maidstone.'

'What for?' She had leapt on to the conductor's platform and now had a foot on the stairs. 'To enjoy myself, I suppose. What else? Good-bye.'

'Enjoy yourself? With whom . . .? Tess . . .'

But the bus had started again and carried her away. Fingers fumbling together, Stanley stood at the corner, watching the bus till it was out of sight. 'That's what a whore is... a whore.... Do I put up with this . . .? God, I don't think I do . . . No, I'm damned if I do. She doesn't know *me*.'

§

From that day, fascinated by a pain almost unbearable, and so seeking it, he watched and waited for a sight of her at the hours when he believed she might emerge from the camp. After his working hours in an orchard were finished at six he would hurry, even run to the corner from which he spied down the Pine Wood Road. This tossing aside of him by Tess, who'd been his one fugitive healing, left him with a final hatred of all men and all life. He now imprisoned himself within himself, never speaking to anyone if speech could be avoided, and half longing for death—dreaming of it—as the only imaginable substitute for that girl's false love—what else was there any-where? His only pleasure—if pleasure it could be called—was

E   57 this brooding on his wrong, and his only avid interest was to angle for these glimpses of her that would pour their vitriol into his wound.

One evening, peeping from his end of the road, he saw her come out with three other girls and walk to the distant bus-stop. A second time, a Thursday and her 'day-out', he saw her emerge alone and walk to the bus-stop. Only the third time, soon after six in the evening, did he see her come out with Bombardier Crabtree, their fingers linked and their hands swinging happily. Here was the pain he sought because it was unbearable. And it was more than he sought because they turned towards his point of observation, so that he was obliged to withdraw from the corner and peep from there. And he saw her lead him with loving fingers into the timbered garden of the empty mansion and away behind it—to the very place which he himself had found and chosen for their hidden love together. His fists clenched, the nails driving into the palms, as he stood there and tormented himself by imagining her now in the possession of another man, there where she used to be his, among the great forest trees. With mouth grimly set, teeth biting his underlip, he vowed that next time she came from the camp alone he'd ease this heart's-death by unloading his wrath on her again. 'She doesn't know *me.*'

§

Nine days after that parting by the bus-stop Police Constable Leaver, walking along Wash Green Road, saw a soldier come out of a lane and begin to walk towards him. The man's uniform was bedraggled enough to arouse some wonder, and a sudden suspicion was stirred by the man's abrupt halt, as if he'd a mind to turn back at the sight of a policeman. But apparently he decided to walk on with a parade of carelessness, as if a young policeman passing by was of no interest to him. Perhaps he was the more ready to do this since P.C. Leaver knew well that his own face looked all too young and fresh for his smart new uniform and peaked cap: it was not a year since he'd been a cadet. And now they were approaching one another.

P.C. Leaver's suspicion heightened. Had they not all been

under instructions for weeks to look out for a gunner who'd 'gone absent' from Battery 917 in Claverton Fields? Of course it seemed ridiculous to suppose that a deserter who'd been absent from his unit for weeks would still be in its neighbourhood. Wouldn't he try to merge himself among the millions of some city far away? But this dishevelled and stubble-chinned soldier—it *could* be the bloke. He was young, tall, and dark, as the description said. Some interest had been added to the search for this missing gunner by the information that, though still of the lowest rank, he was a Member of Parliament's son. It'd be fine to be the constable who had found and arrested so interesting a deserter; and, moreover, there were arrangements under the law whereby the justices could recommend a reward to any police officer who apprehended a deserter. A small reward, only five or ten shillings if the soldier was in uniform and apprehended near his quarters. Still a dollar was worth having and a commendation by the justices worth more. But, Lord, the whole country was full of soldiers young, tall, and dark. Probably all this was only a pleasant dream that would vanish with the first words spoken by the man.

He stood before him. 'Morning, mate. Sorry, but I got to ask questions of people. Got to do my job same as you do yours. May I know who you are and where you're coming from?'

There was a second of hesitation—perhaps two seconds—before the man answered. 'You can certainly know all you want to know. My unit is Battery 917, but, as a matter of fact, I've just come from Mr. Wakeman's at Buckmead Farm, where I've been working for him, fruit-picking. There are a lot of us doing it.'

P.C. Leaver observed at once that this was a 'gent's voice'—what he called a 'la-di-da voice'. It could well be the voice of an M.P.'s son. Excitement touched his heart. Was this really the mysterious deserter?

'What? Finished your job at hah-past ten? Must be a soft job, or have you been at it all night?'

'I was at it yesterday and I slept at the farm. Quite a lot of us soldiers are helping with the fruit harvest,' he repeated.

'I know that, guv'nor. May I see your pay-book and papers?'

'To hell, why?'

'Because I'm authorized to do so when I think I oughter.'

The gunner fetched his pay-book from a breast-pocket and said indifferently, 'There you are. I can't suppose it'll be of any interest to you. But take what you want from it.'

P.C. Leaver looked at the soldier's name and number, and the excitement lit up in his head like a shaft of sunlight in a shadowy room. 'I'm afraid it's of the greatest interest, mate.' And he dropped into a constable's official manner. 'We've reason to believe that you've been an absentee from your battery for several weeks.'

'True enough,' said the gunner with his gentlemanly drawl. 'But actually I'm now in the process of returning to my unit.'

'You ain't going in the direction of Pine Wood.'

'Obviously not, since my battery happens to be in Claverton Fields.'

'So it is, guv; but I'm afraid you'll have to come to the station first.'

'Oh, well . . . if that's the way, let it ride. Which damned police station?'

'Our chief copper-house, of course. Croome City.'

'All right. As you say, you've got to do your duty. This is an arrest, I suppose?'

'Yes, guv'nor. 'Fraid so. As far as it goes.'

'Oh, well, lead on. I don't much care what happens at the station, one way or the other.'

'I expect the Chief Inspector will want to have a talk with you.'

'I see. And what then?'

'Then I suppose we'll either have to bring you up before the beaks or hand you back to your unit.'

The man shrugged helplessly—or, rather, heedlessly—and they walked back together in the opposite direction from which the constable had come, he more delighted to be the one who had found the deserter than his native decency would allow him to show. He saw to it that they talked together as a pair of strangers might, walking the same way. It was all of two miles out of the country roads and into the heart of Croome City, and so far as P.C. Leaver was concerned, this was the most satisfying walk in his brief career. But he tried to make friendly conversation with his prisoner. No easy task, for the man tended to be moody and silent for long spells, even though, apart from a strange trembling now and then, he seemed indifferent to all that was happening to him. When addressed, his answers came readily enough, though fragmented at times by stammerings and catches in the throat. In answer to his studiously amiable companion, he described life at the battery, at Pine Wood gunsite, and in the orchards among the fruit pickers.

At the station P.C. Leaver, on the instructions of a station sergeant, led his prisoner to a cell and parted amiably from him, seeing no need, since he had some sympathy with runaway soldiers, 'to be beastly to him'. He said, 'We shall have to store you in here safely for the time being, mate. Just till they send an escort for you, the sergeant says.'

'When will that be?' asked the man, sitting down on the rough mattressed bunk, and sighing as he saw the white-tiled walls, the w.c. pan in the corner, and the high window with its panes of heavily protected glass.

'Almost at once, I expect. We shall be getting in touch with your battery.'

'What will the escort be?'

'Probably just a bombardier and a gunner.'

'All right. Let them get on with it. Here I am; for them to do what they like with.'

'You've had your breakfast, have you?'

'No, as a matter of fact, I haven't. I came straight from where I was sleeping. I was going to get something when you met me.'

'What a pity I met you! Well, I'll bring you a cup of char and a cheese sandwich. Will that do?'

'Thank you. But I can do without it, if it's any trouble.'

'Don't you do without it. Get from the Government all you can. I'll bring it in half-a-mo.'

But P.C. Leaver had hardly clicked the cell door shut when Detective Sergeant Gowers, a detective old and grey in the business, came through a door into the cell corridor. 'Come,' he

61

ordered. They passed through this door that shut off all the cells and, clicking it behind them, stood, so to say, in the world of the free. 'We don't want him hearing nothing,' the Sergeant explained with something that might be called enthusiasm but was certainly excitement. 'Here! The Chief's quite a lot interested in the boy you got there. Wants him for interrogation right away. Could be you've brought off a more sensational arrest than you thought for, my young feller. Could be you've been lucky on your very first year. Quite a nice break for a young blue-bottle like you.'

'Why? Why, Sarge?'

'Wait a minute. Could be you've copped someone much more interesting than you know. What's a deserter these days? Ten a penny.'

'You mean he's an M.P.'s son?'

'Nah!' The Sergeant tossed this idea away from him contemptuously. 'What's an M.P.'s son? Hundreds and hundreds of them. Cheap as daisies. Forget it. And now tell me all about this bloke. What was his attitude when you nabbed him?'

'Well, not all that pleased at first, natcherly. I seen happier guys, but I can imagine 'em a sight unhappier. He soon accepted the fact that he was properly knocked off, and more or less shrugged his shoulders over it. He said something like, "Oh, well, there it is."'

'But he talked a bit as he came along?'

'Not much more than answering me decently as a gentleman should: he's every inch a gentleman. But I wouldn't say he was in love with life by any means. Natcherly after being knocked off by a lousy cop, so that he could be court-martialled and given months in the glasshouse, he was a bit mumpish with the world in general. But not with me. He was matey enough with me. I quite liked him.'

'You did, did-jer? Well it'll probably interest you to know that he may be a——'

'A what?'

'Well it's only a guess. But this cove was the boy-friend of a girl who was done in last night. We've identified her as an

A.T.S. private from Pine Wood, and Bill Sams has brought back a tidy packet of information from other girls there.'

'Done in? How done in?'

'Stabbed.'

'Hell, where?'

'In an orchard where they found her about two hours ago.'

'But are you suggesting this chap done anyone in? He never stabbed no one, or I'm a Dutchman. He's a bit depressed and fed up with the world, but a decent bloke in his way.'

The sergeant shrugged and lifted empty hands. 'Of course I'm not saying anything's certain. It's only that the girls say he and she had long been sweethearts and that she chucked him for a bombardier. The bombardier agrees and says he warned her against having anything more to do with him, being as he was a deserter. So she sent him about his business. At least there's a motive there. But you never know. She may have had other boys and done the dirty on them. She certainly had two going on at the same time, the bombardier and your friend.'

'Yes, but, Sarge, this chap's the son of an M.P. He's not one of your violent types.'

'Hah do we know? What's he doing, going absent and sleeping rough in haystacks and outhouses?'

'The poor bugger had nowhere else to go. Things aren't too easy for a deserter. Deserter or not, he's a gentleman. I'd say he was Oxford or Cambridge or something posh like that. A bit la-di-da, you know. Gor lummy, we'd be kep' busy if every gentleman who's had the go-by from his girl-friend decides to do her in.'

'All the same, there's something exceptional about him. He was known as "Misery" among his mates in his last days at the battery.'

'Was he ever violent with any of 'em?'

'No. Not a bit. It was just that he never spoke to anyone. The only person he was seen in a rage with was this girl; and that's interesting. Seems he come back to these parts because he was missing the girl.'

'A pretty daft thing to do.'

'Yepp; unless he'd persuaded himself that his battery had

forgotten all about him. He comes back, and nothing can alter the fact that the poor girl checked out of her camp at six or so last night and was due back at half-past ten, but she never booked in at the guard room and was marked absent. Another gunner fancies he saw your boy with the girl at about ten o'clock. But the road was very dark then under the trees and he admits that, knowing he had been her boy, he might have imagined this. Certainly it was a tall figure but also it was some way from where she was found in the orchard. You can see why the guv'nor wants to know exactly what his movements were last night. Better fetch him along.'

'But I've just promised to take the poor blighter a cup of tea and a bite of something to eat. Can't I give him that first?'

'Yes, give him that and then yank him along.'

'Okay, Sarge; but you'll find it difficult to persuade me that this pretty decent sort of fellow had anything to do with a murder. I'll stake my boots that he never stabbed no one.'

8

The Alamein Bells

The report of a young A.T.S. girl found murdered in a Kent orchard earned no great place in the newspapers that evening or the next morning. The War had provided events of far larger interest, worthy of the tall headlines and the long inches of space. Grace sat alone in their large drawing-room which was their cosiest and favourite living room, reading for a brief hour their *Daily Telegraph*. The lead story of the day told how the greatest force of heavy bombers ever launched in daylight from British fields, more than a hundred B 17 Flying Fortresses and B 24 Liberators, had showered bombs by the hundred thousand from high levels on steel and locomotive works in the Lille area of France, while five hundred Allied fighters had made diversionary raids on a hundred-and-fifty-mile front from Dieppe to the Dutch islands. 'Four of the bombers are missing.'

Oh, of course it was wrong to feel this happy relief that Liberators and Flying Fortresses were American bombers, and that if the Allied fighters included some British, they could not number Everard among them, for he was in Bomber Command; utterly selfish and wrong, but how could one do anything else? One could only make amends for this momentary pleasure (it was hardly less) in the loss of other young men than one's own son, by dropping the paper to her lap and praying (though she pretended to no religion) 'Oh God, let some of them be safe. Safe as prisoners of war to return to their mothers one day.' And to this she added, 'Keep Everard safe. And Stanley too.'

Sighing for the easiness of this escape from selfishness, she picked up the paper again. And almost at once, like a punishment, her eyes fell on a smaller headline, '*Daylight Attack by R.A.F.*' This was a surprise because she had understood that the British bombed by night, and the Americans by day. 'Daylight attacks were made by aircraft of Bomber Command yesterday on several places in Western Germany more than a hundred miles inland from the Dutch frontier. Two bombers and three fighters are missing.' Two only, and the British had thousands of bombers now. Then the odds were thousands to one that Everard's plane was not involved. So do not worry. But here was the selfishness again, so she prayed again to the God she could not believe in, 'Grant that some of them may be safe as prisoners of war. Everard too if he is among——'

But here was something happier to read. '*Good news of the Harvest*. The Minister of Agriculture announced in the House yesterday that the total tillage under crops had advanced in one year from nearly nine million acres to fourteen and a half million. The only acreage that had neither increased nor decreased was that under fruit.' This had little interest for her, and her eyes passed quickly from it leaving only the thought that Rodney, who was in the House yesterday, must have sat listening to this—if he hadn't, as seemed more likely, got up and left the Chamber, for he always said that, as a 'sadly limited urban production', he was disgustingly ignorant of, and lacked all interest in, agriculture. It was while she was thinking this that her eye picked up a brief paragraph low down on the opposite page. Extraordinary, she thought, how often, if one's thoughts had been directed to a subject seldom considered, or perhaps never known before, someone referred to it almost at once or it leapt out of a paper to catch one's eye. '*Mystery of a Girl's Body Found in a Kent Orchard*. Yesterday the body of a young private in the Auxiliary Territorial Service was found by fruit-pickers in one of the Kent orchards where the fruit harvest is being gathered. Foul play is suspected because the girl appears to have been stabbed. A man is helping the police with their enquiries.'

'Thank heaven they've got the murderer,' she thought, for Grace always assumed that the man in the hands of the police was the guilty man. Normally she was too impatient to treat him as innocent till time should prove him guilty.

Her mind passed quickly from this. It stirred no memory of

Stanley who, morose and silent, had never told them that his gun-site was among the orchards. And it seemed but a small matter, this one poor body added to the hundreds lying dead in factories and homes after these raids on France and Germany, and the hundreds of young airmen—British, American, and German—who, as the days went by, were being gathered up, burned or smashed to death, from the wheatfields or pastures on which they had fallen.

§

A morning, three days later; Rodney and Grace were seated in their small breakfast room, idling with newspapers and talk over a late breakfast, when they heard a ring on the front-door bell, and the steps of their old Irish maid, Patricia Corrigan, going along the hall to answer it. Both, listening, heard her voice in conversation with a man's. She came in. 'There's a policeman at the door, ma'am, and he says he'd like a word with the Master.'

'What, a policeman again?' laughed Rodney. 'Lord, what have we done now? Show him in, Pat.'

'But he said he kind of wanted to speak to you alone, sir.'

'Me alone? Must be something the mistress has done. Or you. Have you been up to anything lately, Pat?'

She laughed dutifully. 'No, sir.'

'Then it must be Cook. Yes, it might well be Cook. I can easily imagine it's Cooky. She's been on a shop-lifting spree. Tell her I'll go bail for her up to a thousand. Or you'll have to cook for us, Pat, and Lord save us from that. But not more than a thousand. I am but a poor man. What sort of policeman is he?'

'I should think he's an awfficer, sir. He looks more than an ordinary policeman. Very smart . . . like.'

Grace ventured, 'Could it be that nice Inspector again, Roddy?' Her mind had leapt at the idea that he might be bringing news about Stanley, but she couldn't speak of this in front of her maid.

'Tall?' asked Rodney.

'Yes, quite as tall as Master Everard or Master Stanley.'

67

'With gloves? Did he carry in his hand a pair of brown gloves that have never been worn in this life, and never will be—gloves carried just for show?'

'I think he did, sir.'

'Then he's probably our Inspector. Leave him to me, Pat.' And he went from the room into the hall while Patricia returned to the kitchen.

In the hall, tall and smart with gloves in his hand, stood Inspector Garrett. 'Good to see you again, Inspector. What can we do for you now?'

'I thought I ought to tell you, sir, that your son, Gunner Merriwell, has been found and of course—inevitably—arrested by the Kent police.'

'As a deserter?'

'No, no. Only as an absentee. Nothing more than that. I don't know if you would wish Mrs. Merriwell to know all the facts.'

'She'll have to know them in time. Best come in, Inspector, and let her hear all. You'll find us at a lazy breakfast. After all, it *is* Monday morning.'

He brought the Inspector into the room. 'A friend you will recognize, Grace. With news of Stanley. Nothing too bad. Actually she guessed it was you, Inspector. Do sit down. You look rather enormous, standing there.'

The Inspector having sat himself sideways at the foot of the table, told them, with some sympathetic hesitations, that Stanley had been arrested four mornings ago, held in custody for four days, and then handed over to the military the previous afternoon.

'But . . . Inspector . . .' Rodney, seeing the distress and dismay in Grace's eyes, concealed that his own heart was sinking, and probed for information that might bring some comfort to her. 'You told us the other day that if he was found by the police, he would be delivered at once into military custody. Why was he held for four days?'

From Grace, spoken in shocked tones, came the words, 'Four days in a police cell? Stanley four days in a *cell?*'

'I suppose so, madam.'

68

'But why?' she demanded.

Rodney echoed her. 'Why?'

The Inspector remained silent for a few seconds. He seemed reluctant to answer. His eyes had turned away, and his fingers beat upon the table. Rodney surmised at once that he knew more than he wanted to divulge. When at last he spoke it was to say, 'In the nature of things our information is limited. What little we've been told will probably surprise you. It seems that your son has been, as they say, "sleeping rough" for a fortnight or more in the vicinity of his battery.'

'Sleeping rough?' Grace frowned, bewildered by the phrase.

'Sleeping in the open air or in sheds, madam. While he earned enough money for his food in the orchards around.'

Stunned into a kind of gaping silence, neither Grace nor Rodney could speak at first, till Grace, speaking mainly to herself, bewailed, 'Oh, I don't know what's happened to him—what's come over him. He never used to be like this'; and Rodney managed to ask, 'But why on earth should he stay for weeks in the neighbourhood of his battery, where he was almost certain to be picked up? He must have been mad.'

Inspector Garrett just shrugged in an equal surprise. 'Perhaps he had no money to go elsewhere. It looks like it, since he was sleeping rough.'

'But there's such a thing as hitch-hiking. And, anyhow, is it a crime to sleep rough?'

'No sir, but it so happened that a serious crime had just been committed in that neighbourhood—an unhappy coincidence, no doubt—and inevitably the police want to interrogate all who've been near the scene of the crime, and of course your son, as bad luck would have it, had been behaving—shall we say?—somewhat irregularly.' To this he added quickly, 'But the fact that they handed him over after a few days showed that they had no evidence against him.'

'I should think *not*,' muttered Grace. Not for a moment had she associated this story with a small paragraph she'd read three days before.

'What was the crime?' asked Rodney.

'It looks like a murder. Of a local girl.' The Inspector supplied no more.

And Grace only pursued her angry protest. 'Four days in a cell like a convicted criminal. Just because he'd been sleeping in the open instead of in a house. My son is no murderer.'

'By God, he isn't,' said Rodney.

'No,' the Inspector agreed. 'It's just that they have to suspect everyone more or less till they're sure they're on the wrong tack. They'd treat him fairly enough while they kept him. Obviously they found they had nothing to charge him with. And in any case we're not allowed to keep a suspect in custody for more than four days without charging him in a magistrates' court. So it's plain'—he repeated the previous words for their comfort—'they found nothing they could charge him with. They had nothing against him except that he was an absentee.'

'And what now?' Rodney asked. 'He's in the hands of the military. What follows? Will there be a court-martial?'

'Only if his C.O. decides that his summary powers are not enough to deal with the case, which I don't think is likely. A C.O., you see, can only award a punishment of up to twenty-eight days detention. A court-martial could do much more, and commit him to a civil prison.'

'Then the charge will be "absent without leave", you say. Not "desertion".'

'So I should suspect, sir, since "desertion", as I told you, would involve all the heavy paraphernalia of a court-martial, and with the many hundreds of absentees in the country, no one's very keen on a court-martial for any particular one of them. At least, that's what I should think, sir.'

'Shall we know what the C.O. has decided?'

'Only if it *did* come to a court-martial. You won't be troubled if it's a mere detention. But I myself will undertake to keep you informed so far as I can. My Chief Inspector is in touch with the Chief Constable at Croome City, which is where they are investigating—where they held him at first.'

§

They heard nothing more from their friendly Inspector and

so concluded that Stanley's commanding officer had contented himself with the maximum twenty-eight days, or less. They did not dare to write to the C.O. because they knew that neither of their two independent sons liked any interference from parents in his career. Either of them, at twenty-one, could be very sour if any such meddling was attempted. When nearly all of the twenty-eight days had passed without news Grace was able to think that Stanley was now free of his detention (whatever that implied) or about to be free. Nor in those twenty-odd days did any dreaded telegram come to report that Everard was 'missing'. So Grace was able to think that Everard must have returned safely from any raids and nearly completed his second tour of operations.

It was now the twenty-third of these silent days, and again they were sitting at breakfast with their newspapers open before them. And today large excited headlines glared at them: '*Greatest News of the War*'. At last after three years of war the newspapers could announce a victory. Rodney, after exclaiming 'Oh, my God!' and 'Grace, my pet!' and 'God alive!', said, 'Listen, woman, listen,' and read out from his *Telegraph,* 'Great news was given in a special Middle East Joint War communiqué last night. It said, "The Axis forces in the Western Desert, after twelve days and nights of ceaseless attacks by our land and air-forces, are in full retreat. Their disordered columns are being relentlessly attacked by day and night. So far we have captured over nine thousand prisoners, destroyed more than two hundred German and Italian tanks, and captured or destroyed at least two hundred and seventy guns. In the course of these operations our air forces, whose losses have been light have destroyed or damaged in combat over three hundred aircraft and put out of action a like number on the ground. The Eighth Army continues to advance."

'Oh, my God!' repeated Rodney; and 'Did you ever?' And again, 'Listen to this from the special correspondent.' He seemed unable to believe that Grace's more frivolous paper would deal with the matter as properly and as fully as his. ' "This is complete and absolute victory. The Bosche is completely finished in these parts." With these words the G.O.C.

Eighth Army announced the outcome of the El Alamein battle in an address to war correspondents at his desert headquarters. He said, 'It has been a fine battle. Two nights ago I drove two armoured wedges into the enemy and I passed three armoured divisions through those places. They are now operating in the enemy's rear. Those portions of the enemy's army that can get away are in full retreat. Those portions still facing our troops will soon be in the bag. But we must not think that the party is over. We have no intention of letting the enemy recover. We intend to hit this chap for six out of Africa . . .' "' Whereon Rodney added his own comment: 'Bright fellow, this G.O.C. Who *is* he?'

Grace had no answer to this; she was possessed at the moment by a strong need to give him in her turn succulent morsels from her paper; and she read out: ' "The King has sent a message of thanks to the army for this 'brilliant victory'." That's what he calls it. " 'This victory has caused a stir all over the world. A marvellous military feat,' said the United States Secretary of State. The Germans who were predicting an Axis victory two days ago are now pretending that this headlong flight is a voluntary withdrawal according to plan——"'

'They would,' Rodney agreed happily.

'Yes, but let me finish. My paper gives more prisoners than yours. It says, "The prisoners taken up to now amount to thirteen thousand. The number of Italian divisions deserted by the Germans is five, not three, as earlier reported. They are scattered about the desert between the Quattara Depression and the coast, waiting to be taken prisoners." '

'Well, I hope that's all true,' Rodney demurred, 'but I always suspect your paper takes more prisoners and destroys more divisions than any other. It's all for popularity. I know all this El Alamein area. Don't forget I served in Egypt during the First War.' His excitement was now such that he had to rise from the table and abandon the food on his plate, even though it included the luxury of a war-time egg with his meagre slice of bacon. He had to walk up and down, declaring, 'If you ask me, Grace my much beloved, the war has swung right round. From being badly underneath we are now right on top. I'd say it's only a matter of tim now.' Proud of his knowledge he set the El Alamein scene for Grace: a dry desert of sand and scrub and outcrops of rock lying between high rocky hills on the sea coast and the famous Quattara Depression. Proud also to seem an expert, he expounded learnedly, as he walked up and down, that the enemy had been caught between these two, the hills and the Depression, and the British, blowing a gap in his forces, had driven their armoured divisions right through it into the open desert beyond, so that, as the G.O.C. said, they were now operating against the rear and flanks of a routed army.

Grace, no less uplifted though she kept to her chair, asked, 'But dare we really hope that it'll all be over soon? If Everard is rested for six months, could we hope that it'll be over before his rest is over?'

'Oh, dear me, no. Not as soon as that.' Though an inveterate optimist himself, he had to display a masculine sanity and discourage too much optimism in a woman. 'This is only the beginning. I reckon it'll take us another year at least to make the Huns realize they can't win now, and bring them to the conference table.'

'But we've had three years of it already.'

'I know, and we shall need another year. It's asking too much to expect the end before, say, Christmas 1943. But we've plainly got air superiority now; and that's the trump hand. In the House they are saying that the Chief of Bomber Command is convinced that he can win the war with bombers alone, pounding and pounding the Huns till they're forced to call it a day.'

'Oh, but that's just what I'm afraid of. That'll mean more and more raids for Everard after his six months' rest.'

'It may not be so. Only the other day the Air Minister told me that after a bomber pilot has done as much as Everard has done he's often grounded for good.'

'Yes, but you know our Everard. He'll insist on getting back to an air-crew.'

'Maybe, but his A.O.C. can be tough too and insist that his rest is permanent.'

'What would they do with him then?'

'Probably send him to an Operation Training Unit to teach other chaps, upgrading him a rank. If so, we shall see our Everard as a squadron leader. A squadron leader safe for the rest of the war. Or as safe as we are.'

Sadly Grace murmured, 'I suppose we shall never see Stanley as more than a gunner, after this last disgrace,' adding for her comfort, 'But what'll it all matter if the war is over soon? Another year, you say? Oh well, what's a year? A year can pass quickly. The last three years seem to have gone by in no time, though I've never ceased from worrying. But if in this next year both my boys are fairly safe . . .'

On the Sunday in November, when the full story of El Alamein had been told, the King and Queen went to a victory service in St. Paul's Cathedral, and all over Britain the church bells pealed, not, according to the original plan, to announce the invasion and summon all to action stations, but to sing a paean in honour of El Alamein, while the B.B.C. broadcast their chimes to the world. And because of the bells Rodney and Grace went to that same place on the Spaniards ridge which they had visited two months before, and there, looking down again upon the vast city in its misty river basin, they tried to believe that among all the clangour of the nearest bells they could distinguish, far away, those of Westminster's clock tower, Big Ben and his sisters, and, alongside of them, the splendid carillon from a tower of the Abbey.

> Gay go up and gay go down
> To ring the bells of London Town

But it was on this Sunday afternoon, when the bells were silent, that their friend, the Inspector, appeared at their door again. To Rodney who opened the door, Patricia, the maid, having her 'afternoon out' and the Cook her Sunday siesta upstairs, the Inspector apologized for disturbing him on a Sunday but explained that he had wanted to come while Rodney would almost certainly be at home.

Rodney asked at once, 'You have some news of our son?'

'Yes,' said the Inspector; and for the moment no more.

'Is it good news?'

The answer was only, 'I'll tell you, sir; and Mrs. Merriwell too, if you would wish it.'

'Of course.' Rodney, hiding alarm, brought him into the drawing-room and, when he was seated, asked again, 'Well . .?'

The Inspector still hesitated, glancing at the nails of one hand; then nervously began, 'I told you that, directly we had any news from the Chief Constable at Croome City, I'd come and tell you.'

'Yes?'

'Well, sir, the news is not happy. May I say that I'm quite prepared to believe there's been some grievous mistake, but of course I know nothing beyond the bare facts we've been given.'

'And they are?' asked Rodney, Grace in her alarm being able to do no more than gaze at their visitor, lips apart.

'You will remember that after four days at the Croome City police station, they surrendered him to the military. A bombardier and a gunner came as his escort.' Almost it seemed that the Inspector had supplied this unnecessary detail because he didn't want to come to his climax too quickly. 'His commanding officer did not, as we had imagined, content himself with a summary jurisdiction but decided that this second apparent desertion was matter for a court-martial——'

'But you told us,' Rodney interrupted, 'that if it came to a court-martial we should be informed.'

'So I imagined. But it may be they've been waiting till a date was fixed. The Army moves slowly at any time, and just now when it's busy with other things——'

'Then they'll tell us in time?' Rodney interrupted again.

'No.' The Inspector shook his head significantly—and, for their sake, sadly. 'Because there'll be no court-martial.'

'No court-martial! Then what are we talking about?'

The Inspector only repeated—as if to gain time before continuing with unwelcome news, 'Yes, I'm afraid there'll be no court-martial.'

' "Afraid"? What do you mean?'

'It appears,' said the Inspector, after a brief sigh which seemed sympathetic in its intent, 'that while he was at the police station they not only interrogated him about his move-

75

ments but examined every inch of his body and his clothes, and took his fingerprints—all largely, you will understand because he'd been wandering in a strange way near the scene of a suspected murder. Our conclusion was that they'd found nothing to justify any charge——'

'Of course not.' It was Grace who interrupted now, hotly resenting even the suggestion of such a charge. 'I should think *not*. How dare they even hint at it?'

'So they handed him over to the military,' continued the Inspector. 'But now . . . well now, after nearly a month, a Detective Inspector Castleton, of Croome City, has been to the barracks and charged him with—with the murder.'

'*No!*' cried both Rodney and Grace. '*No!*' and Rodney declared angrily, 'My boy never murdered anyone.'

'Never, never, *never*!' Grace echoed him. 'They must be mad. It's impossible. He's been going through a difficult time, which we don't understand, but he's quite incapable of that. He's just been thoroughly unhappy; that's all. That's why he wandered about. Oh, Roddy, what are we going to do? We can't have our boy charged with a murder. Stop it. Can't you stop it?'

This question being, alas, as futile as it was wild, Rodney could not deal with it. He asked only, 'When was he charged?'

'This morning.'

'Well, thank God it's Sunday and there can be nothing in the papers today. What sort of supposed murder was it?'

The Inspector, looking down upon the floor, said after a pause and unhappily, 'There was a stab.'

Again Grace cried '*No!*' loudly, 'Oh, *no!*' and then, sharply but more quietly, 'Well, that proves it wasn't Stanley. No boy of mine is capable of taking a knife to someone. If there's anything certain in the world, it's that. There's some dreadful mistake. Roddy, see about it.'

Rodney asked, 'Why should they even suspect him of this?'

The Inspector answered gently, 'It was a girl he knew.'

'And what is that?' Grace demanded. 'Others knew her, I suppose? Heaps of others.'

'She was a young A.T.S. girl.' The Inspector spoke this so softly as to be hardly heard. 'And a girl he had once loved.'

Rodney rose from his chair, and the rising amounted to a hint that they would wish to be alone. 'Thank you Inspector for coming and telling us all. I will get in touch with the police at Croome City at once. Everything I've got is at the service of my son.'

9

Croome City

Again and again throughout that night, Grace, lying at Rodney's side cried out in her sleep, or between sleeping and waking, 'Oh, what are we to do?' or 'Oh, what has happened? It's wicked, wicked—what can we do?' And later 'He's not bad. He's only for some reason miserably unhappy. He's not bad; how can they accuse him of a thing like that? Stabbing. Stabbing.' Once she spoke into the darkness of the room those words of the Inspector, 'There was a stab.' And again and again Rodney, when he thought she was half awake tried to comfort her with the assurance, 'I'm going down there first thing in the morning, sweetheart. Don't worry too much. Don't worry too much.' Once or twice he passed his hand caressingly over her hair, 'Don't worry too much, my darling.'

In the morning at the breakfast table he searched through his *Times* but found only a small paragraph at the bottom of a column on an inner page. 'Man Charged with A.T.S. Girl's Murder' was the headline in lower-case type; and the words beneath were no more than 'Stanley George Merriwell, a gunner in the Royal Artillery stationed at Claverton, Kent, was yesterday charged with the murder of Theresa Frances Christie, a private in the A.T.S., aged twenty, whose body was found in the orchard of Wash Green Farm near Croome City four weeks ago. He will appear before the magistrates today.'

Small though the paragraph was, the sight of it pierced him like the lunge of a spear. He turned from it quickly and did not show it to Grace. As soon as it appeared a natural and easy request, he asked Grace for her paper, the *Daily Express,* which, for its liveliness she had always preferred to his sober *Times.* With an assumption of carelessness he said, 'I'd just like to see what it says about yesterday's church bells,' and with the same feigned ease he searched through it. Again only a small paragraph far down on an inner page and with words almost the same as those in *The Times*. No 'story', boldly featured. The report from Press Association or Exchange Telegraph palpably 'played down'.

Then instantly it struck him that since these morning papers must have been 'put to bed' last night, and Fleet Street which always knew everything must have learned by that time from its correspondents that this 'Stanley Merriwell' was the son of Rodney Merriwell, M.P., better known than many backbenchers because of his long service in the House, then Fleet Street, so often attacked for its indifference to personal suffering, was showing for once, by this deliberate omission of any reference to the charged man's father, the mercy which often it would practise too.

He returned the *Express* to Grace nervously, and marvelled that not once did she appear to expect a report about Stanley. How different, he thought, was a woman's use of her paper from a man's. Grace glanced seldom at the news pages and barely at all at the political columns; generally she turned at once to the feature articles.

After a hurried meal he rose saying, 'I'll be off at once, darling' and went out to the Wolseley limousine in his garage. This, no recent model, since it was five years old, but one of his loves and prides—he called it 'James' after the two first letters, J.A. on its number-plate—would devour the miles between Ridgeway and Croome City in less than two hours. But as he drove through London he stopped the car in Waterloo Place before his club, the Athenaeum. The club was hardly awake, the cleaners still sweeping and dusting in its great rooms; but he was able to enter and he hurried up the Grand Staircase to the long drawing-room which is the club's glory. Here a woman was still sweeping, but the porters had already laid out on a central table all the morning's papers. All were there, tidily arrayed, from *The Times* in its dignity, to the highly popular journals which strove not at all for dignity. He scanned them all; and this did not take long for they were but half their normal size 'in conformity with wartime economy standards'.

No mention of Gunner Merriwell's father in one of them. Not even the *Daily Worker* mentioned the relationship, though it had only just been released from its wartime 'suppression' by the Home Secretary and therefore, presumably, had small love for M.P.s as such. Of course, if the accused man was committed for trial, and in due time the trial began, everything would have to be given the full light of day, and in most of these popular papers the fullest blaze of publicity. For the present, however, no one knew what would happen. So could it be that they had all resolved not to wound a prominent and popular figure too soon?

He hurried back to his car and began his speedy drive to Croome City, hoping to see Stanley before his case was heard at the magistrates' court. There was no hope of bailing him out since the charge was murder; a remand in custody was certain. Here, long before noon, he was at the Croome City Police Station and was glad to see that it was a large, modern red-brick building, both police station and magistrates' court. A uniformed sergeant in the entrance office received his name and request with obvious sympathy, picked up a telephone and, after talking with someone in the bowels of the station, said, 'Yes, sir, the Guv'nor's in his room and willing to see you at once. It's this way, sir.' And he led him along an angular corridor and, after several angles had been turned, opened the door of the Chief Constable's office. Rodney had expected something larger and finer than this. This room was but a small, simple, business-like chamber, with the Chief's large desk, two comfortable chairs for visitors, a safe, some filing cabinets and a wardrobe against pale green walls.

The Chief Constable sat behind the desk, a dark, slim handsome man looking much younger—even as his office had looked much humbler—than Rodney had foreseen. He looked to be well on the easy side of fifty but was probably more. However there was nothing subordinate or humble about his uniform with the high insignia of laurel wreaths and crossed batons on its shoulders.

'I am Stanley Merriwell's father,' Rodney began.

But the Chief Constable stopped him quite cheerfully. 'I

know, sir. We were expecting you. Do sit down. Anything we can do to help you, we will.' He moved a box of cigarettes towards his visitor. 'Smoke?'

'No, thank you.' Could anyone feel less like nonchalantly smoking? 'All I want to ask is, Have I any chance to see my son, or is it already too late?'

'Most certainly you can see him. He is here. The cells are just above.'

At the word 'cells', spoken casually but unavoidably, an anger that was like a bodily pain, seized Rodney's heart, though the Chief Constable was proceeding in the kindliest voice. 'He has already appeared before the magistrates, but that was all over in a few minutes. The chairman told him that there was no need at this stage for him to plead one way or the other, "Guilty" or "Not Guilty", but he chose to speak out. He said sullenly—if you'll allow me to say so—"Whether it's necessary or not, I certainly plead 'Not guilty' to a nonsensical charge".'

'Of course he did.' The boy's angry words were a temporary balm for the ache at Rodney's heart. 'I should think *so.*'

The Constable, allowing this to pass, went on, 'The chairman then told him that he could have a defence certificate, but he only answered with a shrug of indifference, which the chairman chose to regard as an acceptance——'

Rodney intervened, 'He will need no defence certificate, if that means what I take it to mean. Obviously I will do everything for him.'

The Chief Constable nodded. 'Yes, of course. We all knew you were coming but it was not the magistrates' business to mention that. They remanded him in custody for eight days. There was nothing else they could do. So we have him now here, awaiting transport to Groomgate.'

The name of Groomgate Gaol fired Rodney's anger—or pain—again. 'I know that was all they could do; but I'm sure you realize that I entirely support my son's statement. I find it absolutely impossible to believe this charge against him.'

The Chief Constable answered sympathetically. 'Naturally

you do. And equally I must admit that the responsibility was mine for sending a detective inspector to Hounsland Barracks to arrest him on this charge and bring him here. You will see that I must have felt there was evidence enough for such a charge.' Here, hardly aware of what he was doing, he picked up some foolscap sheets on his desk, folded them down the middle, and laid them down again. 'I'm not going to say it was conclusive evidence. Truly I can say I hope it isn't.'

'But what evidence? What evidence?'

'I don't know that it's my business to disclose it at this stage, sir. You will of course instruct counsel to appear on his behalf?'

'The very best we can find.'

'Then everything will be told to them. And every help given to them. For the present, the fact remains that I decided the evidence was enough to justify a charge.'

'Whether or not you thought that,' answered Rodney, barely able to contain the smouldering impatience, 'and whether or not you are prepared to tell me the evidence, I am fully prepared to say again that I have no doubt whatever of my son's innocence.'

With a kindly, tolerant smile, the Chief Constable replied, 'And I am fully prepared to say, sir, that I sincerely hope it can be proved. People like to say that the policeman's one interest is to secure a conviction, and this may approach the truth about some of us, but with the best of my boys it is certainly not true. They are taught that our sole interest should be to present the evidence and get at the truth. So therefore I am able to repeat that I wish you every success. You would like to see your son now, I expect?'

'If you please.'

By way of answering this, the Chief Constable picked up his telephone and spoke through to the station office. 'Sergeant Hodwin, please . . . Is that you, Sergeant? Good. I have here the father of Gunner Merriwell. Mr. Rodney Merriwell, M.P.' Was it possible that for all his high position and the sanity which controlled his speech, there was still within him somewhere something sufficiently commonplace and young to be not without pride in a distinguished visitor? 'Will you come and take him to—I think the detention room would be best—and bring his son to him. Give him all the help you can. Thank you.'

Quickly a sergeant in uniform, grey-haired, big, and plump, who looked much older than his Chief, appeared in the room, and the Chief said to Rodney 'Sergeant Hodwin will look after you. Don't hesitate to ask him anything you want. He will bring your son to you. If you care to come and see me afterwards, I shall be here.'

'Thank you, Chief Constable.' Rodney imagined that, on the analogy of 'Thank you, Prime Minister', this was the proper way to address him.

The big grey-haired sergeant led him along more angular white corridors and through a spacious charge room to the long narrow passage that ran between the cells. Rodney noticed quickly that there were two women's cells on one side and several more men's cells on the other—which seemed to make a statement about the incidence of crime. Indignant that his son should be immured in one of these tainted places he asked the sergeant suddenly, 'Could I see what a cell is like?'

'Course you can, sir, if you want to. But there ain't much to see. There's more pleasing sights in the world than a copper-house cell, if you take my meaning.' Wherewith he looked through a peep-hole into the nearest cell and, having reminded himself that it was empty, unlatched and flung open its door.

Rodney saw the high, narrow, heartless room, with its cold white tiles reaching well above a man's height, its wooden bunk with a pile of worn brown blankets, its w.c. pan, and its heavily protected window far too high for any incumbent to be able to look out at the world of the free.

Thinking of Stanley in such a pitiless human 'safe', he felt driven to say, though with a forced smile so as not to offend, 'You know, I always thought we prided ourselves on the fact that in our country an accused man was presumed innocent till he was proved guilty. But these horrible places look no sort of quarters for a good citizen possibly innocent. They look as though you're pretty sure that anyone lodged here is as guilty as he can be, and the more scathing his treatment, the better.'

'Well, sir, they mostly are,' said the sergeant with the confidence of one announcing a fact of nature, and quite unmindful of the fact that this was the last thing he ought to have said to this gent.

Rodney remembered just such words from Grace, always less instantly liberal than he.

'We get some very rough types in here—' the sergeant was continuing—'you'd never believe. This one's for the drunks. That's why the floor's of wood.'

'I see,' said Rodney with a sigh, and left it there.

The detention room into which they now moved was next to the cells and, while slightly broader, was very like one of them: it had of course no bed and no w.c. pan, but the same white tiled walls, the same high window, and for furniture a small table and two common chairs.

'Jest sit down, sir,' said the sergeant, as friendly as ever. 'Jest take a chair, and I'll bring your son to you. Won't be half a mo. He's in the cell next to the one we looked at.'

And it was less than half a minute before he came back with Stanley walking in front of him. To Stanley he said, 'There you are, mate. There's your guv'nor for you. Jest sit down and talk to him as much as you like. I shall have to stay here, but I won't be listening, like. Jest standing 'ere and thinking me own thoughts and not paying no attention to you. Say whatever you want, son.'

And for the rest of the interview he stood there, between Rodney and the door, a big tall figure in uniform, trying to appear as inanimate as a wax-work model.

Stanley, his face a pale mask emptied of any expression except indifference, said only as he took the other chair, 'Hallo, Dad. Good to see you.'

Rodney who had not seen him for more than a year was alarmed by the look of him. Here was a handsome young man, his face an exact replica of Everard's—but it was Everard's with all the lights extinguished. It was the face of a young man who'd lost the ability or the desire to smile. In the emptied eyes there lay neither love nor hate any more; and no fear, no horror of his present position, but rather a kind of living deadness to the world of men.

From Rodney's heart there rushed out to this pale youth an ache of love not less than that which would have poured from Grace's heart; a love that longed to rescue him from whatever sea of misery had overwhelmed him, and to surround him with an impervious protection. But he said only and uncomfortably, 'Yes, it's good to see you, Stan.'

'Yes,' said Stanley, in a low, weak agreement.

And Rodney went on, 'I want you to know, Stan, that neither your mother nor I believe one word of this nonsensical charge against you.' Unconsciously he had echoed the words which his son, according to the Chief Constable's report, had used before the magistrates.

'Of course you don't. Who could? Of course it's nonsense. The biggest bloody nonsense ever.' Stanley was now leaning forward with elbows on his knees, and his hands clasped. Rodney noticed that occasionally the clasped hands trembled. Sometimes they unclasped and clasped again.

'You shall have the very best counsel—I'll see Fred Nicols about this at once. He'll brief two of the best, and they'll satisfy any jury that some ghastly mistake has been made.'

Stanley didn't seem to have paid much attention to this. Rodney doubted if he had heard it. The boy was looking down at the clasped hands and saying, 'All I know is I wish to God the blasted cops would get on with it. Four days they kept me in the police station, four months I've been kept at the barracks, and now I gather they're going to keep me for weeks and weeks on remand at Groomgate. It's like being a bullock in its pen at a slaughter-house. I'm tired of it. I'm not afraid of a trial. They'll never prove anything against me.'

'But, Stanley, what on earth was the evidence they thought they'd got against you?'

Without changing his posture over the clasped hands, Stanley just lifted his shoulders. 'It's just acting on suspicion; that's all. Of course they suspected me from the first—I can understand that—because I was a deserter—and that's crimi-

85

nal—and because I knew the girl, and because she'd thrown me over. That was a first-class motive for stabbing her, wasn't it? What more could anyone want? It doesn't take much to satisfy the cops that they've got the right man.'

Not a sign came from the tall sergeant standing near the door that he'd heard this, or if he'd heard it, that he disapproved of it. Let the lad say all he wanted to.

'At the police station, if you'll believe it, Dad, they stripped me stark and searched all over my body, even taking a specimen hair from my head. Maybe it matches a hair on her body. Likely enough. They searched my clothes and found a hair somewhere on my uniform and solemnly preserved it. Maybe it was one of the girl's—more than likely because we'd made love often enough—I've never denied that—and what else it proves perhaps you can tell me. I wouldn't mind betting there are hairs from her head or her body on a few other uniforms walking about at Pine Wood. I should think they could make quite an interesting collection.'

It touched Rodney's heart that Stanley, who according to all reports had for long avoided talk with anybody, was now doing the opposite; in his father, so long unseen, he had found a vessel into which he was willing, eager, to pour out at last the long stifled emotions. The love that ached at Rodney's heart was increased by this gush of filial confidence.

'But let me tell you this, Dad: they never found a single bloodstain on my uniform or any trace of blood on me anywhere, and how you can stab a girl to death without getting blood on you I don't know. Mind you, I'd slept that night in an old shed and so had had no time for a wash—I was, in fact, walking to a barber's at Lyneham when the policeman arrested me, and I suppose with a two-days' beard and my clothes all messed up I looked capable of anything. Then I was idiot enough, or unlucky enough, when I'd got a bit annoyed with this frisking of me, to say "What the hell are you looking for. I haven't done any murder"; whereupon the chief C.I.D. bloke chipped in with "Who said anything about a murder?" No one had said anything about a murder the night before, so this was enough for them to assume that I'd guilty knowledge. The remark was really a wretched sort of jest. I should have thought that to anyone of sense such a remark would have suggested innocence rather than guilt. How's Mum?'

'She's well enough, but naturally she's upset and properly furious on your behalf.'

'And she may well be. I don't want her upset but I'm glad she's angry.' Only now did Stanley raise his eyes from his joined hands as he spoke. 'Tell her it'll be all right. My view is that the police, if they're in a spot, would rather arrest somebody instead of nobody so as to keep an impatient public sweet.'

Still not a sign, not a word of shock or protest, not even a tolerant smile from the sergeant standing on duty there. Let the poor lad say what he liked.

'That's about all there is to it, Dad. The very fact that it took them four weeks before they could bring themselves to charge me suggests that the evidence they think they've got is pretty thin. My guess is that the murder was done by some stranger whom no one knows anything about. Soldiers aren't in the habit of murdering their girls, and I'm certainly not. Good lord, if I'd stabbed a girl, I'd hardly have been fool enough to toss the knife only a few yards away, in the same orchard. Sort of thing a half-wit would do.'

'A *knife*?'

'Oh, yes, didn't they tell you? They found a bloodstained knife. The second day I was in the Chief Man's office they showed it to me. The Chief pulled it out of a box where it was preserved like some precious piece of jewellery. It was that old-fashioned kind of clasp-knife with more than one blade and a corkscrew and a tool for fetching a stone out of one's horse's hoof. Any working man might have possessed such a knife to cut his bread and cheese with in his lunch break, or any tramp when he's eating an apple by the roadside. There are all the apples a tramp can want lying about in the orchards just now. They asked me if I'd ever seen it before—another daft question because if I'd used it I'd have certainly said "No". I did say "No, never" but I added honestly that I'd had one like it, but not at all the same, some time ago. You may remember it. Of course they asked where was it now, and I only said I wished they could tell me. I hadn't seen it for weeks. Months.'

'But surely all this is nonsense, Stan. Were there no finger-prints on the knife to show it wasn't yours?'

'I suppose not, or they wouldn't have continued trying to plant the business on me. I imagine the cove had enough sense to wipe it before he tossed it aside. Any man nowadays has the sense to do that. Probably he shoved it deep into the earth before he flung it away.'

'But you said it was bloodstained?'

Wearily Stanley answered, '*I* don't know . . . Suppose I should have said it had traces of blood on it. In the hinge as likely as not. I don't know. All I know is it was never mine. How's Everard? Is he still flying and is he still all right?'

'So far. But we're hoping that he'll soon get his six months of relief or, better still, that he'll be told that he needn't go on ops any more.'

'Doubt if he'd ever settle for that. He always seems to me to enjoy risks. I suppose I used to once.'

'I think it'd be truer to say he both loves and hates the danger, but the love is that much stronger and wins.'

'Could be. Perhaps you're right. Does he know all about this nonsense?'

'I don't know. There was a very small report in all the papers but it looked as though they had been careful not to identify you as my son.'

'Gentlemanlike. What did it say?'

'Just "Stanley Merriwell, a gunner in the Royal Artillery, stationed at Claverton, Kent——" '

'But, God, if Ev's seen that, it'll be enough for him. For heaven's sake write and tell him it's all a put-up job. Tell him all I've told you. Heaven knows what they'll let me write from prison. They black out most of it.'

By now, though this unhappy boy before him was his son and his heart was aching with a desperate and frustrated love for the tall, handsome, downcast youth; though ever and again the love was recalling Stanley as an infant riding pickaback on his shoulders, turn-and-turn about with Everard when both were tired after a family walk—by now Rodney was longing for this interview to come to an end so that he could escape from it. Every question, every answer, every weary, casual remark had been heavy with embarrassment. And now in one sickening moment—one only—a new thought had approached, only to be driven violently away and out of sight. With ninety-nine parts of his mind he could only believe that Stanley, his son, Grace's son, Everard's twin, however unhappy, had been incapable of the crime with which he was charged, but now the remaining hundredth part, a first tiny lack of conviction had dared to approach the door of his mind. But he didn't allow it to come near. He slammed the door on it. And never, never, would he tell Grace or Everard that this dark thought had drawn near with an intent to knock and ask for admission. In their boyhood Stanley and Everard had told their lies to escape disgrace or punishment, but neither had ever been an easy liar. No, no, the unthinkable couldn't be true. What had flung this horrible, this single, seed of doubt into his mind? Was it perhaps those careless, strange words about a bullock in its pen waiting for the slaughterer? Or that mention of driving the knife into the earth? Did they suggest that Stanley knew he was living nearer the scaffold than he chose to pretend? No, no, not for another second would his father harbour even the smallest doubt about his son's innocence. Stanley? Oh, *no*!

Nevertheless, shaken by this moment of sickness, he arose slowly and said, 'I suppose I mustn't keep you, Stan. I gather they want to take you to this Groomfield——'

'Groomgate,' Stanley corrected.

'Groomgate, or wherever it is. Meantime I'll go home and arrange everything. We'll get the finest defending advocate there is. Two of them, if necessary.'

'Thank you, Dad. But don't upset yourself too much or go spending too much. I don't care a lot what happens to me. I know they can't make this absurd charge stick, but, when it fails, I'm up for desertion, and God only knows what that'll imply, but whatever it is, I don't seem to care much.'

'You mustn't talk like that. We all have these dark moods sometimes, but they pass.'

'Do they? I wonder. I've felt pretty hopeless for over a year now. But never mind me. Give my love to Mum. And to Everard.'

Only smiling his assent, Rodney went out of the room with the Sergeant, who, without fully closing the door, asked 'Had all the time you want, sir? No need to 'urry, though there *is* a car waiting to take him to Groomgate, but that don't matter. Cops can wait. That's what they're doing most'a their time. Patient blokes. I can assure you, sir, he'll be treated very decent at Groomgate. After all, no matter what you say about our cells, which aren't all that agreeable, I'll allow, he's nowhere near being treated as guilty as yet. You and his lawyers'll be able to see him as often as you like, and get all the meals he fancies sent in to him. There's worse places than Groomgate to spend a week or two. Better than a haystack or a hedge.'

Rodney thanked him for these comforting words, and the sergeant, opening the door wider, said to Stanley, 'Okay, that's that. Your guv'nor's done with you so . . . well . . . come along of me, brother. There's a carriage waiting for your 'ighness.'

Through the open door, Rodney, before hastening out of their way, had seen, in a last farewell glimpse that Stanley was still sitting in the posture he'd maintained through most of his father's visit: arms on knees, hands clasped, and head bent over them: a figure that Rodin might have modelled as Despair.

10

Magnanimity

Again on the following day the newspapers reported under an inconspicuous heading, *Murder Charge*, no more than that 'Stanley George Merriwell . . . was remanded in custody till 15th November.' But when, two weeks later, the magistrate committed Stanley for trial at the Old Bailey, it was no longer possible, though the papers still did not mention his father's name, to mask his identity from the world. Everyone had heard now that he was the son of Rodney Merriwell, the M.P. for Ridgeway. All Ridgeway knew it. Everard reported that all at his airfield knew it. Monty, speaking with the frankness of a greatest friend, admitted that all whom he met, colleagues, patients or friends, knew and spoke of it.

But so far no one else had spoken one word about it to Rodney. Everyone so far was according him the mercy of silence. In the House, whether in Chamber, Lobbies, Committee Rooms, or Smoking Room, he could apprehend that all knew and were feeling sympathy, but that all, in a kind of universal magnanimity, had decided that he must be left to say the first words.

For a few days after Stanley's committal he had stayed away from the House, afraid to face any of his six hundred fellow-members, but after four such apprehensive days, he had gathered his courage together and forced himself to be in his place and to face whatever awaited him there.

It was with an unsteady heart that he had passed along St. Stephen's Hall and entered the Central Lobby, that soaring circular cathedral, with its clustered columns, lofty perpendicular windows and white staring statues, the very heart and hub of Parliament and of the whole Palace of Westminster. Fortunately for him on this day it was packed and noisy with marchers who had come from somewhere, an army with banners, to protest against something. Elsewhere on the fringe of this demonstrating army little groups of constituents were talking with their members. All these seriously national activities seemed to diminish his story into a matter merely personal, local and small. Unobserved, he walked into the Chamber, once the Chamber of the Lords but now occupied by the Commons since their own Chamber had been bombed and partly destroyed sixteen months before. It was still far from full and he had no difficulty in taking his most usual place in a back row near the Throne—though the magnificent Throne was now railed off and dimly deserted, the Speaker's Chair and the Clerks' Table standing at the further end.

Gradually the Chamber filled, awaiting an important statement by the Prime Minister, and one or two members near him gave him a friendly smile, one or two others offered a few commonplace words but most, as he could well see, had resolved that words would embarrass him and silence was best. Some members on the opposite side of the Chamber did glance at him curiously, but quickly and considerately turned their eyes away. From all these symptoms he could have no doubt that in the four days of his absence the House had been buzzing with his story.

He sat in his place for a long time, determined not to appear too ashamed. The Prime Minister made his statement and received an ovation with cheers roaring and order papers waving aloft, because its substance had been exciting and exhilarating and its delivery graced with fun and mischief and wit. When the Prime Minister had finished and gone, many members left the Chamber, but others came in for other purposes, to none of which Rodney could give much attention. The attendance kept dissolving and changing its character but he stayed in his place desiring to be seen there by as many as possible. Wearying at last of this strained and embarrassing occupation, he too left the Chamber and walked nervously for a further trial of his courage into the Smoking Room. It was crowded to stuffiness because the Prime Minister was seated at one of the tables sipping his brandy and surrounded by members who were as eager to listen to him as he, still flushed with his recent triumph in the Chamber, was eager to talk and laugh and discuss further the great story he had told. He sat hunched over the table with his shoulders nearly as high as his ears so that his face seemed to have more than ever its bulldog cast, round cheeks, brief nose and protruding underlip; but today it was that of an old bulldog fully satisfied, and happy among friends.

Rodney went to the bar and ordered a sherry from the woman there, one of his good friends with whom, over the years, he had exchanged many an amiable joke. She allowed nothing in her eyes to suggest that she knew anything, but he could almost, nevertheless, discern her knowledge as, smilingly, she served him.

As he came away from the bar, hoping to find a seat at a table somewhere and continue his present performance among the members there, the Prime Minister observed him and instantly called out with deliberate merriment, 'Rod! Come on, Rod. Bring that glass here. We're discussing the great news, surely the only great news to come out of France since she fell. And that's two and a half years ago. Make way for Rodney, everybody.'

'Thank you, Prime Minister.'

The great news had been in the later newspapers that morning; Rodney had seen it in a late edition, but heartening though it was, he had been so preoccupied with the self-imposed assignment before him that he'd been unable to delight in it properly—or even to read it fully. The Germans, believing that the French fleet in Toulon Harbour was making ready to escape, had descended in the darkness upon the town with a view to seizing all the warships there, some sixty of them. But before they could reach the harbour water the French admiral had ordered all his captains to scuttle their ships, and the Germans could only stand and watch an armada go down.

Rodney stood with the others around the Prime Minister's table, and the P.M. talked of this fine action so enthusiastically, since it appealed to both his romantic relish for the heroic and his romantic love for France, that Rodney's trouble seemed to

93

grow small again, compared with the sinking of sixty majestic ships.

'It's the greatest scuttle in history.' The Prime Minister had emptied his glass of brandy and was lighting a long cigar. 'Greater even than the scuttling by the Germans of all their captured ships at Scapa Flow after the last war. Though that was a pretty magnificent effort,' he allowed, always generous to a beaten enemy, 'but this French action is grander. The Germans scuttled *after* their surrender; the French, God bless them, have scuttled rather than surrender.'

'How many really big ships were there, Prime Minister?' asked a member. 'Were there many?'

'Oh yes . . . oh yes. As far as we have heard, there was one battleship, two battle cruisers, four heavy cruisers, some medium cruisers, an aircraft carrier, and of course, several destroyers and submarines. Nothing like it; nothing like it in all history. And all the captains were on their bridges as the ships went down, some of them dying with their men.'

There were tears in his eyes and a gulp in his voice as he said this, for he resembled Rodney in that he couldn't tell a great story of heroism or self-sacrifice without a struggle to control the mounting tears in his throat. While he got himself into control Rodney offered a comment, a singularly uninspired one, but it was spoken chiefly to show that his voice in this company was not too ashamed. 'It is a truly terrific story, sir.'

'Yes, yes, Rod; and "terrific"'s the word.' One could see that he was glad to be speaking in comfort again, having mastered his weakness. 'It was not only the ships that went down. The naval arsenal ashore and all the coastal batteries and all the munition depots blew themselves up. Blew themselves up in the faces of the Germans. The German tanks and armoured cars had rushed to the Milhaud docks and the Vauban basin, but they were too late. Just too late. They were met by explosion after explosion. The first was from the battle cruiser *Strasbourg*; the next from the twenty-six-thousand-ton cruiser, *Dunkerque*; then the other cruisers followed suit, the *Foch* and the *Algeria* and the *Jeau de Vienne*. Some of the ships were not quite ready for scuttling, so the crews opened a furious defensive fire on the enemy till they were ready to sink. What do you say to that, Rod?'

This deliberate addressing of his words to Rodney, and this deliberate use of an affectionate diminutive by the greatest figure in the House had done everything in a single moment, Rodney thought, to make easy his position among the six hundred fellow members. Those words 'Make way for Rodney, everybody' rang and rang in his mind.

'It's glorious, sir,' he said, having nothing better to say.

'Yes, this is La Gloire come back again. All those great ships, I'm told, are now lying on their sides in the water under clouds of drifting smoke. They may be on their sides but French honour stands erect again. These sunken ships and ruined arsenals have redeemed it. From these mighty flames in Toulon we have our assurance that France will rise again. And we'll see to it that she can and does. Strange, but the loss of a whole fleet, and the total disablement, as I understand it, of Toulon harbour, is really a victory . . . a great victory . . . a great naval victory . . .' but he was in difficulty with his tears again, and he puffed at his cigar to hide this awkward fact.

11

Monty's Silence

Monty sat with Rodney and Grace in their drawing-room. It was the evening before Stanley's trial began, a day in January '43, nearly two months after his committal to the Old Bailey. They sat there after dinner and over their coffee, Rodney having begged Monty to 'come and be with us. Your presence will help my poor Grace. And me too because, dammit, I don't know where we are in this matter or how things have come to this pass. Anyhow my Stanley has two of the finest counsel in the country to defend him: Mordon Graeme, and Bill Whitton. I feel all must come right. It must do.'

He was repeating this now in the presence of Grace. 'It must do. It *will* do, won't it, Monty?'

Monty had no immediate answer ready, being never a man to speak, merely for the sake of comfort, words to which his reason could give no certainty. So Rodney, laying down his cup after a silence in which no one had spoken, drove on anxiously, 'They *can't* convict. They can't possibly. Where is there any evidence against him except that the wretched girl had been his mistress and had jilted him, and that some fruit-picker found, thrown aside in the orchard where the poor creature lay, a bloodstained knife like one he was known to have possessed?' In loyalty to his son Rodney had dismissed firmly, penitently, fiercely, that seed of doubt—shameful doubt— which had been flung into his mind for a moment by some words of Stanley's about 'waiting like a bullock for the slaughterer'. And some words about thrusting a knife-blade into the earth to clean it of blood. 'Why, God help us, Monty, *I* used to have a clasp-knife like that with its several blades and a corkscrew and so on. They were common enough once and may be so now. As young men we used to love them and be proud of them. Or, come to think of it, Stanley's knife which some other fruit-picker saw him using to cut an apple may have been my actual knife. I don't know what became of it but I know he always liked it. But—Monty—as he said to me, he'd hardly be such a fool as to toss away among the trees a knife which he knew fruit-pickers had seen him using. He may have done many foolish things but he's not such a fool as that. And the fact that he'd deserted and was sleeping rough has no bearing on the charge at all.'

'None at all.' Monty was glad to speak words that were genuine and would probably comfort. 'There are probably many other deserters sleeping rough all over the country after three years of war. It did no more than throw suspicion on him, and it'll throw suspicion on the prosecution if they try to use it now. You can imagine how Mordon Graeme'll deal with *that*. He'll throw it back at them.'

'Yes, and, Monty, you're a doctor and will know the answer to this: can you stab anyone deep enough to kill without getting a single spot of blood on your jacket or your sleeve or somewhere? They searched and searched and found no blood anywhere.'

'I should have thought it was impossible.' Again Monty was happy to be able to reply like this, and honestly. 'It's a strong point in his favour.'

'Oh, they'll get him off!' Grace exclaimed confidently. 'They're bound to get him off. He couldn't have done it. Whoever heard such impossible nonsense? Stanley stabbing someone? And a girl too. It's quite impossible. It's inconceivable.'

To this Monty said nothing.

Fortunately there was little time for his silence to be noticed because Grace's indignation surged on quickly and passionately, 'The girl was a hussy with other lovers among the soldiers, some of them rough types, probably, who'd stab easily if a girl doubled-crossed them. Killing's their business at the moment. Stabbing belongs to simpler types than Stanley. Has anyone ever heard of a boy from a good home, who'd been to a good school and the university, taking a knife to a faithless young woman? Monty, you do think they'll get him off, don't you? Sir Mordon Graeme'll know how to show a jury that the whole charge is ridiculous and impossible.'

'He's certainly one of the finest defenders we've got. If anybody can do it, he will,' Monty allowed, but at first he conceded no more. Then he added words that he knew were true and would be comforting though his reasons lay hidden from both his hearers. Let them have their comfort, unaware of the thoughts that had determined the words. 'I haven't the slightest doubt that he ought to get off.'

'Of course you haven't. Who could?' Grace demanded; while Rodney burst in, 'And surely, Monty, the fact that the knife was just thrown carelessly aside tells in Stan's favour rather than against him. It looks like the work of an utter simpleton, as Grace suggests; or, worse, of some cretin or congenital idiot.'

Monty nodded; but he alone knew that the nod was less one of instant assent than of slow contemplation. Better that they should read it as agreement, since what he was thinking would be of small comfort to two dear friends. He was thinking that the 'mental fragmentation', his own words for all that Stanley had been suffering from during a year and more, was a condition for which no certain cause had yet been found, and no name finally attached to it except that frightening one of *dementia precox,* given it because it struck in adolescence or early adulthood. No respecter of persons, it visited rich and poor, men and women, those of high intelligence and those of low, requiring only that they be young. Once it had struck its victim, his behaviour might be quite unpredictable. In its catatonic form a sufferer might alternate between periods of sluggishness to the point of stupor and moments of extreme violence. The knowledge that Stanley, despite his intelligence and education, had taken so easily to aimless wandering like a drug addict or a meths drinker suggested that other characteristics of this cruel visitation might be present in him: negligence, manual clumsiness and bungling, all of which might—possibly, only possibly —explain the careless tossing aside of a knife after carefully wiping it. 'Inconceivable', Grace—or Rodney—had said. To Monty not wholly inconceivable; it could be a typical mixture of rational care and irrational bungling. But this was a thought and no more; and certainly not one for submitting to Grace and Rodney. Like Rodney's fellow-members in the House, but for his own very different reasons, Monty judged that silence was best.

12

Closing Speeches at the Old Bailey

Sir Mordon Graeme, K.C., leading for the defence, had called no witness other than Stanley, the prisoner, thereby securing for himself the right of addressing the jury after the prosecuting counsel and so getting the last word except for the Judge's summing-up.

Counsel for the prosecution had finished his address to the jury the previous afternoon and the Judge had adjourned the case till this morning. It was still only eleven o'clock, so it was possible, if the summing-up was not too long, and the jury did not take too long in reaching a verdict, that the trial would end today. The January day was cloudless and bright, and the sunlight streamed through the glass dome into the panelled courtroom, falling with an inappropriate happiness upon the large square pen which was the dock and the ranked seats for counsel, jury, press and public. Twenty or thirty barristers in their wigs and gowns had come in from the corridors and were standing in the gangways between dock and seats to hear Sir Mordon and learn which of his famous methods and skills he would adopt in striving to save from the gallows the son of a well-known M.P.

In a bank of seats reserved for privileged guests and well placed behind counsel's pews Monty sat with Rodney on one side of him and, on the other, Everard, granted compassionate leave. Monty wondered how many among the public recognized Rodney as the prisoner's father; a few did so, he was sure because they gazed at him with some fascination and whispered to their neighbours. For his part, and because of his professional assessment of Stanley's sufferings, his eyes tended to swing between the scarlet-robed judge on his elevated throne representing the State (which still lacked, in Monty's view, any adequate appraisal of its prisoner's condition) and the prisoner himself, once his happy young friend, seated in the large dock between the warders.

Throughout the trial Stanley, except when he went into the witness box and denied all knowledge of the murder and the many-tooled knife, had sat with his head drooped forward over fiddling hands, and hardly ever raising his eyes to see a new witness enter the box. He seemed the least interested person in the crowded court; in a sense one could say he was hardly there in the court, and all that was happening in it mattered nothing to him. For three and a half days this had been his attitude. Jury, judge and spectators had found it easy to accept the answer which one witness gave to Sir Mordon in his cross-examination; it had been Sir Mordon's final demand of him. 'Mr. Beck: you were a bombardier at the Pine Wood gun-site when the prisoner was stationed there. Would you tell us what was his nickname among the men and women in that camp?'

'Yes, sir. "Misery".'

'Thank you, Mr. Beck.'

And Sir Mordon had allowed a moment to elapse before he sat down. He knew how to use a pause if he wished to emphasize an answer.

Short and slight in figure but splendid in face, it was a custom to say in the criminal bar that Sir Mordon's grand nose, high brow, strong mouth and waved silver hair deserved at least ten inches more of height. He rose now without his spectacles on his nose or his papers in his hand, but standing very erect and staring very straight at the jury, while his hands gripped his silk gown as if half aware that this was his robe of authority. A pause; and then after the formal 'May it please your Lordship' he began. 'Members of the jury it is my task to explain to you exactly what is the defence in this case. The defence is that the prisoner, Stanley Merriwell, did not commit the murder; that he was never there on the site of the murder; that the knife we have been shown was never his; and that he never met or touched the girl, Theresa Christie, since the day they parted for ever.'

Having said this much, he put on his glasses, adjusted them and picked up a sheaf of notes. Adjusting the glasses yet more comfortably, he declared that, in his submission, the prosecution had entirely failed to prove that the accused had anything to do with this cruel and stony-hearted murder. They had suggested that he had a strong motive for such a savage act, but this, gentlemen of the jury, was utterly treacherous ground. Many others, as they have heard, might have had the same motive or a stronger one. To offer such a motive to a jury was but to invite them to indulge in speculation and suspicion; and it was their bounden duty—their sworn duty—that if the charging of the prisoner was a matter of mere suspicion—even if they themselves felt a suspicion, and perhaps a strong suspicion, that the prisoner was one of many possible murderers—to bring in a verdict of 'Not Guilty'. The burden of proof rested entirely on the prosecution. It was not for him to prove innocence. Enough to prove doubt. No more. Only some doubt, gentlemen. It was sometimes said that the prisoner was 'entitled to the benefit of the doubt'. This was an unfortunate phrase; it suggested a privilege but the consequence of doubt was no privilege; it was a *right*. (Here one of the celebrated pauses.)

My Lord, he continued, would tell them that the charge must be proved beyond all reasonable doubt. And in his submission, never in the many cases in which he had played a part had there been more 'reasonable doubt'. Had the prosecution produced any circumstantial evidence against the prisoner? Had a witness been produced to say he'd seen her with the girl? Had any evidence been produced to show that there was one trace of blood on his clothes or his body, and this though he had spent the night before the murder in an empty shed where there were no washing facilities, no mirrors, no means of examining himself or his bedraggled uniform. He had no other clothes, as they had heard. Yet in the morning he emerged from that empty shed and was arrested in the very clothes he'd worn the night before. He was sleeping in the vicinity of the murder, said the prosecution. But then, gentlemen, so were five hundred other people at least. 'Vicinity' was no safer argument than 'motive'. Indeed his learned friend, the prosecuting counsel, had very properly said that if the prisoner was where he swore he was at the time of the murder he could not have been the murderer. That knife. In his submission, it had certainly not been identified as Merriwell's knife. They would remember that one fruit-picker whom he had cross-examined had answered very fairly (here Sir Mordon read from his notes) 'I cannot say that the knife produced was the same as I saw the prisoner using. It was only very like it.' Doubt, gentlemen. Doubt. (He flung the notes down on his desk, as if he were flinging away all certainties, and all possibility of a conviction; then waited and spoke again.)

'I submit that the proximity of the knife to the place of the murder argues the prisoner's innocence rather than his guilt. Can you really believe that a man of his education would have been so foolish as to fling the knife a mere score of yards away instead of burying it deep in some distant field or perhaps throwing it down a drain in some distant street? The presence of that knife in the place where it was found, under a tree, suggests to me, not merely a man of exceptional simplicity, but an imbecile; it suggests a village idiot, and I should have thought that the business of this court was to consider sending him, not to a gallows, but to a lunatic asylum.'

Beyond question the pause after these last two words, as Sir Mordon gathered up his notes again, was studied and calculated. And it was at this point that Monty began to suspect that Sir Mordon was pleading with all his skill, and no little pity, two contradictory causes: the one that Doubt entitled his client to a verdict of 'Not Guilty', and the other that, if he *was* guilty, then he would be entitled to the merciful verdict of 'Guilty but Insane'. From now on Monty listened to Sir Mordon's speech with a deepening interest and wonder. He surmised that, despite all his brave and well-acted efforts to secure the 'Not Guilty' verdict, he really believed in the guilt. And a deep gratitude and liking for this merciful man began to grow within him.

After those loaded words about an asylum, and the weighted pause, did not Sir Mordon add, casually, quietly, pretending to be no more than thinking aloud, 'It was mad enough to come back to the place where he was known as a deserter, but this carelessness with the knife surely strains all belief.' Why these words?

His speech lasted for over an hour. There had been parts of Stanley's coldly unconcerned and often stumbling evidence in the box that needed the most skilful efforts to make light of them and dissipate their damage, and bravely he went about this, though he must be thinking all the time that the final speech of the day was not his but the Judge's, and that my lord would certainly reassemble all the damaging points he had tried to disperse—probably after paying a courteous tribute to 'Sir Mordon's valiant endeavours on behalf of his client'.

Sir Mordon's closing words, spoken with his glasses off again, his notes laid aside, and his eyes fixed on the jury, rang so quietly and yet effectively in a crowded chamber, rapt into silence, that Everard leaned across Monty and whispered to his father excitedly, 'I believe he's got him off!' and Rodney, who'd never attended a trial before, nodded and murmured, 'I think so. I think so.'

Everard turned and said the same words to Monty. Monty kept silence.

The last words were, 'Let me repeat that the onus of proof is on the Crown, and in my submission that proof has not been forthcoming. You are left with too great a burden of doubt. And let me remind you before I end my task and offer you my last words that the duty of coming to a decision on the facts of this case is not mine, nor my learned friend's, nor even my lord's; it is yours; yours only, and when I say "yours" I mean each individual one of you. I cannot stress too greatly the extremity of care, the overwhelming sense of duty, with which each individual one of you, acting as it were alone, should discharge your task of declaring a verdict that really accords with the amount of evidence available. I suspect that this is the first time in your lives that you have been asked whether a man should live or die; and it is not a little thing, gentlemen, to send a man to his death, if there lingers in your mind even the smallest element of doubt. If any one of the several doubts that I have put before you—any *one* doubt—stays unresolved in your mind then I ask you to give the full effect to it, which will mean that you are constrained to find my client "Not Guilty".

'Gentlemen, I leave his fate with confidence in your hands.'

A hubbub of conversation arose from all parts of the court-room, some of it like plaudits, some like disagreement, more like wonderment, and it continued so that the usher had to call twice and again for silence. Monty heard people behind him saying what Everard had whispered, 'He's got him off!' and others urging 'Wait and see. It's not finished yet.'

By now the usher had enforced a silence and the Judge began to speak. He began with dignified, grave, but, as it seemed to Monty, remarkably unnecessary statements of facts with which the jury, after hearing the case for four days, must have long since acquainted itself: such as 'Members of the jury, the prisoner, Stanley George Merriwell is charged with having murdered a young woman, Theresa Frances Christie, on a day in October, 1942. Before you find him guilty the Crown has to satisfy you of two things; first, that this young woman was murdered, and secondly, that, if she was murdered, she was murdered by the prisoner.' Having said which, he told them again, but in more verbose and resounding phrases, what Sir Mordon had told them, in simpler terms, a few minutes before. He was a small man, as was Sir Mordon, and Monty guessed that, like many small men (though not Sir Mordon) he liked his phrases large. 'You must understand that any opinion which I may hold, or appear to hold, on questions of fact in this melancholy case does not matter at all, or concern you at all. It is you, the jury, whom the country has empanelled, who carry now the solemn but inalienable obligation to state your minds on the questions of fact, uninfluenced by any opinion that you may suspect the Judge, for his part, entertains.' These facts and principles being now safely understood by all, he set about his reviewing of the evidence in minutest detail. He had not been speaking for more than fifteen minutes when Monty heard untroubled whisperings behind him, probably from those who thought themselves wise and well-informed in these matters: 'He's summing up for a conviction.' 'Yes, obviously.' Or a kinder voice, 'Yes, I'm afraid so.' 'Why "afraid"? If ever anyone was guilty . . .' Monty hoped that neither Rodney nor Everard, staring fascinated at the Judge who probably held Stanley's life in his hands, had heard these low-voiced comments.

The Judge, at the moment, was conceding Sir Mordon's affirmation that even the strongest apparent motive was not necessarily evidence of guilt, but he qualified this by contending that evidence of motive combined with evidence of opportunity did 'constitute considerations that they should not completely cast aside'. But these were matters for them, members of the jury, not for him. He allowed too that the fact of Stanley's having spent the night before the murder in a disused hut not a mile from the scene of the crime provided them with no more than suspicion, on which alone they must certainly not act. Nevertheless, for what it might be worth, it did afford some evidence of opportunity. The absence of any blood whatever on the prisoner's clothes which he could not have cleaned during the night would 'seem a powerful argument in the hands of the defence', but he must remind them that the Home Office pathologist, after defining the nature of the wound, had insisted that, if the knife had been held in a certain way, there might be no blood at all on the prisoner; and the other doctor called by the prosecution had supported him in this. He could not accept, said the Judge, that, in the words of defending counsel, the knife, old-fashioned and unfamiliar as it was, could be 'thrown out of the case'. The evidence that the prisoner had been seen in the orchards using one very similar was circumstantial evidence into which they would be wise to probe deeply. 'My learned friend, Sir Mordon, has said that a highly intelligent man like the accused, could not have done anything so abysmally silly as to leave the knife on the scene of the murder. But, gentlemen, the most highly intelligent men in the country occasionally do abysmally silly things—' here came some laughter from the public seats, and the Judge paused to say, 'I will not allow any laughter in this court; we are not offering you an entertainment; let that be clearly understood—I was suggesting, members of the jury, that probably not one of you, nor I myself, nor my learned friend could maintain that he'd never once done an unimaginably foolish thing. But all this is for you to consider and carefully weigh. It was perfectly fair of Sir Mordon to submit this point to you, but I must differ from him in suggesting that it is a matter which can be thrown aside.'

Before he came to those words and acts of the prisoner that were most damaging to the defence—and it was almost, Monty thought, as if, like a good artist, he was keeping these most pungent thrusts till the last—he did say, 'I was somewhat at a loss to understand what point Sir Mordon was seeking to make when he closed a cross-examination by establishing before you that his client was nicknamed by his comrades on the gun-site "Misery". I am not clear what relevance this has to his guilt or innocence. If it was an appeal for pity we can only assume, since Sir Mordon's case is that his client is completely innocent of this charge, that it was designed to explain such unhappy acts of the prisoner as deserting from his battery and sleeping in haystacks or in some ruined shed.

'I can only suppose that this is what my learned friend had in mind.'

'No, I believe he had more in mind than that,' was Monty's thought. 'I believe that a compassionate man, privily confident that the verdict would be "Guilty", had resolved to summon up among the jury a reasonable pity for an unhappy man committed to his care.'

The Judge had just come to the most damaging evidence; he was saying, 'Now I come to the remarks made by the prisoner to Detective Sergeant Maitland, on the occasion of his first arrest as an absentee after he had—' when the air-raid sirens began. From close at hand they began their loud ululating lamentation. The Judge paused in his sentence; he looked up at the glass dome above the court; he listened to the first firing of distant guns; then said, 'Gentlemen, I think, especially as there is one person among us who is denied all freedom as regards his movements, that he should be taken down to the comparative safety of the cells below; and it may be that you and others in this court—' here he gave a genial smile to all in the room—'may prefer to go lower down in this building. I will therefore adjourn this hearing till the All Clear is sounded. But first allow me to apologize for this intervention from abroad in the due process of our British law, and this unmannerly disruption of the judicial calm in which we would wish to see it conducted.'

A little smiling bow to all, and he passed out through his private door.

Monty was surprised how few in the room, whether barristers or press-men, police or public, accepted the suggestion that they should leave this glass-roofed chamber and get themselves downstairs. Some did; far more didn't. Monty who slept nightly in his stout shelter, would have liked to go down as deep as he could—he had in mind, as a prudent Jew, unashamed, the Gentlemen's lavatory deep down in the building's basement—but since neither Rodney nor Everard showed any sign of moving, he decided, though it was against his nature, and though some nearer guns were firing now, that he could not get up and leave two good friends in this, their dark hour. So he remained in his place, between the two, listening to the guns, glancing through the dome at the blue battlefield of the sky, and wondering, as so many had wondered before, if there was not something a trifle mad about these island Anglo-Saxons.

Some of those who had gone downstairs and had returned to places behind him were reporting that, raid or no raid, crowds were massing in the street to hear the result of the trial and police were marshalling them away from the doors of the Old Bailey.

Meanwhile he sat there somewhat envying Stanley in the top security of the strong cells far below.

This daylight raid was not prolonged; the guns stopped; the 'All Clear' sounded, and the Judge was back in his place; the jury too.

'I was about to deal, members of the jury, with the prisoner's remarks to Detective Sergeant Maitland, when these German gentlemen interrupted me. These remarks were spoken after he had been thoroughly searched and examined at the police station for anything that might associate him with the murder. You will remember that his clothes were removed and searched for bloodstains, his fingerprints taken, his finger-nails examined, and even some hairs taken from his head; and that, after this surprising treatment for a mere absentee, he said to Sergeant Maitland, "Now what's all this about? None of it was necessary if you have arrested me merely as an absentee from my unit. You must have been examining me for something far more serious. Was it for that murder?" At least that is what the Sergeant has declared under oath that he said. Of course all the police promptly asked him, "What murder do you mean?" To which he replied, "Wasn't it in the orchard of Wash Green Farm?" Now, members of the jury, the prosecution has made it clear to you that the murder had only been committed during the night before the prisoner uttered these words. Only a few hours before. And naturally the prosecution suggest that this careless, impatient, and possibly unconsidered utterance proved at least that the prisoner knew all about the murder—not only that it had happened but where it had happened.

'The prisoner's answer to this contention, you will recall, was, first, that he said "a murder" and not "that murder", and, secondly, that Police Constable Leaver, who arrested him as a deserter, had mentioned the murder while they were walking together to the Croome City police station; but P.C. Leaver, in his evidence before you has declared that nothing of the sort happened; and you may think that this young man was a fair and excellent witness. Further to this, Sergeant Gowers has deposed that the young constable himself knew nothing about the crime till he arrived at the station with his prisoner. In rebutting this evidence, so damaging to his case, learned counsel for the defence has argued once again that a man of such education and intelligence as his client could hardly have blundered so hopelessly as to uncover within hours of the murder what could only seem guilty knowledge of it. But perhaps I once again may suggest that the wisest of us in times of distraction—and a man arrested for desertion in time of war may well have been distracted—are capable of astonishing and even monstrous blunders. Still, as I have said, it is for you alone to choose between the sworn evidence of the prisoner, and the sworn evidence of two detective sergeants and the young P.C. Leaver.'

He paused on this injunction, and during this small pause Monty was thinking, 'It's those few desperately ill-considered words of poor Stanley, "Was it for that murder" which will hang him. Hang the son of my best friend. All the other evidence would have been insufficient. This is the evidence which closes the vice. What can Rodney and Everard be thinking?'

The Judge had been phrasing his Charge to the Jury for nearly two hours, and he now closed it with a half-minute summary, all of which seemed to Monty to have long been as clear as the daylight in the room, and to require none of this rehearsal, unless it was addressed to a dozen of the mentally void. 'Members of the jury, the Prosecution say that these words could only have been spoken by the murderer himself or by someone who was cognisant of the murder. They say that the knife, exhibit six, was almost certainly the prisoner's. They say that his conduct in the hands of the police was that of a man whose conscience was accusing him of the crime. They have sought to show, not merely that the crime *could* have been committed by this man, but that it *was* committed by him If you agree with them, it will be your duty to find him guilty. On the other hand, if you disagree with them, it will be your duty to acquit him.'

And, having explained this somewhat obvious situation to them, he instructed them to retire, consider the evidence, and 'come and tell him how they found'.

There had been an adjournment for lunch, so it was now past three in the afternoon, and the jury did not return till long after four o'clock. All this time, while the court-room buzzed with chatter—and even laughter now and again—Monty wondered what it could be that was delaying them. The silence between him and Rodney and Everard was not once broken. Presumably they could not bear to ask him what he suspected. And he could not bear to tell them. There were moments, as he waited, when he found himself wishing he was not an 'unbelieving Jew' but one who could pray and pray to some God to help them, to invest them with the strength to bear what was coming.

The jury returned, and the chattering in the room was at once converted into a silence. A staring, waiting silence. Some eyes swung to Rodney in his seat. The wigged barristers standing in the gangways were probably in no doubt as to the issue, but they were waiting there to see the end. Someone knocked three loud raps on the door through which the Judge would return; three loud knocks that brought the whole room to its feet. For the ordinary spectators those knocks were thrilling drama; to Monty they were horrible drama, and not less: Judgment coming through that narrow door—too narrow a door?—to lay its rod on Stanley and to rend the lives of Rodney, Everard, Grace.

The Judge bowed, all sat again, and now, into the silence, came the usual exchange between the Clerk of the Court and the foreman of the jury.

'Are you agreed upon your verdict?'

'We are.'

'Do you find the prisoner, Stanley George Merriwell, guilty or not guilty of murder?'

'We find him guilty.'

'And that is the verdict of you all?'

'It is.'

The Clerk turned to Stanley. 'Prisoner at the bar, you stand convicted of murder. Have you anything to say why the Court should not give you judgment of death according to law?'

Stanley's only answer was a shake of the head, a small, helpless, uninterested shake which suggested that he was as indifferent to what was happening now as he had been to all that had happened during the trial's four days.

The usher called 'O yez! O yez ! O yez!' almost as if he were answering the Clerk's question instead of the prisoner. 'My lords, the King's justices do strictly charge and command all persons to keep silence while sentence of death is passing upon the prisoner at the bar, upon pain of punishment. God save the King.'

Formally the Judge, black-capped now, and with a chaplain

at his side to say 'Amen', began his pronouncement, but before he came to the sentence of death he did say, 'Stanley George Merriwell, you have been found guilty of a terrible crime. No doubt investigation will be made by the proper authorities as to whether there is any medical explanation of your act'—and Monty's heart, which for much of the Judge's Charge, had been occupied with doubt and criticism, leapt with a new sudden hope and with warm approval. The Judge continued, 'In the meantime it is my duty to pass upon you the only sentence known to the law . . .'

In the meantime!

13

Monty Speaks

Monty broke his silence that evening in the presence of Rodney, Grace and Everard. The three men had returned from the trial in Rodney's car, but maintained a silence from the gates of the Old Bailey to the door of Rodney's home. Not one single word came from Rodney and Everard. At Rodney's request Monty had telephoned the verdict to Grace but with the comforting words, at his suggestion, 'Don't worry too much. This is not the end.' This silence of his two companions in the car was pregnant, Monty thought, with grief and with things that could not immediately be spoken. Only the privacy of a homely room could contain them. On their arrival at the house they walked into the drawing-room, and now they were all there together just as they had been on the evening before the trial began.

Rodney spoke first. Grace could not yet speak. Everard, not usually of a retiring habit, did not presume to speak till father or mother had spoken. Rodney walked to the cocktail cabinet which would have been for the most part empty, had not Monty been less inhibited than Rodney, a member of Parliament, in dealing with wartime's 'grey market', and sent them on the trial's eve an under-the-counter bottle of whisky and another such of brandy. If ever two sick people needed some grey market whisky, he had decided, it was his best friends next door.

'Whisky, Monty?' Rodney asked. 'Some of your own whisky?'

'A small one, Rodney. Thank you.'

'Everard?'

'Yes, Dad. For God's sake.'

Against the background of silence Rodney poured out whiskies for the two men, a sherry for Grace, and a neat brandy for himself, to combat a faint sickness. Bringing his glass to a chair, he sat down and asked, 'The truth, please, Monty.' He asked it wearily.

'I do not know the truth.'

'Then the truth all of you think . . . please.'

But before Monty could tell exactly what he thought, Grace cried out, 'Oh, it's all wicked. Absolutely wicked. He didn't do it.' But was this not a cry expressing a desperate hope rather than a certainty? 'Roddy, you know he didn't do it. He was incapable of such a thing. My Stanley never took a knife to a girl. Never, never, never.'

'Yes, sweetheart, he did.'

Monty, astounded by this answer, bewildered by its firmness blent with tenderness, could only stare at Rodney, and wait.

And Rodney said, 'He lied from beginning to end, darling. Chiefly for your sake. Which at least shows to us that there was one place in his poor disordered mind where he was still capable of love and loyalty.'

Grace's face had blanched, her lips were parted in gaping confusion. 'Roddy, what are you saying? He can't have done it. Oh, no!'

Monty, perceiving that Rodney had acquired the answers somewhere, said, 'Tell us all, Rod.'

Everard, as astounded as the others, remained a silent listener, his gaze frozen. Monty suspected, for Everard had told him many things he'd never told his parents, that, behind this frozen glance there were thoughts of a girl, Jeanie, now temporarily lost to him at a distant station, and a wonder what mood would be his if she had sharply thrown him aside for another man.

Grace was sitting on the settee, and Rodney left his chair, sat beside her and picked up her hand. 'Sweetheart, I was allowed, after it was all over, to go down and see Stanley in the cells below the dock. He was sitting there as he had sat all the time in the dock, or as he was sitting when I first saw him in Croome City, with his head down and his hands clasped, indifferent to everything. When I began to speak he interrupted me, saying, "I don't mind the verdict, Dad. Why should I mind it? I don't care what happens to me. Give my love to Mum and Ev."' Here

Grace buried her face in her hands, and Rodney put his arm round her. 'He didn't protest that he was innocent and wronged as he did at Croome City, but told me the truth, that he'd lied all along for your sake, and I suppose for mine and Everard's. Now let's hear what Monty says, darling. Since the verdict was a just one, let us hear how one who was not the boy's parent reads these terrible events. I will accept his views because I am defeated; I do not know what to think.'

'I too,' muttered Everard.

And Grace could no longer say 'But never me. I will never believe . . .' She could only weep. And say, 'It's too awful to think he could have done this terrible, this wicked, thing. He couldn't have known what he was doing. He didn't.'

'Come, Monty.'

A hesitant pause, and Monty spoke. 'I'm afraid, my dears, that I've been pretty certain for some time that the truth was just what Stanley confessed to Rod so honestly. All that careless blundering with the knife and with his words at the police station, and his lies everywhere, fitted well enough with his condition, as I think I understand it. It is a state in which a blind stupefaction is possible and an incredible reasonless bungling, because he's indifferent to everything, including truth. Why worry about truth? They were actions outside the pale of any normal sanity. But don't let these words frighten you, Grace dear; it's just that we all know now that there are vast regions of inadequately explored conjecture about mental derangements that can sometimes be only temporary. You see, I was soon pretty sure that Sir Mordon, who seemed to me a good man, believed he could have secured for Stanley a verdict of "Guilty but Insane" but he was precluded from this because Stanley insisted on a plea of "Not Guilty". Counsel cannot go against his client. He could only hint at the more merciful verdict, which he did more than once, and I blessed him for it. But all this means, Grace dear, that there's much which can now be urged in Stanley's help.'

'You mean that there's a chance he may be reprieved,' Rodney asked.

'I mean exactly that. And I suspect too that the Judge was

thinking on those lines. He had to sum-up for a verdict of "Guilty", since that was the palpable truth of the matter, but he went out of his way, generously, I thought, to suggest that there might be a mental explanation of Stanley's acts, and that there would certainly be an inquiry into this possibility. Which means we can hope for a reprieve. The judge who has conducted a trial is always a powerful voice in such an inquiry.'

'But then Stanley, my son, will be imprisoned for life,' Grace protested.

'Not really for life, dear. For a few years.'

'And that poor girl can never be brought back to life.'

Since this was something that none could bear thinking about Rodney diverged from it. 'But what is the method by which a reprieve is secured? How do they go about it?'

'Yes, how?' Everard asked, glad to be in an area of thought less unbearable. 'You know all about forensic medicine.'

'Well, it's all rather odd and typically English, in that logic is laid aside and a practical issue is arrived at by a compromise between the Law and Common Sense. Strictly a jury alone can decide on the fact of a man's mental derangement, but once the trial is safely out of the way, and the Law has been properly honoured, it requires no more than a certificate from two prison visitors that they doubt his sanity for the Home Secretary to get busy considering a reprieve. He gets two or more doctors to report on a condemned man, and if they decide he's insane, the reprieve is likely to follow. It's all hopelessly illogical, and, I should have thought, illegal, but who minds so long as a humane decision is reached?'

'Good,' Rodney murmured. 'Splendid. And do you think this could happen in Stanley's case?'

'I think it's what ought to happen. But . . .'

'But what?'

'But there is much opposition among the sterner judges and K.C.'s and M.P.'s—as a good Liberal like you, Roddy, must know—against all us interfering psychiatrists, and especially against our intervening in the processes of law. A recent committee argued that if an offender escapes punishment by "dubious and unprovable doubts about his mental condition the observance of the law is gravely hindered." We are not the most popular breed in the Law's sacred chambers, and maybe it's partly our fault because we often differ so widely and noisily from one another. As I've often bewailed to you before, there are almost as many sects among psychologists as among Christians, each with its own prophet, and probably with its own Holy Writ; the sacred books of Freud, Adler, Jung, Fromm, or whichever. But I imagine we're all agreed on one thing, whatever our particular faction . . .'

Monty stopped. He suddenly feared that he was touching too fluently, too easily, on the less promising truths.

'Go on, Monty. We must know all.'

'Well . . . the so-called "Judges' Rules" on what can support a plea of insanity are exactly a hundred years old this year, and psychological medicine has advanced far in a century. The modern view is that unsoundness of mind is not simply a disorder of the intellectual faculties but something much more profoundly related to the whole organism—a morbid change of the emotional and instinctive activities, with or without much intellectual derangement. Thus we all believe these "Judges' Rules" to be far too narrow in their vision and hopelessly out-of-date. But the judges still harp on them, and insist on them, in their Charges to juries. Only the other day, as you may have seen, there was a stormy row between defending counsel and one of our most illiberal judges, Wilford Hardings, who'd demanded of him irritably, during his examination of a witness, "Mr. So-and-So, must we go through all this psychological clap-trap again?" Hardly a judicial comment from a judge's throne. That is what we shall have to fight. And only yesterday I was arguing with a famous and usually lenient judge, having Stanley in mind, that there *can* be something in a man sufficiently unhinged that we can only call an irresistible impulse. His answer was that if an impulse was so powerful as to be called irresistible there was all the more reason that we should not withdraw any of the safeguards against such impulses. An answer that seemed to me less reasonable than it sounded.'

There was silence again when Monty had finished. Then

117

Rodney said, 'Thank you, Monty,' and pursued, 'If the Home Secretary is approached about a reprieve——'

'As he will be——'

'—how long will it be before we know his decision?'

'That I can't say. Some weeks, I suppose.'

To which Rodney could only murmur impotently, 'Oh, God . . .'

And Grace, out of her hopelessness, and probably picturing with an utter heart-sickness a rope, a noose, and a trap, could only say, 'They *must* reprieve him . . . Stanley, my boy . . . They *must*. Monty, they *must*.'

§

The trial had ended on the 21st of January, and the papers did not fail to report two days later that the date appointed for Stanley's execution was the 16th February. If the press had been magnanimous in the first days of Stanley's arrest, deliberately omitting his father's name, no single paper could spare Rodney now. The publicity was the more widespread because the condemned man's father was a well-known and popular name in Parliament—the more popular and well-known, perhaps, because of his loneliness as a Liberal. The copy of *The Times* which reported the date of execution Rodney took quietly out of the house that Grace's eye might not fall on it. He pretended he was going to Westminster but this morning he could not face his fellow-members. If there was a reprieve he would take his place among them again. Somehow it would be easier to appear before them as a man whose son had been reprieved than as the father of a son awaiting execution. He just got into his car and, heedless that he was using the last of his wartime petrol, raced it anywhere—he did not care where. But it was difficult to shake off the vast spread of London, and when at last he found himself in open country and between hedges, he realized that he was on the Dover Road and approaching the orchards of Kent. He observed behind the wintry hedges, for the first time, their long serried rows of naked trees. Instantly he swung the car round to get away from them, and drove back till he was in a stretch of landscape between Shooter's Hill and Oxlease Wood.

There he stopped the car, and now that it was still, and his eyes and hands unoccupied, he took one more look at the brief statement in *The Times* and remembered Stanley once again as a three-year-old infant sitting pickaback on his shoulders, or batting to his bowling at ten or eleven-years-old in their small London garden with Everard alert in the covers. Of the two boys it had been Stanley whom he'd thought the more likely to play one day for Middlesex and perhaps for the Gentlemen. At first he struggled with his tears, biting his lower lip as far as his chin, but abandoned the struggle, since there were none but speeding motorists to pass him by, and they would not see in a closed limousine a complete and unmanly breakdown. He let the sobs shake him and the tears flow as they had not flowed since childhood.

'There must be a reprieve. God make it that they give him a reprieve. Please, God, hear me in this; forgive my sins and let my cry come unto thee. Stanley. O God, I commit him to thee. Stanley . . .'

The tears spent at last, the sobs quelled, he started his engine, let in his clutch, and drove slowly home to Grace.

In the afternoon he did go furtively to the House, which was in session again after the brief wartime recess, but he did not go into the Chamber. He passed rapidly and guiltily from sight of all in the Lobby and found cover in the Library. Here he was glad to find himself alone, as he had foreseen. In a Statute book he found with difficulty the Criminal Lunatics Act, 1884, and read in its stilted and involuted lawyer's language exactly what Monty had told him.

'In the case of a person under sentence of death, if it appears to the Secretary of State, either by means of a certificate signed by two members of the visiting committee of the prison in which such prisoner is confined, or by any other means, there is reason to believe such prisoner to be insane, the Secretary of State shall appoint two or more qualified medical practition-ers . . .' and so on. He closed the book and sat beside it where it lay shut upon the table.

Then, after prying, like a guilty schoolboy, to make sure no one was approaching and his retreat was safe, he came out of the Library, trying to live with hope.

'There *will* be a reprieve. Even the Judge was in favour of it. And they are treated kindly in a mental hospital—' not even here alone, walking along St. Stephen's Hall, could he speak the name 'Broadmoor' to himself—'and possibly after some years he will be fully cured by those advances in psychotherapy which Monty described, and "at His Majesty's pleasure" he will be set free. He will still be young. This is what I must keep before Grace. I will keep her hoping.'

But the days passed, two weeks passed, nearly three weeks, and it was only two days before the date of execution that an announcement appeared. Headed 'No Reprieve for Merriwell', it stated simply that the Home Secretary, after causing a special medical inquiry to be made into the sanity of Stanley George Merriwell, and after careful consideration of the reports submitted to him, had decided that he was unable to advise the King to use his prerogative of mercy. 'The Law must therefore take its course.'

Without showing the dreadful paragraph to Grace, Rodney hurried to Monty and to him alone, asking, demanding, repeating the burden of his question again and again, whether the fact of Stanley being the son of a well-known M.P., whom simple people might imagine to have a power above ordinary citizens in such a matter, could have weighed in the scales against the granting of a reprieve. 'Justice must not only be done, but must be seen to be done by all,' he argued. 'No one must seem to be privileged. Crimes are far less pardonable in the privileged classes who've enjoyed every advantage. And if a boy's father's an M.P. enjoying the friendship of the Home Secretary . . .'

But Monty would not allow that any Home Secretary would suffer such an irrelevant factor to decide whether a man should live or die. All he could say was that if only this were happening in ten or twenty years from now he felt sure that Stanley would be reprieved; because by then his present mental condition would be more deeply understood and more generally accepted. There was little comfort in this, and Rodney argued wearily, 'Yes, but all I am suggesting is that if the odds were swinging evenly against a reprieve, this was an odd that tilted the scale down.' No matter what Monty might say, he could not shake himself free of the fear that his prominence in the country had played its part in denying life to his son.

And he never did.

§

Early in the morning of the execution, just before its hour struck, Rodney was sitting on the drawing-room sofa, side by side with Grace (all thought of a meal being impossible). He was holding her hand and spasmodically pressing it fiercely. Everard sat with them on a neighbouring chair. He had been granted leave to be with them by a patently sympathetic if undemonstrative Station Commander, to whom he had said, 'I think, on the whole, sir, perhaps it might be easier for them if they had one son with them.'

Rodney, glancing at the small clock on the mantel, even suggested softly that they might kneel and pray—as he had prayed in his car, but Grace said, 'I will not.' She said it passionately, and continued passionately, finding relief in words. 'I have no belief in God. I never have had, and I have it less than ever now, since Stanley has been so cruelly struck down. I've often sat down and tried hard to believe, but it's no good. None of it makes sense to me. When I read that our sun is ninety million miles away and anyhow is only one of the smaller stars in the Milky Way in which other stars have their solar systems around them, or that our own solar system started two thousand million years ago, why, what's the good of telling me there's a Creator who's interested in my little troubles and will do anything about them? And then tell me that he's a God of love! *Love*, when all this has happened to a boy of mine! I didn't bring my Stanley into the world for this. Of course it was terrible what he did, but it was not his fault; Monty said it was not his fault. You pray to your God, if you like, but I'll not say one word to him, ever.'

Rodney offered nothing in answer to this tirade; it was no

hour for argument, so he just pressed her hand again, and said, 'All right, my dear.'

Everard had nothing to say either, but he rose from his chair, kissed his mother's limp hand, and returned to his seat.

The clock on the mantel struck its mild notes, each note wounding Rodney like a stab at the heart. When all must be over in the prison far away, he raised Grace to her feet and gathered her tight against his breast but all he could think of to say was 'He's at peace now.'

And she, speaking to herself rather than to him, trying to teach herself the ever imperative lesson of acceptance, said only, and in part defiantly, 'Oh, well . . . there it is . . .' But the defiance couldn't last. She dragged herself away from him, dropped to the sofa again and dropped her face into her hands that the tears might gush, while she cried through them, 'Stanley, Stanley, Stanley.' And again all he could do was to draw her close against him, press his lips upon the bowed head, and murmur, 'Just think that he's at peace, beloved.'

14

Everard over Hamburg

Everard had been rested on the ground much longer than he
had expected, and this in spite of his requests, as the later
months went by, to be put back on operations. It was only in
the summer of this year that he was 'back on ops', with the
rank of squadron leader. He was back in time for the terrible
mass-raids on Hamburg, Germany's second greatest city, in
the black 'Hamburg Week' of July 24th to August 1st. Probably the mounting loss of pilots had made the A.O.C. ready
at last, and very ready, to accede to his requests. On August
4th, after a few last dwindling raids on the dying city had
petered out, he came home on leave, and told his parents the
story of Hamburg.

They thought he looked pale, tired round the eyes, and
thinner, like a youth worn in face and frame to the point of
exhaustion.

'It's been going on for days, day after day, or rather night
after night, as far as we are concerned. The Yanks go in by
day. The heaviest raids were on Friday last, and on Sunday a
week ago. On Friday the whole dockland area was laid waste
and a great part of the city too. On Sunday the Yanks with
their Flying Fortresses went in during daylight and then we
followed, eight hundred of us, just as the dark came down. We
bombed and bombed for a solid four hours, coming in over
the target area at the rate of ten a minute. There's no doubt
what we're doing: we're laying the whole city flat, bombing it
flat and setting it ablaze from end to end, civilian areas as well
as military targets, and never mind if the civilians are men,
women, children, or babies—or even if they're our own
prisoners-of-war in the hospitals. We're given area after area
of the city to plaster night after night, till the whole place

is dead. That's our policy. Bomber Harris has said so. He said——'

'Bomber who?' Grace had to ask.

'Harris. Bomber Harris. C. in C. Bomber Command. He said, "We're going to scourge the Third Reich, city by city, and ever more terribly. That's our object." Well, we've done it now. We've dropped, so they tell us, eighty thousand H.E.s——'

'H.E.s?' Grace pleaded for clarification.

'High explosives, eighty thousand incendiaries, and five thousand phosphorus bombs. When we went in before dark a few nights ago we could hardly see a wall standing; the whole place was a bloody wasteland, and "bloody" is probably the exact word. In the docks there are great ships lying on their sides, and U boats too. According to a stoker type who—very wisely, I thought—deserted his ship and got himself to Stockholm, the death roll was then estimated at forty thousand, of whom five thousand were children. But it must be a lot more now. There were about one and a half million people in Hamburg, and I should think all of them are done in except those who took to the woods outside the city, and are living like gypsies there. There must be thousands now lying buried beneath the universal ruins. I can tell you, Mum, your London Blitz lasted for more than two months, but it didn't do one hundredth part of what this week on Hamburg has done. I suppose they deserved a lot, and I'm all for destroying ships and U boats and setting the oil refineries and the flour-mills ablaze, but I don't think I'm for destroying and setting children and babies ablaze. I don't know what you think about it, Dad. I have to do it, because I'm ordered to, but—' he shrugged—'between you and me, I'm supremely happy bombing all the military targets you like, but the whole civilian population—God, no! It's the kids that worry us, and the old and the helpless too, I suppose. . . .'

'But you've been all right all the time?' Grace besought him.

'So far. A few pin-pricks on my starboard wing three nights ago. That's all. I have the luck of the devil. And this particular little job's done now. Hamburg's dead. They'll bring it to life again, but not the five thousand kids. Dad, I sometimes think I'd never have pestered them to put me back on ops, if I'd known I was going to be told to play this filthy game, but one can't back out now. Orders are orders. . . .'

Very plainly he had been longing to vent these harrying doubts within four loyal walls of his childhood home. This familiar and comfortable room with its ever-silent walls, their backs turned upon the world outside, were but an extension of his private mind.

'Quite a few of our chaps don't like it. But they say the only thing they can do is to try to forget it. Tell me what you really think about it, Dad. I mean, what can I do? Just damn-all. Disobedience of a lawful command given by a superior officer is mutiny.'

'I know what I think about it,' said Rodney. 'I think it's gross and awful and wicked. But I don't know what you can do. Disobedience to a *lawful* command . . . I suppose one could argue that the organized killing of civilians isn't lawful and refuse to do it, but——'

'But that's much easier said than done. I'm not hero enough for that. I'll face old Jerry's flak—I can't say I love it, but I somehow enjoy it—the excitement gets you, but there's no excitement in facing a firing squad. Besides, they'd have shot me before some clever bloke proved that it was all illegal, and I was right and they were wrong. And a fat lot of use——'

At these words Grace cried, 'Oh!' and 'Don't say things like that . . . *please*. Roddy, for God's sake, don't encourage him to do anything rash. How can you run an army and a war, if the boys are to decide which orders are legal, and which they'll obey. If it's all a crime, then the criminals are those who order the boys to——'

But she could not speak the word 'murder'.

Quickly Everard said, 'You needn't worry, Mum. I'm just not equal to doing anything brave like that;' and one could see that he regretted recalling to them both, in a heedless effort to speak smartly, their dark hour of seven months before. He turned them quickly away from that terrible memory, and himself away too, asking almost laughingly, 'What about you,

Dad? What about you doing something as an M.P.? What's the good of being an M.P. if you can't let them have the whole ghastly truth? Yes, I think that's a wonderful idea.'

'My God, I wish I could,' said Rodney, 'but it'd need a brave man to do it properly, and I'm not much of a hero either. Indeed, as I've often told you, I'm a coward when it comes to making a big speech in the House. I sweat with fear about it for days and nights before. And this, I should think, would be about the most unpopular speech I could make, and I hate being disliked. Quite simply, I'm lacking in moral courage.'

'No, you're not,' said Grace, 'and I think you should do just what Everard said. It would be a wonderful thing to do. I think it's just what you ought to do.'

So easy, thought Rodney, with lips compressed but not unhumorously, so easy for a woman to talk like that, who hasn't got to do it, who doesn't realize, though I've told her a hundred times, what it takes to do it, who's only to sit at home or in the Distinguished Strangers' gallery and rejoice in a husband's fine action; and so like a mother to seize upon and urge a son's counsel at the expense of her husband. I did say months ago that I wished I could do something about it, and she only discouraged me, saying 'What'd be the good? You wouldn't achieve anything. I should keep quiet and do nothing unwise.' But now Everard has spoken, and his is the truth.

Everard caught his mother's new mood and endorsed it cheerfully, 'Yes, Dad, you have one hell of a raid on your old House of Commons. Do 'em a world of good.'

'But steady, steady, both of you,' Rodney complained. 'You talk as if one can get up in the House and speak about anything one fancies at any time one likes. One can't.'

'Then what's the good of being an M.P.?' Everard demanded again.

'That's what I sometimes wonder.'

'Surely there's some way of doing it,' Grace persisted.

'I can think of only three ways.'

'And what are they?' both asked.

Rodney was pleased to be asked this. Like any other man

he was always proud to be an expert delivering erudite information to the ignorant; and the more unfamiliar and resonant the technical terms, the better. 'You might get your speech in by opening the Motion for the Adjournment, but you'd have to win the ballot to do that, and as it comes at the end of the day's business, there'd be precious few to hear you.'

'Well, that's no cop,' said Everard.

'Or you might do it during the Supply Debate on the Air Estimates.'

'Obviously the time,' Everard acclaimed triumphantly.

'True enough, but that chance won't come till the spring of next year when the war'll probably be over, and, anyhow, there's no assurance you'd be called. Just the same applies to the Debate on the Address—the King's Gracious Speech— a long way off, and no certainty you'd catch the Speaker's eye. The only way to make certain of being called would be to put down a Motion for an Emergency Debate on a Subject of Immediate Interest.'

'Well, let's do that,' said Everard. 'This is of immediate interest, if ever anything was. Yes, I'm all for that.'

'You may be, but there's no certainty the Speaker would grant an Emergency Debate; indeed the odds are he wouldn't.'

'Good God,' sighed Everard. 'Why does anyone want to be an M.P. when you can stay at home and water the garden?'

15

Uproar in the House

Rodney rose from his back bench. The Commons, since the bombing of their Chamber in '41, had sat for a while in Church House, and sat now (as has been told) in the House of Lords. But the Lords' Chamber, while serving as a home for the Commons, had been turned, as it were, head to tail, the King's magnificent Gothic throne being railed off from any trespassing by his faithful Commons, the Woolsack removed, and the Speaker's Chair, fine but humble compared with His Majesty's, erected at the opposite end. Today the tiered benches, upholstered in their royal red, were fairly well filled, spectators were looking down from the brass-railed galleries under the soaring stained-glass Gothic windows, and probably never, within these glories, had a speaker been more nervous than Rodney when he rose.

It was his first speech for more than a year, and certainly his most important. After the execution of a son he had allowed weeks to pass before showing himself in his usual place. Yet when he did take his seat again his reception by members of all parties had been notably generous, many making it their business to address kindly words to him, never mentioning an execution, nor alluding to his absence.

And now he had to rise and address them. As always nervousness shook his heart, and he was glad that the missing of several heart-beats was known to none, and that the red bench in front of him, to say nothing of the gentleman sitting on it, concealed a quivering of his right knee.

But, partnering the nervousness, there was something else: a longing, a determination, to overthrow these disabilities and discharge a task his conscience approved. And beneath both the nerves and the longing, there lay a hope of comfort. Knowing himself, he knew that, if the opposition to what he had to say was loud and rude enough, a daemon of indignation would take fire within him, a certainty that he was right would fan the flame, all fears would slough off him, and he would speak with the rushing ease (and the comfort) of anger. As a 'pure Liberal' he was usually hampered from hot fighting by his toleration of all opposing views; but if an unarguable principle seemed at stake, why, then . . . then this most diffident of Liberals might shed all weakness and speak fire.

Grace knew this too, and ever since her conversion by a son on leave instead of a daily husband, she had been badgering him to get up and tell the House his mind, as Everard had wanted him to do. 'It's your duty to do what the boy says. All these boys being forced against their will to massacre women and children—it's wicked. And you should tell them. Tell them so.'

'But I'm no good at it, as I keep on telling you.'

'Oh, yes you are. You are when you're angry. I've heard you on platforms when some idiot has properly annoyed you, and you've been splendid. Exasperate them, exasperate them properly, and then they'll exasperate you, and you'll fairly let fly.'

'Well, as long as you're not there listening perhaps I could have a try at it.'

'You can, and you will. I insist upon it. Just remember Everard and let go. You know, and I know, that if only you were not so wretchedly at the mercy of your nerves and could trust yourself to the moment, you'd be as good a speaker as any in the House. And better than most I dare say, because you've a real gift of eloquence. Speak the truth, make them angry, lose your temper properly, and then see what happens.'

'But *you* mustn't be there. I shall be nervous enough without being infected half the time with your nerves up in the gallery.'

So Grace was not in the gallery today, and his hour had come.

'Mr. Speaker, I move that this House do now adjourn to debate a matter of urgent public importance. What I have to say will not, I fear, commend itself to many in this House, but a long searching of my heart has decided me that it is my duty to speak. Before I say a word I would remind you that I have been an opponent of the Nazi regime in Germany since it first disclosed its full quality ten years ago—and this, honourable members—' here he attempted a disarming smile—'was rather sooner than some of my friends opposite.'

The conventional words were flowing well; they could not do other, because he'd been learning them by heart during a week and more of doubts and birth-labours, rehearsing them in his empty study, in the street as he walked, and in the darkness before sleep, beneath his bedclothes. His only worry at the moment was a trembling of the hand that held his notes. He hoped no one noticed it. His eyes were good, so it was possible for much of the time to keep the trembling notes behind the head of the gentleman in front. Unfortunately, however, there were members on either side of him, turning to watch him as he spoke, and they were not denied a sight of this ineptitude. Possible too that they could detect the trembling of that knee. Still, the reception of these early words was warm-hearted enough, murmurs of encouragement and friendly smiles supporting him. Nine months had not enabled the House to forget that this was a father who had suffered Heaven-knew-what one morning. . . .

'I must declare at the beginning that in what I shall have to say I am intending no criticism of our pilots and air-crews who are but obeying their orders and performing their allotted tasks with a courage that almost transcends belief.'

'Hear, hear's' from all parts of the Chamber.

'Perhaps in this context I may add that my own son is a pilot who has done many tours of operations and is now, at his own insistence, flying again because he deemed this his duty in the present hour.'

More 'Hear, hear's'; greatly approving 'Hear, hear's', though he could detect in them a wonder as to what it might be that he was about to say.

'Mr. Speaker, at the outbreak of war, the Governments of this country and of France made a declaration of their intention to conduct hostilities in such a way as would—in any bombardment by Army, Navy, or Air Force—attempt to attack only military objectives and spare, so far as possible , all non-combatants. It is true that our Government qualified this by an announcement that—' here he was glad to be able to raise his notes visibly and read from them—'that in the event of the enemy not observing these restrictions our Governments reserve the right to take such action as they considered appropriate.'

This drew such an abundance of 'Hear, hear's', some of them hotly combative, and directed towards the absent enemy rather than to the present speaker, that they served as a warning of what he must expect as the speech proceeded. Fortunately this began the process of stripping away the nervousness and stirring up the so helpful impatience. 'Yes,' he said, 'we know that the enemy has not spared civilians anywhere; we remember London and Coventry, Warsaw, Belgrade and Rotterdam; I don't forget the Baedeker raids, Exeter, Bath, York—' a voice: 'I should think not'—'but my submission today is not for us to make the Nazi barbarians our exemplars and to compete with them, as we are now doing, in these monstrous cruelties——'

Now came the first notes of intolerant and incensed opposition; cries of 'Oh, rubbish!' and 'War is war' and 'Let 'em have a taste of their own medicine'. One angry voice even mumbled, 'Oh, sit down;' while a milder voice, talking to itself, was content with 'Stop? At this stage?' and 'sentimentally absurd'. A last straggler supplied, 'Bilge'.

And thanks to these voices Rodney was now fully alight, and healed of fear; timidity gave place to ease and power; indeed there now followed, often independent of his precious notes, the only speech he'd delivered with ease and delight during the twenty-five years he'd been in the House.

'Honourable members may hoot as much as they like; I hold to what I say. If we conquer the enemy by imitating everything we've violently condemned him for doing, we may win this war in a material sense, but he will have conquered us spiritually.'

'Rubbish,' 'Stuff and nonsense,' 'Oh, come off it,' and 'He's asked for everything he's getting.' A rumour that a scene was developing in the House must have run to lobbies, library, and smoking room, because members were now straying in, or hurrying in, to take their usual places or stand beside the Speaker's Chair and watch and listen.

And surprisingly, gloriously, the sight of them all, instead of renewing the nervousness only swelled a desire to say all his stuff to them (the more of them the better) and loosed, when necessary, a whole flow of new, excellent, and unpremeditated words.

'Let us look at the things we have done and are proudly proposing to continue doing. I assert that they are beyond the limits of justifiable war——'

'No!' 'No!' But these 'No's' only strengthened his fighting arm. They and other protests might beat about his head but he went on with ever greater assurance, 'Hamburg is—or was—Germany's second largest city. It has—or had—a population of nearly two million. It has—or had—industrial, military and naval works, all of which are legitimate targets——'

'Quite so.' 'Hear, hear.' 'So why not shut up?'

'I have no intention of shutting up. What did we do? For seven or eight terrible days we set about the complete obliteration of the city with no limitation to justifiable targets. This was openly announced as our policy. A Government spokesman told us—proudly: "It is the proclaimed intention of Bomber Command to proceed with the systematic obliteration, one by one, of the centres of German war production till the enemy's capacity to continue the fight is broken down—"' voices: 'Quite right too'—'and the Chief of Bomber Command rephrased this more picturesquely, "One by one, we shall pull out every town in Germany like a rotten tooth—"' 'Good' and 'Hurray' and 'What's wrong with that?' and 'Quite right too.'

'What's wrong? Only that, in pursuance of this policy, we have set about destroying civilian homes as well as military objectives. I am informed—' no mention of Everard—'that in Hamburg at least forty thousand civilians were killed and some seventy thousand in Berlin—thousands of them children. And this is to go on, we proudly proclaim, until, quoting the Chief of Bomber Command again, "the heart of Nazi Germany ceases to beat". So there it is; and for my part I have judged it time for me to stand up and say this is something I will not be associated with. I am glad I belong to no section of any party that believes in this. I love my country with the best of you, but there can be a larger loyalty than love of one's country; and it is loyalty to humanity as a whole. Mr. Speaker, I remember one summer day last year when I stood on the sandy ridge of our Northern Heights, which gives its name to my constituency, and looked down upon the whole of London with pride because I was seeing her as the capital, not only of England, but of every country in the world that was fighting for humanity. But, alas, it was just about this time that the great raid on Lubeck and the thousand-bomber raid on Cologne introduced me to our new terror bombing; and if I pass that way now I look down upon her with sadness. It seems to me—and I'm choosing my words deliberately—that we, who have heard with horror of the Nazi's so-called "Final Solution" for the problem of the Jews by destroying them in millions, are attempting some sort of "Final Solution" of the German problem by a kindred method——'

This was the sentence that provoked the uproar. Members sprang to their feet, shouting angrily. For a minute or more the chorus of protests continued. 'Disgraceful,' 'Outrageous,' 'Withdraw,' 'Bloody treason——'

'I shall not withdraw,' he strove to insert into the din. 'Not one single word.' But no one listened; the fury beat about his head, till one of the 'pure Liberals', rising beside him, managed to catch the Speaker's eye. Rodney gave way to him, temporarily sitting down, and looking towards him.

He was one of many Liberals, pure or impure, and indeed of other parties, who had supported Rodney's request for an emergency debate, possibly in a puckish mood, some of them, because the Member for Ridgeway, the Lonely Incorruptible, was so popular, in a humorous way, among them.

'Mr. Speaker—on a point of order—the Honourable and Gallant Member for Goldstone has just, in my hearing, offered a remark, and I suggest he repeat it, so that we can be told if it is in order.'

'I said "Bloody treason".' The Honourable and Gallant

Member was happy to repeat his offering. Certain enough, thought Rodney, that no 'honourable and gallant' member would tolerate what he'd just said.

Not surprisingly the Speaker ruled that the words were unparliamentary and the Honourable and Gallant Member must withdraw them.

'If it was not a parliamentary expression, Mr. Speaker,' said the offender, 'I will of course, in deference to you, withdraw it, only maintaining that, parliamentary or not, the statement remains, in my view the truth.'

'Hear, hear' from several.

And everyone seemed satisfied with this counterchange, this due demanded and paid to the parliamentary courtesies, so Rodney was able to proceed. Heated and indignant, and certain he possessed the truth, he was well away now.

'You do not like what I say. I cannot help that. For me it looks too much like a truth, and no amount of opposition will stop me saying it. I will allow that this "carpet bombing" is less terrible than the Germans' massacring of the Jews, since it is at least an act of war—however blind and wicked I may think it—whereas the other is just coldly organized genocide, having no necessary relation to a war. None the less our obliteration bombing, differ as it may from the Nazi's "Final Solution", is still something very difficult for humane men to live with; and, in my eyes, we are all degraded by it. Up till now, like a civilized people, and like all our forebears in the past we have honoured, I should have thought, the Laws and Customs of War which declared that the slaughter of non-belligerents out of uniform was, so far as possible, unacceptable to all and mutually forbidden. But, quite apart from the legitimacy of this saturation bombing, I am going to make the point that it will defeat its own ends. What was the result of the indiscriminating Blitz upon London? Upon Coventry? Upon Exeter and Bath and the other cities? Simply that the whole people woke up to the fact that this was *their* war. I suggest that a precisely similar result must be happening in Germany. By our massacre of civilians we have probably achieved more than the Nazis achieved by tyranny and terror. We have gone a long way towards uniting the German people behind their Nazi masters. Since Alamein the tides have been setting towards our victory, so where's the sense of delaying it by murderous nonsense like this? Note that I said "gone a long way to uniting the German people". Thank God there remain in Germany a great number who oppose the Nazi tyranny. Not for a moment am I denying the responsibility of most Germans in their acceptance and toleration of this monstrous regime, but it is necessary for all sensible men to distinguish between the German people as a whole and their Nazi state——'

Many cries of 'No!' and 'Not any longer.' One member managed to rise and, Rodney giving way to him, to assert that from the dawn of history, from the times of Julius Caesar even, the Germans had shown themselves as a bellicose people, ardent for war, easily disciplined in hordes for it, and ever pitiless in it.

'Then what about you?' Rodney retorted. 'You are probably proud to be an Anglo-Saxon, descended from the Saxons and the Angles who came from Schleswig-Holstein and the Rhineland five hundred years after Caesar—which means that you, and probably fifty-per-cent of the members listening to me, are just as Teutonic in extraction as any of these Germans you are condemning.'

No doubt this was a fair debating point, and it pleased him not a little, but it was certainly the most unpopular and unwise remark he had made. It had mildly offended the majority present. A kind of sneering silence met it, which was much less helpful and invigorating than the loud hostility. It knocked him off his stride, and it was only after stuttering and stumbling that he recovered some ease and power.

Weakly, he resumed, 'Oh, but come, come. Of course we must distinguish between seventy million Germans and their temporary Hitlerite state. There's no sense in crying out "No!" and "Not any longer". That's on a level with a schoolboy's thinking. Look at facts, not at your over-heated prejudices. What about the thousands and tens of thousands of anti-Nazis in the concentration camps, many being killed or tortured there? What about the brave Confessing Church of

Germany which opposes the Führer's National Church and has issued a Confession of Faith that the only word they will listen to and trust and obey in life and death is the Word of God. In life and death. For many it has been death. Here are thousands of Germans who might be on our side, and we are driving them to despair. The Minister of Propaganda in Germany is using our saturation raids to tell the German people that if we get into Germany we shall hang and torture and burn them alive, and it is likely the simpler Germans believe him. Where's the sense of trying to help Hitler win his war?'

When the murmurings of dissent and ridicule allowed him, he came to a simple peroration, read from his notes as quietly and calmly as his previous words had been unrestrained and provocative. 'After victory there must come peace and gradual reconciliation, so today I, as one who has sat among you as a Liberal for so many years, beg to submit, with all the earnestness I can command, that it should be our task to serve and not frighten, to encourage and not discourage, the large Liberal forces that are undoubtedly to be found among the seventy million German people.'

§

The silence was complete as he sat down. It was a remarkable and, to him, a distressing silence: no muttered jeers or disapproval; not a voice anywhere. It persuaded Rodney that in all the large audience, seated or standing, there were but a few who fully agreed with him, and they were stilled by the silence of others. It was a silence that seemed to hold a cold hostility in the many, and discomfort in the few; it was like a winter-frost which can seem at times to silence all the world around it. Instantly the ease and power with which he had fought for his creed against cries and sneers was gone from him again, dispersed like a transitory enchantment, and he was converted into his normal self, a nervous man easily enslaved by apprehensions and doubts. His knees knocked where he sat, and a sweat formed as usual on the nape of his neck. A high Tory member rose, undoubtedly to berate and ridicule him;

and he did not wish to hear the man. He had said his piece, taken his punishment, and that was that; he wanted no more. He would have liked to quit the House there and then, in despair and disgust; but as mover of the motion he must stay in his place till the debate's end. The moment it ended, however, he rose to escape from the Chamber and be alone. Other members went out with him, but they gave him not a word. They carried the Chamber's hostile silence with them.

He walked quickly out of the precincts into New Palace Yard, his mind reiterating all the time phrases he had used when he was afraid of no one, and wondering how general was the disapprobation and dislike. He shivered away from dislike. Too shaken to drive his car which was in the Yard, he left it there and walked alone along the Embankment, looking at the river till his disarray should have settled a little. He was in better control of himself by the time he reached Hungerford Bridge, but, even so, he dreaded going back into New Palace Yard lest he met members who passed him in silence or turned uncomfortably away.

16

D Days and V Days

It was late in '43 when Rodney, his heart-beats irregular and a sweat forming on his nape, attempted this denunciation of area bombing and ended by hearing himself for the first time shouted down and visited with almost universal scorn. He never spoke again in the House—except for an infrequent question or intervention. Thereafter he just voted in the Lobbies for the true Liberal attitudes with the dozen other incorruptibles, a lonely band mostly from Scotland and Wales. If silent in the Chamber, he often spoke hotly in Smoking Room or Dining Room about his country's part in the continued obliteration bombing, which had been affected not the slightest by his daring speech, despite his labour pains before it and the sufferings after it.

Sometimes a doubt would assail him as to whether he had been as completely sensible as he had supposed. You could argue that this war was no longer a war between armies in uniform but a war between whole peoples, everyone helping it except the whole-hogging pacifist and conscientious objector. Then it looked as if the only logical position was 'Be a conchie and then alone you'll be talking sense.'

But he could never get his heart to believe this, whatever his head might say. He remained at one with Everard, hating the thought that a son of his should be forced under orders to inflict agonizing pain or death on women and children and babies. Somehow and somewhere here, his heart maintained, there must be a wrong.

In '44 came the D Days, the days of 'Operation Overlord', which was the invasion of Normandy and the sentencing to death of Germany. In his breakfast room at nine in the morning he and Grace heard the simple announcement, 'Communiqué No. 1 from Supreme Headquarters, Allied Expeditionary Force, states, "Under the command of General Eisenhower, Allied naval forces, supported by strong air forces, began landing armies this morning on the northern coast of France."' In the House, packed, expectant, and chattering like an excited cage of monkeys, he sat waiting for the Prime Minister to come in and tell them more.

The P.M. entered just before noon, his face so white and drawn that some members wondered if things had gone ill. But, ever mischievous, he began by talking at length about the recent fall of Rome and its complete occupation by the Fifth Army 'in a most timely and successful operation', which was given a suitable but somewhat frustrated cheer, because it was not what every man in the Chamber was restless to hear. Having tormented them a little like this, he paused, picked up a sheet of notes, and with no more than a tremble of the lips, hardly amounting to a smile, said in unemotional voice, 'I have also to announce to the House that during the night and early hours of this morning, the first of a series of landings in force upon the Continent of Europe has taken place.' So delayed was this news that the House did not immediately cheer; and he went calmly on: 'Between midnight and eight a.m. five thousand tons of bombs were dropped on the coastal batteries. The bombing was supported by a bombardment from six hundred and forty naval guns, ranging from sixteen inch to four inch. Battleships, cruisers, monitors, destroyers, and specially designed close-support vessels were engaged. Hundreds of mine-sweepers went ahead of the invading armadas and swept the channels and marked them. The landings, which involved the use of four thousand ships, with several thousand smaller craft, were made under cover of the most gigantic air umbrella ever seen.' Here the rapturous cheers really broke in upon his speech; and his smile enlarged. 'Berlin Radio says that the landings—' as if he didn't know—'were made at about twelve points along a hundred and sixty miles of coast from west of Cherbourg to Le Havre.'

§

It was only six days later that at last the Germans' long-expected 'secret weapon' appeared in the sky over London, a small unpiloted wasp of an aeroplane which brought a jet of fire behind it and two thousand pounds of high explosive in its head; the V1, or 'retaliation weapon', *Vergeltungwaffe*, as they called it. It sped towards the heart of London at three hundred miles an hour with a hoarse asthmatic roar, and when its fuel was exhausted, its engine cut out, and it dived to the ground exploding with a lightning flash and a dense plume of smoke on some random building, garden, street or green. Rodney, more fascinated than frightened by these horrid visitors in the daylight sky would sometimes go to his chosen spot on the Spaniards ridge to watch them coming over. He was unaccompanied by Grace who was terrified by the disgusting things. But he couldn't feel other than exhilarated by the splendid attention given to them by London's anti-aircraft guns and her new rocket batteries, by the fighters of the Ninth Air Force whose new 'sport' was to chase and shoot them down, in the Bomb Alleys over Surrey and Kent; and by the sight of London's barrage balloons all rearranged and massed on her farther side to serve as a screen of taut cables protecting the city. When hauled down and collapsed on their sites these balloons looked like swollen and clumsy dead elephants but when they were slung across the sky, and across the path of these inanimate miscreants, they were silver, graceful and beautiful in the sunlight of June. He was told there were soon to be two thousand of these balloons aloft as London's last line of defence.

At night one would awake in bed to their hoarse accelerating roar and their menacing cut-out which always seemed to have occurred at just the right place for them to dive to earth in the neighbourhood of your house—if not through its very walls or one of its windows. There was a night when Grace was absent from home on a summer visit to her sister in Sussex (very glad to have a few nights away from these too-frequent terrors) and Rodney sleeping alone in their bed, was awakened at about two o'clock by the approaching roar of one of these 'buzz-bombs', as the people frivolously dubbed them. All the front rooms of his tall Victorian home had bay windows with two narrow lights at the sides and one wide light in the centre.

Each of these lights was a clear sheet of glass uncrossed by glazing bars. Louder and louder, and therefore nearer and nearer, came the flying bomb's roar, and to Rodney it sounded as if it had been directed from its launching pad at Peenemünde in the Baltic straight at his house with intent to cut out near by and burst through that central pane of his bay window. So certain did this pointed direction seem, for the light from the mindless brute's fiery tail was now visible through the window curtains, and so idiotic can one's sense of self-preservation be, when one supposes a shell to be coming towards one, that he pulled all the bed-clothes over his head as some protection from the results of a detonation on his bedroom floor. Between the cut-out and the explosion he had time—since thought flies faster than any bomb—to think that if Grace had been in the bed beside him he would have thrown himself on top of her to shelter her, as far as possible, from splinters or blast or death; that he was glad she was not lying here in danger of immediate death; that it would be strange if he was killed and would never see Grace again; that she would suffer deeply at first because of his death, inserting in *The Times* and *Telegraph* 'beloved husband of Grace and father of Everard and Stanley'; yes, she'd never leave Stanley out . . . 'Everard and Stanley' to-gether—but at this stage the bomb burst fairly near, but not near enough for even its blast to disturb the virgin purity of that central window. He rose, put on some clothes, and hastened out to the 'incident', wherever it was, that he might minister, where necessary, to the needs of constituents.

§

Everard, after a night of double raiding, on Berlin and Ludwigshafen, in November of the previous year, had been rested on the ground again and it was not till these D Days, eight months later, when enormous demands were made upon the R.A.F., and especially upon Bomber Command, that he was yet again 'on ops'. A late July evening, while it was not yet dark, he as squadron commander accompanied his team of great bombers from the perimeter track of his new Lincolnshire airfield, Waggon Fold, on to the runways. Very different these great four-engined Lancasters from the Wimpeys of those earlier days. Assembled on the perimeter they might have been so many gigantic winged reptiles from pre-history. In the pilot's seat of his own great bird or reptile, waiting for the take-off, there sat in fact the two Everards, the wondering introvert known only to himself and the boisterous extrovert known to his crews and messmates. Sweating in his flying kit and Mae West, with his oxygen mask hanging loose from his face, he looked down at his ground crew who'd finished their jobs and stood waiting to see him take off and disappear, a fast-diminishing bird, in the distant sky. And one part of the more wistful Everard was thinking that hardly a man among them was without a hope that he'd done his part properly and left nothing undone that would ensure the safety of a ship that both crews, ground and air, had grown to love, and of a pilot and crew that were his mates. And probably not a man but was wondering at times if he'd see this bus and its crew again, and knowing that hours of the night must pass before their dread was allayed.

Grand fellows, his ground crew. Round them stood a ring of other watchers, such as always gathered to see the planes away, and their hopes and fears, in all likelihood, were hardly less, though the ship was none of theirs. One face was missing from that waiting crowd: Jeanie's. Jeanie now laughing and joking perhaps with other girls on her distant field, and not thinking of him at all, for once in a way; not picturing him, seated and waiting, in the cockpit of his Lancaster.

'Well, we'll do our best to come back and please you all, be sure of that. Jeanie, I'll come back. I always have. . . . And one day, perhaps. . . .'

Then came the old thoughts again. Their target tonight was Stuttgart in Wurtemberg, and their task no less than the city's obliteration. Thirty thousand heavy incendiaries and tons and tons of high explosives would be dropped by Lancs and Hali-faxes on the people of Stuttgart—and it was now eight months since his father's doughty but wholly futile attack in the House upon this manner of waging war. Not only had that speech been fairly well reported, a 'scene in the House' being always

a sure-fire headline, but he had been given by his father the
full substance of it, and he was telling himself now that he
'agreed with every bloody word the old boy had said'. Indeed
had he not told the old boy what to say? 'And damned well
did he say it with all his stops out and all the knobs on. I think
he did me great credit.'

But here he was—ready to take off and obey his orders to
distribute death and torture among the people of Stuttgart.

His eyes swept the airfield as he waited, and he wondered if,
thirty years on, a greying and middle-aged man, driven as
greying men are by a nostalgia for the sites of their youth, he
would sometimes come back to look again upon Waggon Fold,
if it was still there, and to remember and relive these great
days, roaming sadly around.

But against this the odds were long. All his old friends on
that Wimpey, J for Johnnie, all except one, had gone. Gone for
a Burton. Nick and Rory Longden and Tim Betts and
Jacamac, the Wop—no, Rory was the Wop—and Tony
Downes. Only Chiefy Betterson was still alive, too old now for
ops. Of Tony Downes it was written 'Missing believed killed',
but 'believed' was the truest word there. The others had been
seen to go down with their wings or fuselage aflame and be
incinerated like so much rubbish in a bonfire. This brought
back the old thought that though he was still only twenty-four
these crowded and heightened days had matured within him
a secret wisdom above his years, and it would be rather a pity
if this were wasted in death.

But Time now. 'Time, gentlemen, please.' Okay. So here
goes; and he went first into the dusk with a long white vapour
trail pencilled across the sky behind him.

§

Through the first dark hour of that night these thoughts had
recurred within him, one after another, with only the roar of
his four engines and the empty skies for their background, till,
suddenly, all was action.

'There's the bloody target,' shouted Ham Mac (Hamish
McLeod), the flight sergeant at his side.

'Yeah, that's it,' Everard agreed, his mask now in place. Was it possible that his magnificent bird had devoured three hundred miles and more in so brief a time? 'The Pathfinders are doing their stuff.'

'I'll say they are,' agreed Ham.

For nowadays Pathfinders flew ahead of the streaming bombers, and tonight, still far in the distance, their brightly coloured flares were falling so that half the horizon seemed alight. These target indicators in their different colours were landing all round the city and burning for several minutes while the searchlights of Stuttgart raked the sky to find their sources.

'Don't like those searchlights,' said Everard. 'Rather too many of 'em.'

'Hell, yes,' came a voice on the intercom, Fred Brewer's, the mid-upper gunner. 'Dodge 'em, skipper.'

And Ham Mac offered the comment, 'Well, either they'll get us or they won't.'

To which Everard added, 'Nothing could be more intelligent than that remark, Ham. I congratulate you.'

'I'm bright at times,' Ham allowed.

It seemed many crawling minutes before they were among the searchlights and the flak. The flak was all around them, coming up at them in threads of changing colour, yellow and red and green, while heavy guns, plumbing the dark, freckled the whole of their sky with crimson flashes, and the searchlights fingered it to get hold of them.

'I'd say they've got five hundred guns at work,' Everard lamented.

'Could be something like that. They—' Ham began, but at that moment the searchlights found them. One after another converged its beam upon them till they were wheeling, dodging and pitching in a cone of searchlights. But the cone did not let them go. It moved with them. It held on to them with twenty trembling fingers.

'Christ, they've got us,' said the wise Ham.

'You're telling me,' muttered Everard; and a voice on the

intercom objected, 'Why on us? There are hundreds of others flying free.'

'They just love us; that's all,' Everard explained.

Splinters from the flak came gashing into the fuselage, and the Wop behind Everard shouted, 'Freddie and Jim are both hit, skip. Jim badly, I think.' Jim, the tail-gunner. 'He's lying moaning.'

'Hell and damn.' The shivering aircraft was now listing this way and that, tumbling hither and thither, like a bird madly drunk, high in the air.

'Bombs gone yet?' asked Everard of the bomb-aimer under his feet. 'Let 'em go when you can, for the love of pity.'

'Bombs away, skip.'

'Praise God.' And instantly Everard struggled up to ten thousand feet from their low bombing altitude. His team had been on a special mission, all the planes flying low under his direction instead of operating independently at a great height, in a radio silence.

Now began an old familiar exchange on the R.T. which he'd heard many times before. But it was for him to lead it now. He called up Tom Jakes, his second-in-command, 'Hallo, M for Mary. M for Mary. Can you hear me, Tom?'

'Getting you loud and clear, Leader.'

The old phonetic alphabet had been changed in the previous years, but Everard and his team deliberately maintained it among themselves, for the fun of it, the love of it, literal obedience being no first priority in the R.A.F.

'Are you all right?'

'All okay so far, Leader. A hole or two but that's nothing. And they've punctured poor old Mike, but not too badly. Otherwise we're fine.'

'Good for you. Keep okay for God's sake. We seem to have bought it properly. Two of us are badly wounded. Not me. I'm still intact. Stand by to take over if we're for the chop.'

'Okay, Leader. But make it if you can. You always do.'

'Don't think I can this go, Tom. We . . . good luck to you, old boy. We're——'

And as he said this the nose of his ship pitched forward and the plane, riddled with shell-fire, was spinning vertically down. Everard was not hit, but Ham Mac was dead at his side, slumped forward with a hole in his head. From his height of two thousand feet Everard could have bailed out, but how bail out with two of his crew lying wounded? No, it was just the tedious old story, he told himself with a last laugh: a captain goes down with his ship. 'Bail away, lads,' he called to those who could. 'Go on. Hop it. 'Bye for now.' He fought to hold the falling plane in some sort of posture from which they could jump and be safe. They did so, but the old kite went pitching on and was soon far too low for him to jump, had he wanted to. He did not; and Everard's last thoughts, as his ship went down with black smoke streaking behind it, instead of the white vapour trail, were strangely at odds, two of them relevant, one vaguely irrelevant. In that brief journey he remembered—faster than a falling plane—other aircraft which he'd seen crash on a field and burn up in one quick explosion of orange flame that lived but a few seconds and yet lit up the whole world for the bright moment in which his friends had died; he remembered words of the Prime Minister, reported to him by his father, 'I no longer feel bound to deny that victory may come soon'; he thought, 'So at least I can know we've won'; and then the last inappropriate words that stood in his mind, as he saw again that orange flame, sprang from boyhood days with Stanley in their school chapel. He had thought them rather beautiful then, but had not heard of them or read them or thought of them again till this moment: 'Let there be light'. This was the strange last thought of the secret Everard, before another brief blaze of light illuminated the darkness for seconds only. In it Everard went the way his friends had gone.

17

The Messenger

The telegram came when Grace was out of the house. As W.V.S. organizer, she was getting her mobile canteens with their hot meals to the rescue workers and the tenants of a large block of mansion flats, one corner of which had been hit by a V1 that brought the corner down in a cataract and blasted out, or in, or both, nearly all the windows of the flats otherwise undamaged. In hands that quivered and fumbled Rodney held the telegram, unable to lay it down, while he walked aimlessly about the house, resolving not to speak of it to Grace till he should have recovered enough to support and strengthen her in her suffering.

When in the afternoon he heard her key in the door, he pushed the telegram out of sight under books on his desk. Not yet could he speak. How begin? 'Darling . . .' but no words were comfort enough. 'Dearest, listen . . . I . . .' but no; he could build no sentence that would not strike her down. What to do? He could only act before her a serenity, never allowing her keen wifely eyes to detect that his heart was sick and help-less within him. In later years he liked to wonder if Providence —or God—had used his timidity to keep him dumb during all these hours. For when evening was near to night and he had not spoken, there came a knock on the door. He himself went to the door, restless for something to do. He opened it, to see a young R.A.F. officer waiting there, a youth with a pleasing boyish face who might have been a year younger, or a year older, than Everard. The single wing on his uniform, with an S at its base, showed that he was a wireless operator—what Everard would have called a Wop. 'Sir, our A.O.C., Group Captain Collynge, has sent me.'

'Yes?' inquiringly.

'You will have received a telegram——'

'I have.'

'Well, sir, the A.O.C. is of course writing to you, but he thought I ought to come at once and tell you things that would be of some comfort to you.'

'Yes?'

'He knew I was one of Everard's greatest friends and that I would like to be the one who would come and do this.'

'Yes? . . . but come in. It is most kind of you to come, and of your C.O. to send you. Come into my study.'

'Thank you, sir. I was in Everard's crew once. His Wop.'

In the study the young man sat a little awkwardly, and Rodney with even less ease. 'My wife knows nothing as yet. Do tell me what you have to tell me.'

'I—I did not see him go down—I mean I did not see his plane crash, but my pilot and our second pilot did. And they saw that he must have held his ship as steadily as possible so that some of his crew could jump. None of us have any doubt, sir, that he saved the lives of those who could bail out, at the cost of his own. That is what the A.O.C. wanted me to come and tell you, sir; and to tell you too that Everard will certainly be recommended for a posthumous award.'

Awful to be unable to control one's tears before a strange young visitor. Rodney turned his face aside that the tears might not be too easily seen, nor the shaking lips. He had little doubt, however, that the young man had seen both; and he could only hope—and believe—that a boy so compassionate would understand.

It was the young man who spoke next, possibly to cover the unmanly moment with words. The words were but a repetition of what he'd said before, but they served this purpose. 'Yes, the A.O.C. thought you should know all this before his letter could reach you. Probably we shall get the full story of what happened when we get letters from whatever Stalag Luft the lads who escaped are now prisoners in. But there's no doubt about the recommendation for an award. We hope for a D.S.O. but it might be a D.F.C. He ought to have had a D.F.C. ages ago. I wish I could have come sooner, sir, but it's a three-hour journey from Lincoln. I was told to bring you the sympathy of all of us—of every man at Waggon Fold. He was terrifically popular among us all. There'll be a riot at Waggon Fold if he isn't given a high award.'

The boy had given Rodney time to become master of himself again. 'It was wonderful of you to come, my dear boy, and wonderfully thoughtful of your C.O. to send you. Tell him he couldn't have sent a kinder messenger.' As he said this with a half-smile, Rodney asked himself if the C.O., knowing like all the world about Stanley, had found in this a special reason for sending an instant messenger. 'You will give my very great thanks, *our* very great thanks, to all, won't you? I've not so far been able to tell my wife, but I think you have made it possible. Would it be asking too much if I asked you to come in to her with me . . . and, after I've broken the news, to tell her all you've told me?'

'Of course not, sir. I'd like to do anything I can to help.'

'You've done a great deal already. What is your name?'

'Harry, sir. Harry Nevins.'

'Well, Harry.' He rose and drew the telegram from under the books. 'Come with me. Come and help me now.'

They went into the drawing-room where Grace was sitting on the settee and handling some W.V.S. papers. She looked up and stared in surprise to see a strange young R.A.F. officer with Rodney, and though she did not see the telegram which Rodney was holding behind his back, he observed her stare turned towards alarm. Could it be that she was fearing the truth?

'Darling,' he began, 'this is Harry Nevins, one of Everard's brother officers at Waggon Fold. . . . Darling, I got a telegram this morning——'

'Everard is dead? Everard is dead?'

'Yes, sweetheart. His plane crashed in that raid on Stuttgart last night, but he died wonderfully, and his C.O., of his great kindness, has sent this young man to tell us all about it.'

She did not speak.

'Harry.' With a glance he indicated to the boy that he could do them his high service now.

And Harry repeated his story. With a wisdom beyond what

might have been expected from so young a man he used and stressed the words that would help her most. 'There's no doubt, absolutely no doubt, that he gave his life for others. Tom Jakes, his second-in-command, heard on the R.T. that there were two wounded men in Everard's plane. Ev steadied the plane for others to jump and then stayed with his wounded. I've told Mr. Merriwell that he'll be recommended at once for a posthumous award. Something big, we all hope.'

She had summoned up a splendid mastery of herself, Rodney thought—more quickly and more completely than he had been able to do. There were no tears before this visitor; only a great whiteness.

Like Rodney, she addressed the boy by his Christian name. 'Thank you, Harry. And thank your C.O. too. I'm afraid I've been expecting this for three years, so the shock is less than it might have been. Also I've just come from seeing several dead dug out from a heap of ruins, and I've realized that we're all in this together and must bear it together. I suppose we've been fortunate to have had our son for so long. Thank heaven it looks as if it'll all be over soon now, so I can hope that you won't be in any danger for much longer. Good luck to you. Take care of yourself. We shall never forget your coming—but wait: if you've come all the way from Lincoln to help us, you can't go back tonight. You must stay here.'

'Oh no, Mrs. Merriwell. Thank you very much, but I've booked a room at a hotel.' Rodney suspected that this was no exact statement of truth, but a lie from a considerate youth. They must not have to bear with a stranger in their home on such a night as this. 'And I must be going now. It's getting late.'

Rodney, with a hand touching the boy's shoulder gratefully, took him to the door. He raised the hand in gratitude, as the boy turned round at the foot of the steps; then watched him out of sight, hoping that he would be allowed to live.

When he came back to take Grace in his arms and express by touch and pressures all that he was quite unable to vent in words, there were still no tears in her eyes or sobs shaking her;

there was only the dead whiteness on her face. And only once did she say anything as he pressed her head against his breast, or stroked it; this was when, without looking up at him, her voice hardly audible, she murmured, 'Thank Heaven one of my sons died in a way we can be proud of. . . .'

18

V.E. Days

V.E. Day. May 8th 1945. Victory in Europe Day. The whole country was silent at three in the afternoon while it heard from home radios or amplifiers in the streets and squares, in Trafalgar Square, Piccadilly Circus and The Mall before Buckingham Palace, the Prime Minister's broadcast statement: 'Yesterday morning at forty-one minutes past two, in a small red schoolhouse at Rheims, which is our Supreme Commander's Headquarters, General Jodl, the representative of the German High Command and of Grand Admiral Donitz, the designated head of the German State, signed the act of unconditional surrender of all German land, sea, and air forces to the Allied Expeditionary Force and simultaneously to the Soviet High Command. The evil-doers now lie prostrate before us. Long live the cause of freedom. God save the King.' Trumpets sounded the Last Post, and *God save the King* followed, sung by twenty million in the streets.

Rodney had hurried to the House to hear the Prime Minister make a statement in the Chamber. The members crowding the Chamber, and the Ambassadors and peers packing the galleries above, waited and waited for him, though the official time for Questions had passed. Members asked unnecessary and irrelevant extra questions to kill the vacant time and amuse a multitude waiting. Rodney murmured to Iain McEnders, a Scottish Liberal at his side, 'The old boy is late.'

'Can you wonder,' answered Iain. 'Have you seen the crowds in Whitehall and Parliament Square? It'll take even the P.M. half an hour to get through them for the couple of hundred yards from Downing Street to New Palace Yard. Why, the police had to make a lane through them for me, and I was cheered and cheered as if I was the old man himself, though no one had any notion who I was, but several wanted to shake my hand.'

But now some stir and excitement in the Peers' Lobby swung all eyes towards the door behind the Speaker's Chair; and—yes—the Prime Minister entered, grinning broadly, as every man in the Chamber rose to his feet to acclaim him with a continuous roar, and a waving of order papers or handkerchiefs. In gratitude for this ovation he offered, impishly as ever, no more than an incipient bow, along with the grin, as if today were no different from any usual day. Rodney lifted his order paper with all the others, but could not wave it. None rejoiced more than he in his country's victory, but how wave and cheer if one's thought were tied to two dead sons, and they his only children?

The Prime Minister rose to read from a script much the same statement as he had broadcast half an hour before. Many had heard this already in Smoking Room or Whips' Room but they had not seen him lay down the script and, spreading his hands before all in the Chamber, thank them with tears in his eyes for their support through the dreadful years and for their very great part in the victory. Tears were in some of their eyes too as he assured them, 'In our long history we have never seen a greater day than this.'

This said in a simple and even humble way, he then proposed in the stately and formal words 'that this House do now attend at the Church of St. Margaret's, Westminster, to give humble and reverent thanks to Almighty God for our deliverance.' The motion accepted, all in a hushed silence walked in solemn procession, led by the Sergeant at Arms with the Mace on his shoulder, the robed and wigged Speaker, his train-bearer and his Chaplain, through the Central Lobby, out into Old Palace Yard, and into St. Margaret's, ever the Parish Church and spiritual home of Mr. Speaker and the faithful Commons. After the service in St. Margaret's the Chaplain read the names of the House's members who had fallen in the war, while Rodney's thoughts stayed with Everard. Or with Stanley.

As they came away from the church all the bells of

Westminster were ringing their triumphant carillons down upon the people's heads.

Rodney, having no desire to be alone among the tumultuous throngs, now drifting like full tides between the streets' embanking walls, managed by circuitous routes to evade them and get home and be alone with Grace. For the rest of that tremendous afternoon they were alone in their home, glad of course that in all Europe the guns were silent and no more young men would die, but unable to rejoice with the yelling, dancing, clowning people—many decked with favours and rosettes and comic hats—while they must sit together remembering Everard and Stanley.

At length, however, as the afternoon faded into evening, Rodney said to Grace, who had been sitting silent with her knitting opposite him, 'Grace . . . I think we ought to go out and see it all. I remember 1918 and Armistice Night. It'll go on all night, and I suppose one shouldn't miss it.' Bereaved father he might be, but the quick response to any drama or excitement or event that could move the heart was still alive in him. 'Would you like to come?'

And Grace answered sadly, 'Oh, yes. Let us go.'

Remembering the packed streets, he did not use the car; they took an underground train, itself as packed as in any rush hour, to Leicester Square; and emerged from the station to find London, through which they had often crept with their shrouded torches, sometimes feeling their way with their hands or their feet, now brilliant with ten thousand lamps and with spotlights and pin-lights and searchlights. From then onward, till nearly midnight, they were a hustled pair in the streaming or back-washing crowds, holding each other's hands, partly in a loving support, and partly because only so could they keep together. They wandered—or struggled—first to Trafalgar Square, where pin-lights converged on to Nelson's figure, while below his monument the crowds were disporting themselves on the lions and the statues and the base of the column, or in the ornamental pools. Considerate policemen kept their eyes averted from the boys and girls who were climbing lamp-posts and sitting astride on their cross-bars. Much favoured among the comic hats were policemen's helmets, usually too small for the heads they crowned. The men were quick to kiss unfamiliar girls and women, and the girls to kiss the policemen. Who did not arrest them. The National Gallery and St. Martins-in-the-Fields, floodlit from end to end, made splendid galleries where a mass of spectators could sit and watch the entertainment before them. Irreverence and Impudence sat everywhere, on every ledge and step and sill, happy for this one night and unrebuked.

Neither Rodney nor Grace spoke much, but once Rodney said, 'How Everard would have loved all this,' and Grace added, 'Stanley too, in his old days,' at which Rodney only nodded, and attempted a smile, finding it difficult to speak.

But all ways that evening seemed to lead their crowds towards Buckingham Palace, and soon Rodney and Grace were two among some hundred thousand, or more, packed around the Victoria Memorial and against the Palace railings, while they shouted in unison, 'We want the King. We want the King.' After a while the King and Queen and the two young princesses appeared on the balcony to a tumult of cheers, while a man with a trumpet blew vigorously at His Majesty, 'For He's a Jolly Good Fellow'. 'It must be the umpteenth time they've come,' a neighbour informed Grace. 'Poor souls; but I suppose it's nice to be wanted.'

Rodney and Grace were still before the Palace, and it was about nine o'clock when the rip-roaring, rumbustious crowd went suddenly silent. Somehow it had been conveyed to all that this was the moment for the King's broadcast to the nation. 'His Majesty the King' said the announcer; and the whole of the great hushed crowd heard, coming on to the air, the King's fine deep voice, seldom halted by his stammer, now almost completely conquered. For Rodney his words seemed the more moving whenever, for a second, the stammer tried to take control again.

'Today we give thanks to God for a great deliverance. Speaking from our Empire's oldest capital city, war-battered but never for a moment daunted or dismayed—speaking from London, I ask you to join with me in that thanksgiving. . . .

155

Let us remember those who will not come back; their constancy and courage in battle, their sacrifice and endurance in the face of a merciless enemy; let us remember the men in all the Services, and the women in all the Services, who have laid down their lives. We have come to the end of our tribulation, and they are not with us at the moment of our rejoicing. There is great comfort in the thought that the years of darkness and danger in which the children of our country have grown up are over—and, please God, for ever. We shall have failed, and the blood of our dearest will have flowed in vain, if the victory they died to win does not lead to a lasting peace, founded on justice and goodwill. To that, then, let us turn our thoughts on this day of just triumph and proud sorrow; and then take up our work again, resolved as a people to do nothing unworthy of those who died for us, and to make the world such as they would have desired for their children and for ours.'

While the B.B.C. played and the people roared *God Save the King* Rodney and Grace made their way along Birdcage Walk —where movement was easier than in the Mall—and they came to Parliament Street and Whitehall where surely another hundred thousand were waiting before the vast Victorian grandeur of the government building (which now houses the Department of the Environment), having heard that the Prime Minister with other ministers would appear on its balcony. As they waited there Rodney turned and saw that from the four pinnacles of the Victoria Tower four pin-lights swept upwards in pyramidal lines upon the tall flagmast and its Union Jack, triumphantly broken against the night sky. It was good, also, to see, from the flagmast of the Foreign Office 'Old Glory' flying bravely. To a roar no less than that which had greeted the Royal Family the Prime Minister appeared with some of his ministers and, when he could make himself heard, opened with the same words he had used in the House, 'Dear people, in all our long history we have never seen a greater day than this.'

Higher up the road, where movement was possible, the band of the Grenadier Guards was playing the tunes of the last war, while the crowd standing round them roared out lustily the ever-familiar words, some of them appropriate to this night;

others less so. 'Pack up your troubles in your old kit bag,' they
sang, and 'It's a long way to Tipperary' and 'When this blasted
war is over, oh, how happy we shall be.' Among the less
appropriate, but certainly the most popular, was *Mademoiselle
from Armen-teers* which the older men were singing to its admirable tune, and without omitting—though their voices might
drop—its bawdier words.

> Mademoiselle from Armen-teers,
> Parlez-vous?
> Mademoiselle from Armen-teers,
> Parlez-vous?
> Mademoiselle from Armenteers
> She hasn't been . . . . . d for forty years,
> Inky-pinky parlez-vous.

> The Sergeant-Major's having a time
> Parlez-vous!
> The Sergeant-Major's having a time
> Parlez-vous!
> The Sergeant-Major's having a time
> Swigging the beer behind the Line,
> Inky-pinky parlez-vous!

A whole world came back to Rodney as he heard the older
men, in their late fifties like him, roaring these choruses—the
world of the Somme and the Salient, of Arras and Amiens and
the Poperinghe Road. He remembered young men—in their
twenties like him—singing these words as, loaded like pack-
mules, they trudged up to the Line, unaware, or perhaps suspecting, that they had not long to sing.

> The Sergeant-Major's having a time
> Parlez-vous!
> The Sergeant-Major's having a time
> Parlez-vous!
> The Sergeant-Major's having a time
> . . . . the girls behind the Line,
> Inky-pinky parlez-vous!

Young men and lads to whom the First War was but history,
instead of singing with their seniors, were dancing to the

splendid tune with girls who knew as little of the old war as they. Several American G.I.s, if like these youngsters, they didn't know some of the songs of 1914, certainly knew the Battle Hymn of the Republic when the band burst into it for them, and they bellowed it, glorying, as they danced with their English girls. 'Mine eyes have seen the glory of the coming of the Lord. . . . Be swift my soul to answer him, be jubilant my feet. . . .' And jubilant they were. More softly from one or two came the bawdier variations of John Brown's body a mouldering in the grave while his soul went marching on.

Wearying of crowds at last, Rodney and Grace worked their way by Whitehall Place to the Embankment, and from there they saw in the distance the whole façade and dome of St. Paul's Cathedral floodlit, and, as with the Victoria Tower, throwing up pin-lights on to the cross surmounting the dome where it had remained unshaken during six years of war. Most of the City around it was but brick-rubble and fanged walls, a waste of gutted ruins; but neither the London Blitz nor the pilotless bombs nor the more terrible and annihilating rocket bombs had so much as disturbed that great dome and culminating cross.

Of all the sights of this V.E. night, that vision of the unshaken cathedral down-river was the one that struck most at Rodney's heart, and most rendered him incapable of words, because of the lift of tears in his throat. He could only direct Grace's eyes towards it, press her hand, and think, 'V.E. Day . . . Victory in Europe Day . . . perhaps Everard had helped.'

§

V.E. +1 Day. May 9th. Whatever happened in the red school-house at Rheims at forty-one minutes past two in the morning of May 7th the true and final surrender of all German forces to the Allied and Red Army Commands took place, as the Prime Minister proclaimed it would, immediately after V.E. Day's midnight, in the Berlin suburb of Karlhorst. There in a large bare room Air Chief Marshal Tedder, the British Deputy Supreme Commander and Marshal Zhukov, Russian Commander in the Field, sat waiting with General Spaatz of the United States Army and General de Lattre de Tassigny, representing the French Army. Midnight struck. But not in the first minute past midnight, not till sixteen minutes past—could this small delay be read as a last remnant of haughtiness and hostility?—did Field Marshal Keitel, Admiral Friedeburg and Air Colonel-General Stumpf enter, representing Germany's three armed services. Field Marshal Keitel led them in. His was an impressive figure, over six feet tall, dressed for this hour in full uniform, and bearing his marshal's baton in his hand. Neither in posture nor facial expression did he allow anything of shame or grief to appear; if anything, his expression was one of pride approaching contempt. Erect, unspeaking, he saluted the Allied Commanders with his baton, but this was the salute of an officer to officers, not of a commander to victors, and still less of a friend to friends. Rather did all the pride and haughty assurance of the German Herrenvolk come into this bare room with him; it entered undefeated though this was officially an hour of total defeat. Midnight might have sounded the close of a day for Germany, but it was now sixteen minutes of a new day and a new era which would inevitably see Germany great and mighty again.

The British Commander, Air Chief Marshal Tedder, rising from his chair and lifting from the table a large document, spoke first. He spoke as quietly and calmly as if he were no more than one business man asking a business question of another. 'Have you received this document?'

'I have received it.' Keitel's voice was louder and more peremptory than that of his English questioner. Behind his mask of pride he may have given a thought to the notorious and incomprehensible and unbecoming British phlegm. What were they made of, these British, with their casual, unsoldierly, informality?

'Are you as Commander-in-Chief prepared to sign it and then to execute its orders?'

'I am prepared to sign it and execute its orders.'

'Good. Thank you. If you will just come over here. Just here.'

They all moved towards the end of the long table where nine

copies of the document lay awaiting signatures, three in English, three in Russian, three in German. Keitel laid down his baton, removed his glove, and signed. Having signed, he picked up the baton again, and no one troubled whether he carried it or not. No one demanded that he surrendered his sword or his baton or anything but his signature. His two fellow-delegates signed after him, and this concluded a business meeting. A last quick but wholly unloving salute with the baton and Keitel led them away.

Field Marshal Keitel did not know, as he walked haughtily out, that seventeen months later, after being condemned with ten others at the Nuremberg trials for 'crimes against Humanity', he would be standing on a gallows trap to die hanged by the neck, just as Stanley Merriwell had died.

Nor did General Jodl, second only to Keitel in the German High Command, when he was signing with full authority an act of surrender in the red schoolhouse, know that he would tread the same platform and go the same way.

19

Counted Out

After the V.E. days the Prime Minister suggested that the wartime Coalition should continue till victory over Japan had been achieved. But Labour's leaders, now that victory all over the world was sure, were anxious to break with their Tory partners and to bring in those Socialist policies which throughout the war had stood waiting in the wings. This parliament, they now declared, and rightly, was ten years old and tired. The Prime Minister then suggested a General Election in October, but the Conservative Party managers, in some moment of bright illumination, it would seem, saw a wisdom in having the election as soon as possible while their leader was standing on the top of his glory. 'If our late Labour partners want an early election,' they said, 'by all means let 'em have it.'

Probably the Prime Minister was found to be amenable to this flattering view, for he now ordained that Parliament should be dissolved in mid-June and that the people should go to the polls and declare their pleasure early in July.

So Rodney had to go electioneering again in the Ridgeway streets and halls, and after ten years respite from such an exercise he had almost forgotten how to do it. In '35, ten years before, this odd constituency, which for thirty years had chosen to go its solitary Liberal way, had given him his usual easy walk-over. As in the past Ridgeway's walls and windows had been placarded with the affectionate 'Ridgeway Returns Roddy'. And Ridgeway did. The same posters and stickers went up now, but were they not fewer? Indeed did they not seem notably few compared with the Labour posters? Ten years were ten years, and many of his old loyalists had died or otherwise departed, while many revolutionary youngsters, hostile to the ways of their fathers, had attained their places on the electoral rolls. Many of them, one guessed, were too extreme for Liberal tolerances and their hearts vibrated not at all to this notion that Ridgeway must, as in the long past, return Roddy.

'I can see our result already,' Rodney declared to Grace after a day of canvassing. 'Tom Hemans, the Labour boy, an easy first; Rodney M. a poor second; and Selwyn Jackson, our High Tory, nowhere. And it will be much the same picture in other constituencies everywhere—except that the Liberals won't be in the second place.'

'I can't believe it and I don't believe it,' Grace objected. 'You can't go anywhere without seeing enormous pictures of the P.M. along with the words, "Help him finish the job." Surely that's a trump card?'

'No, it isn't. It can't win a trick.'

'But are you telling me that the people will desert him in his greatest hour?'

'Yes. They will. At least they won't be deserting him but his party. The old man, for once in a way, has got his tactics wrong. He made his tactical mistake five years ago when he accepted the leadership of the Tories. He should have stayed apart, in lonely dignity. The people are all for him personally, but they're sick unto death of his party which for all practical purposes seems to have been running the country for thirty years. They'll do anything but vote the Tories back.'

'But it'll seem like treachery,' Grace maintained, since all this political talk was as nothing to her compared with the wound that would be inflicted on the Prime Minister. For Grace the personal view completely eclipsed the political. 'Why, Roddy, the whole world will gasp at such treachery.'

'Yes, the whole world will gasp because it won't understand. They won't see that it's his party that's badly holed below the water-line and certain to sink. He chose to be its captain and he'll have to go down with it. That's just an inevitable fact, taking no account of how far he's loved and admired. Doesn't matter that he's more admired just now than almost any man in the country's history. He'll go down on his bridge.'

Grace, having no immediate answer to this, and ever un-

willing to take part in a battle which was not going well,
switched to another part of the field where the prospects were
brighter. 'But if his party's going to be badly beaten, won't
that help you as a Liberal? You'll be in opposition to the
Tories, so why need you be so confident that you'll be beaten?'

'Because it's the Socialists' hour. Or, if you like, it's the Red
Dawn. Twenty-seven by-elections in these last ten years have
shown us what's going to break now. The country is in a
feverish state and will go all out for one extreme party or the
other. And the one which will lose out is the one which has
been its master for too many years. It's the wilderness for the
Tories and probably a final squeeze-out for the Liberals. The
country's in no mood for Liberal attitudes.'

'Well, I think it's all grossly unfair to the Prime Minister,'
said Grace, who, in feminine fashion, held to her view, having
barely listened to any unwanted arguments against it.

Partly because he had such small hope of success, and partly
because he recoiled so nervously from platform speaking
Rodney kept his public meetings as few as possible. In the past
they had always been but little necessary, so secure was his
hold on the constituency, and he tried to persuade himself now
that he could rely on canvassing and the personal touch everywhere, in which he had always been as successful as in public
oratory he was, all too often, a weak performer. And in this
campaign there was another factor which, however good it
might be for his soul, did little good to his chances of success.
When he had to speak from platforms in schoolrooms or halls
he compromised not at all in the matter of arguments that he
believed with all his heart to be true but knew to be unpopular.
No Versailles treaties this time, he said. No blind demand for
ruthless punishments of the defeated enemy. These would only
sow the seeds of another war of revenge. He avowed himself as
wholly hostile to the current agitation in some newspapers for
the trial of German leaders and generals as war criminals, and
for the execution of the worst of them. 'Let 'em hang' was the
cry; and the Russians, it appeared, were committing themselves to some such course. But this was no way to heal a world
already debauched by excesses of violence. Magnanimity in

163

victory would do far more to build a world peace, and to res-
tore a sanity among nations, than any recourse to violent
vengeance. It was a difficult policy to preach on platforms
to people bereaved of sons or banished from their ruined homes,
but he persisted in it, partly because of his sincere belief in it,
and partly—perhaps more so—because the memory of his
humiliation in the House when he dared to plead for an end
to indiscriminate bombing still rankled in his heart.

There was a Saturday evening in a bare and dusty parish hall
when he outlined this view to an audience of about forty
people sprinkled on the hard chairs. Though aware that his
words would be unpopular and do his campaign no good, he
spoke them with warmth whenever he was remembering that
scene in the House.

'I believe that my country—may I say my beloved country?
—sheltered as it has always been by its surrounding seas from
the infection of many continental fevers, has developed over the
long safe years political talents that are no doubt far from perfect but above those of any other country in the world; and
that therefore she at this moment is the one country that can
lead the nations—both those larger than she and those smaller
—into wiser courses than schemes of national and racial
vindictiveness. Ladies and gentlemen, what I believe in can be
summed up in a sentence: you cannot defeat evil by
itself——'

'Then by what can you defeat it?' This interruption came
from a woman in the front row who had not risen from her
seat; and plainly it was not a hostile interruption but a bewildered one.

'Only by its opposite, madam. By magnanimity.'

This brought to his feet a young man in the middle of the
hall. 'Sir,' he asked, 'how is it that you who were so hot against
the appeasement of Germany before the war are now so hotly
in favour of it?'

'Yes?' and 'Hear, hear' from several voices.

Never quick on the trigger with quick-fire answers, Rodney
was for the moment at a loss, but after a hesitation he found his
reply and was pleased with it. 'I was never against appeasement

of the German people but only against appeasement of their Nazi tyrants. I wanted no peace with them.'

'Good, sir' and 'Hear, hear' from a few places; this time in his favour.

This encouraged him, and he went on, 'Then as now I wanted to save the world for freedom and decency and humaneness.'

'But, sir,' pursued the young man, still standing and palpably proud of his heckling, 'you seem now to be advocating a tenderness towards the Nazi bully-boys and murderers. Is it your suggestion that we should let them all go free?'

'No, no . . . not quite that . . .' he stuttered weakly, but he could say no more, because another young man, of dark and swarthy appearance, had risen and was asking, 'Yes, and what about the murderers in the concentration camps who massacred the Jews in millions? I am a Jew, sir.'

'Yes, yes, yes?' came from many parts of the room. 'What about those foul brutes?'

The trouble now was that Rodney did not quite know what punishment he would advocate for such undoubted criminals. He could only temporize, 'I'm not denying, sir, for one instant the ghastly crimes committed by the Nazis, and least of all those inflicted on the Jews, in the concentration camps. I think the leaders should be brought to judgment and in some way punished, though I would stop this side of death, since, as you must all know by now, I regard hanging as a filthy and disgusting ritual, and all state murders as wholly wrong. All they do is to teach the world that vindictive violence is a right and proper thing.'

'So it is. So it is,' came the voices. 'So it is at times. Not a doubt of that.'

'So you may think,' Rodney retorted, aware that all this was but a feeble exchanging of yesses and noes, 'but I can only think otherwise; I can only believe it to be utterly and hopelessly wrong . . . always.' Recovering some clarity of thought, he was able to add more firmly and sensibly, 'I maintain that it can never do anything but defeat its own ends, because it merely encourages that which it is condemning and punishing.'

Now came the familiar cries of 'Nonsense' and 'Rubbish'. And Grace, who came always to his meetings 'to ensure', as he would say, 'an audience of one', sat in a middle row with her head bowed, because she could feel his discomfiture and was suffering with him.

An indignant woman was now shouting, 'It says in the Bible "An eye for an eye, and a tooth for a tooth." You can't go against the Bible.'

And as in the House these cries set him happily alight so that he began to speak easily and fluently; and while sure that the things he was saying were likely to harm his campaign he was not displeased to be a martyr. 'Oh, yes, you can, madam. You can go against the Old Testament. Your Lord Jesus Christ did this most emphatically. Your vindictive words occur in the Old Testament, and you may recall that Christ said again and again, quoting once your very words about an eye for an eye, "It was said by them of old time . . . but *I* say unto you . . ."' and he went on to talk about loving your enemies, and blessing them that curse you, and praying for them that despitefully use you. May I refer you to his words, madam? I am not asking you to go as far as he asked you—I dare not do that—I cannot expect as much of you—but I am going to ask you to remember that he also talked about the beams in one's own eyes. God forbid that I should suggest that the massacring of your Jewish brothers, sir, was but a mote—God in heaven, no!—but I do say, let us remember that we are not innocent. I will speak but one name to prove this. Not Hiroshima. Not Nagasaki. Dresden. Just Dresden. Officially the Germans reported that the civilian casualties in that terrible obliteration raid were four hundred thousand. We ourselves have allowed a certain two hundred and fifty thousand dead. But the true number will never be known because burial of the many corpses was impossible so petrol was poured over them and they were burned in vast holocausts where they lay. I spoke against this sort of thing in the House,' he said, not without pride, 'hoping I was speaking the mind of most of my constituents; and, as I said then, I accept that a cold and calculated massacring of Jews is far worse than a wartime action which slaughtered men, women and children by the hundred thousand, but none the less I said then, I still say, and I will say it to my dying day, that the memories of Hiroshima and Nagasaki and Dresden are memories very difficult for us to live with.'

There were murmurs at this: 'Did 'em good' and 'Served them damned well right' and, 'Hell! They arst for it!' and 'Fair learned 'em.' Grace bowed her head lower. But to Rodney's ears a few of the murmurings seemed troubled by confusion as if they were not confident he was wrong. Encouraged by these, and exasperated by the others, he hastened on, speaking Truth as a willing martyr saw it, but Foolishness for a parliamentary candidate.

'Some of you do not want to hear this; they didn't want to hear it in the House; they hooted me down—' more pride than pain in this memory nowadays—'but I shall say it here again, even if it costs me my seat. I'm not wise enough to know what is the right or best way for the victors in a war to punish the defeated for their crimes, but I'm sure we must not allow pure hatred and vengeance to be the motives for our action. I think I would say, "Limit the trials and punishments to leaders only." As for those underlings who simply obeyed the orders of their superiors, I simply do not know what to think. How can I know what to think, when my own son obeyed his orders to take part in the obliteration of Stuttgart, though I, as his father, knew that he didn't believe in such methods. But they were his orders, and he died obeying them.'

Many looked towards Grace as he said this, and the woman sitting next to her laid a hand on Grace's hand. These last words probably recovered for Rodney a little of the popularity he'd been casting away. One of two men departing from the hall, because they were now weary of the meeting, said to the other as they passed through the doors, 'Oh, well, that was only old Rogerum'—a recent nickname for him—'the hopeless sentimentalist.'

The meeting was not ended. Throughout this warm expatiation by Rodney on Jesus Christ and Capital Punishment and the Correct Attitude for Christians in Victory, a parson, short, plump, and black-clad, had been standing with a hand

167

uplifted and a finger impatiently pointing towards the speaker,
obviously thinking that he was the expert in this field and must
be allowed to speak, since he possessed the truth.

Rodney, having said his stuff—and the two deserters having
passed from sound and sight—turned to this eager figure, so
obviously pregnant with words and in labour with them.
'Yes, sir?' he invited.

The parson led the meeting back to that part of the debate
on which he needed to be delivered: Capital Punishment.
'You have attacked the principle of Capital Punishment, sir,
and implied that a Christian cannot believe in it. I desire to
say that I fully believe in it.'

'Oh yes, sir?' Rodney encouraged him.

With the impatient finger sternly directed towards Rodney,
the parson proceeded, 'I believe, of course, in a God of Love,
but I believe also in a God of Justice.' Plainly he took pride in
this statement, and indeed it elicited applause. 'You sentimen-
talists are apt to forget that, besides being Love, our God is
Justice too, and that the New Testament, as well as the Old
Testament proclaims again and again his wrath against sin-
ners. I hold that it is not only the duty of us Christians to act
as channels of his love but also as channels of his judgment. I
think there is not one of his epistles in which St. Paul does not
charge his hearers that this is their duty. Accordingly I con-
ceive that a sentence of death on all murderers, a life for a life,
is fully in accord with the justice of God.'

The parson sat down; and it needed no abnormal percipi-
ence to discern that he was pleased by what he had said, and
eased by its safe delivery. Half the audience seemed pleased by
its delivery too; they applauded it.

Rodney did not answer at once. As usual he found difficulty
in gathering his thoughts together. When he spoke it was to
say, 'Well, I'm only a poor muddled Christian myself, but I
think I can see a little further into Christianity than you, sir.'
(And there goes one vote, he thought.) 'As I see it, you are
putting God's justice on the same level with his love.'

'I certainly am.'

'You certainly are, and I think you're completely wrong. I

would even suspect that you're putting it on a superior level to his love, when I should have thought—but perhaps I am wrong—that it should be the other way round. I have always supposed the whole message of Christianity, and the magnificent surprise of it, was that God had shown that his love is larger than his justice.'

'May I ask, do you ever come to church?'

'Rather seldom, I'm afraid.'

'Well, then, I don't think you're entitled to lay down the law to us on what Christians ought to do.'

'I'm entitled to an opinion and to express it, and I have every intention of doing so, in your presence or anyone else's. It doesn't follow that, because you're an ordained minister, you know what the truth is. If it did, there wouldn't be five and forty differing sects. Sir, I have only just thought of it, but isn't God's love, or anyone else's, bound to be more potent than his justice, because love is creative whereas justice is not more than authoritative?' Surely, he thought, that could be one of the best things I've said for many a long day. Where on earth— or in heaven—did it come from? 'Am I right, sir?' he asked quite sweetly now. 'You know more about these matters than I do.'

These words of Rodney's, coming from he knew not where, and surprising him as he spoke them, produced such a silence in the hall that he could believe the audience was wondering if he had not won on points in this unexpected round with the Church. It was now the parson who, sitting there, had no immediate answer. He just lifted his shoulders doubtingly, lamely, and let the matter rest. Grace's head was no longer bowed. Though she would aver she was no sort of Christian at all, and indeed incapable of any religion or churchgoing, she was looking at her husband proudly.

§

Rodney and Grace ascended the Grand Staircase of Ridgeway's Town Hall. There was apprehension in Rodney's heart behind his handsome green rosette, the Liberal colours. He heard many voices in the Great Hall where the Count must have been long in progress. This was the morning of July 26th for, though the polling day had been July 5th, all the votes cast on that day had been sealed and stowed away for three weeks so that the votes of the Armed Forces could be assembled from all over the world. Now it was late in the morning because Rodney, weighed down with doubt, had not hurried to come. The wide staircase swung round and brought them to the doors of the Great Hall. They entered, and there before them was an old familiar scene. Long trestle tables, in parallel rows, stretched across the floor of the hall, and here the tellers were counting the ballot papers and packing those for each candidate in bundles of fifty. These bundles then served as boulders to build up little piles or cairns. On the stage sat the Mayor as Returning Officer with Town Clerk, Deputy Town Clerk, and other council officers on either side of him. Round the room's four walls sat privileged guests. Candidates with their agents were roaming between the tables to study and compare the separate piles. Though much counting was still to be done these piles seemed already to anticipate the result and announce it. On each table, beside each of the counting assistants the piles for Tom Hemans, the Socialist, were larger than the others.

The only way in which this familiar scene differed from the counts in '35, '31, '24, '22 and '18 was the fact that the Hall was not a flower garden of rosettes, red, blue and green, on fervent breasts. Only three rosettes were in the room when Rodney entered, his and Tom Hemans', and Selwyn Jackson's, the three candidates.

Rodney led Grace to a chair on the far side of the room and, leaving her there, made a tour of the tables and the piles with Bob Challen, his agent. Bob welcomed him with a tight-lipped grimace, an upraising of eyebrows, a sorrowful shrug and a spread of his hands. Apart from these, not a word.

'I quite agree,' said Rodney.

Bob shrugged again, and maintained the shrug for some seconds.

'It's just as I suspected,' Rodney explained.

Bob tried to be comforting. 'The day is still young.'

'Young? Nothing of the sort. It's past middle age.' By a coincidence far from cheerful the big clock on the face of the Town Hall chose this moment to strike the fifteen minutes after twelve. 'There you are. It's quite elderly. We shall have the result in less than an hour.'

'Your votes don't make at all a bad show.'

'No, that's one comforting thing. We shall go down with dignity.'

'Not down yet,' said Bob, but one could see that he had little faith in comforting words.

Rodney went back to Grace and sat by her side. 'It's not worth wandering round the tables any more, darling. The result is on them, staring us in the face.'

'You mean you're beaten?' She picked up his hand.

'Yes. Yes. After twenty-seven years as Ridgeway's member. No doubt they think it's time I was put out to grass. Gosh, I shall miss the old House after all those years; notoriously the best club in the world, if a bit overpoweringly Gothic, and rather too much of a hugely gorgeous rabbit-warren with its endless corridors and stairs and lifts; but I've loved it. And the Terrace. The Terrace of the H. of P.! Is there anywhere in London—or in England—quite like it, with our old grey Thames pouring by, intent upon its own works and superbly indifferent to ours as we sit over our teas and watch it.' And enthusiastically he painted the picture for her: the tugs trailing their barges and steamers their long wake, and murky or beautiful ships coming from God-knows-where, up the tide. 'Yes, I shall miss it.'

Her clasp on his hand tightened. 'Well, you're not to let it upset you too much.'

'I don't know that I'm upset. I was too well prepared for it. All the same, I'm sad. I had hoped to hold the seat at least till the next election, presumably in five years time, and then to——'

But here he stopped. He had meant to say, 'I had hoped, since I should be sixty then, to hand over as safe a seat as any in England to Everard . . . or Stanley.' There had been a time when he had thought that Stanley, the more politically minded

171

of the two boys and at his brightest then, would have been the better candidate.

'But Rodney, you can stand again in five years time. I can't believe that this swing to Socialism will last. I'm sure they'll come back to you. And what is sixty?'

'No, I don't believe they'd even adopt me as their candidate again. Twenty-seven years—no, it'll be thirty-two years then and that's time for a whole new generation to arrive, many of whom'll want a whole new world. They'll want to turn our present world upside down. They won't want a tolerant old sexagenarian who believes in perfect liberty for every faith and denounces all violent action.' This stirred the old memory. 'Besides I estranged some of my supporters by a certain speech I made in the House. I won some friends by it but lost many more, and was hounded down for it.' Always he tended to come back to that day of wounds, and yet of pride. 'They'll be wrong and I shall still be right, but that doesn't mean they'll want me. Ridgeway won't return Roddy again. My day is done. But wait——'

The ballot papers were being passed up to the Mayor on the platform. He rose, hammered with his gavel on the table and, so doing, converted the hum of voices into a hush. All eyes turned to him.

With the figures in his hand he began, 'Ladies and gentlemen, as Returning Officer for this division, I declare the result of the election as follows: Hemans, twenty-four-thousand and eighty—' a roar of cheers and a tumult of clapping from the Socialists—'Merriwell nineteen-thousand nine hundred and three—' and here a strange thing: instead of cheers and applause, a general sigh sounded within the whole of the room; it was almost like the sigh of a multitude which hears announced the death of a popular sovereign who has reigned over them for twenty-seven years. This sigh was a pleasant thing granted to Rodney on that day.

The Tory, though he bore the banner of a great Prime Minister, had but a nugatory poll of six thousand.

Tom Hemans, in a speech thanking the Mayor as Returning Officer and all the tellers at the tables who had worked so hard 'to produce this excellent result' added, 'It's a curious thing but, happy though I am at this moment, I am a little sad also to think of our Roddy as no longer Ridgeway's member. No constituency in this country has had a more popular member. I would like to take this opportunity of thanking him on behalf of you all for twenty-seven—is it?—twenty-seven years of modest but admirable labours for Ridgeway.' (Loud and prolonged applause—and Grace in tears.) 'After all, as a good Liberal somewhat to the left of his party he is next door to being a good Socialist' (Laughter). 'Naturally, I shall try to hold this seat against him next time but who knows . . . who knows?'

Since all eyes were now on him, Rodney shook his head to assure them that he would not be in the field against Tom Hemans next time.

When in his turn he rose to second the vote of thanks and to congratulate Tom on his victory, he got a magnificent reception from every corner of the hall, an ovation not less but more than the victor had received, and one resonant with the old affection and with strong notes of pity too. No doubt some here and there were remembering Everard; others perhaps Stanley. But one and all, applauding vigorously and continuously, were manifestly giving him of their best. The applause was prolonged, and prolonged again, breaking at last into prolonged cheers. As ever, of course, it brought the lumping tears high up in his throat and all too near his eyes.

It was Ridgeway's farewell.

He spoke well enough because he'd been privately struggling with the English language for the last hour, to find good words —and to memorize them. 'Although, Mr. Mayor, ladies and gentlemen, it is impossible for a real Liberal to be a Socialist, as Tom has suggested, I none the less know a good man when I see one, and I know that the member you have chosen will be a good member and a fair member, working not only for the twenty-four-thousand who've voted for him but also for the twenty-five-thousand who've voted against him.' (Loud laughter.) 'We are satisfied with your choice, and wish him a happy and successful term of office. It will always be a wonderful memory for me that I was honoured with your confidence, and accepted as your representative throughout some of the most historic years our country has known. Epic years. I hope I discharged my task in those years, watching the interests of Ridgeway carefully, and I'm now sure my successor, a younger man, will serve you no less well and perhaps better. I commit my trust to him with a heart full of hope and goodwill. So here's all good luck to you, Tom.'

§

It was sad to walk out of that hall and into the streets of Ridgeway, no longer its member but only one of its nobodies. 'It's an odd sensation, being a nobody now,' he said to Grace, after they'd walked quite a long way in silence. 'I'd lost all memory of what it was like.'

To comfort him Grace said, 'But it was a very wonderful reception they gave you when you rose to speak. I had an awful job not to let them see I was weeping.'

'Yes, bless them, and I was abominably near weeping myself,' he said. 'Mercy I didn't have to speak at once.' And then he added with a grin, 'But wasn't it rather a case of "We don't want to lose you but we think you ought to go"?'

'No,' said Grace firmly. 'You're not to think like that. You're always to remember that they were trying to tell you how they'd got to love you over the years and that they would go on doing so.'

To which, after a pause, he conceded, 'Perhaps . . . yes . . . well, perhaps . . .'

20

In the Anterooms

Rodney Merriwell, our late member, was one of those, and they are not few, who would worry, sometimes in secret and sometimes with a show of self-mockery to his wife—though the mockery did not end the worry—whether a small ache or pain was not the first symptom of some dangerous and possibly lethal complaint. Often it was a complaint which he had recently read about or heard described. He would wonder, for example, whether an ache in the small of the back did not imply a degeneration of the kidneys and foreshadow the onset of Bright's disease; whether a tendency to shiver after exposure to cold was not likely to issue in pneumonia; whether an unusual haziness over the distant scene as he walked the Westminster streets might not mean that blindness was slowly approaching; whether a strange aching in one leg under the bedclothes, but not in the other which lay very comfortably, might not involve its amputation, as had happened to his friend, Bill Rossiter. Or paralysis, perhaps, as was the case with Big Jim Burgoyne. There was one day, after a friendly visit to one of the poorer and possibly rat-ridden and flea-ridden homes in Ridgeway, when he was wondering whether a cough with some difficulty in breathing, and a suspected rise in temperature, could be the first symptoms of Bubonic Plague. He had lately read that this plague was conveyed from rats to man, by the friendly brokerage of fleas, and that it could kill you in twenty-four hours. Certainly he was feeling no pain but that was characteristic of Bubonic Plague. And never mind about trying to be funny about 'going down with Bubonic Plague'. Apparently it was quite easy to do.

The saner parts of his mind could laugh at these alarms, either in the privacy of his thoughts or in a merry colloquy with Grace, but they recurred none the less in their various forms.

And then on a day not long after the Ridgeway Count, with its rejection at last of Rodney, three months after it and in the first days of November, certain symptoms attacked him that even these saner parts must regard as serious. And just because this time he really feared them he did not at once speak of them to Grace. He kept them to himself in consideration of her, and was not lightly pleased by this loving consideration. He was now suffering a slight breathlessness after any effort, even if it had been no great effort; his heart palpitated forcing his hand to press on his breast to deal with an undoubted ache there. Yet more curiously this palpitation and ache would begin after anything that excited him, perhaps an irritating political argument with a friend or an extreme difference of opinion with Grace when, in his view, she was being absurdly obstinate, or the receipt of a violent poison-pen letter from one of Ridgeway's dafter citizens who'd been enraged by some of the 'unpatriotic' or 'un-English' things he was reported to have said on a Ridgeway platform. Sometimes a meaningless vertigo overtook him so that he had to touch the walls or the furniture as he walked. Throughout his life, as we have seen, he would perspire freely before a public speech but, like the giddiness, the sweating now formed on forehead and hands for no apparent reason at all. There were times when only a towel could cope with it.

Once when he was alone in the house and in his study everything in the room became suddenly blurred, all sounds in house or street paled into a total silence, he rose to his feet trying to support himself by resting fingers on the desk, but they barely felt the desk beneath them. He managed one step, two steps, towards his easy chair and just managed to reach it when all consciousness left him and he collapsed into it. For the first time in his life he had fainted.

The fainting fit was not long. Soon he knew that his eyes were open and seeing everything in the room clearly. He tried to rise from his collapsed position, found it difficult at first, and then, behold, it was as easy as on any day of the week. Standing erect again, he deliberated whether to tell Grace of this amazing incident, longing to do so, rather proud of something so startling, but deciding to wait and protect her from any excessive fears till he understood better what, in the name of Misfortune, was happening to him.

Feeling completely himself again but thoroughly disturbed and anxious, he went from the house to pay a furtive visit to the Reference Department of Ridgeway's Central Library and consult some of the medical books there. Perhaps they, these silent and secret advisers, who could never divulge to anyone that he had come to their consulting rooms, would tell him what to think about these surprising attacks. He drew off a shelf a heavy green book with the gilded title of *The Concise Home Doctor*. And he sat with it at a table hoping it would tell him concisely—and perhaps comfortingly—all he wanted to know. Since his chief trouble was the aching in his breast he sought some article under the heading 'Heart'. And the first heading his eyes encountered was 'Heart Failure'. This was sufficiently alarming to ensure that he read it at once. And in this excellent but usually depressing book he read, sitting there:

'Heart failure is the ultimate result of all cases of heart trouble which proceed to a fatal issue.' Fatal issue! 'Heart failure, in short, is the failure of the heart muscle to perform its work. The chief sign of its presence is progressive loss of power to respond to calls for effort.' Himself exactly. 'What the patient can do, as measured by the ability of his neighbours, is of no account. The only thing that matters is his power as measured by the ability he formerly possessed, due allowance being made for age and circumstance.' Age? 'Loss of power is invariably progressive when heart failure is the cause.' Progressive! 'Organs other than the heart show signs of receiving an inadequate supply of blood. Thus the lungs may be starved of blood, and the patient, on slight exertion, becomes short of breath. This shortness of breath gets steadily worse as the failure becomes more marked. In the same way the organs of digestion are apt to become deranged through obstructed blood supply and back pressure and stomach and liver troubles are also noted. The brain and muscles may share in the general disaster. When heart failure has set in the case as a rule is beyond hope.'

Now his heart was trembling and his hand on the book shaking, but the wretched book had said 'as a rule' and not 'always'. As a rule. He read a little further. 'All that can be done is to restrict activity and protect the patient so far as is possible from stress and shock. These cases may pass gradually to death or the end may come suddenly——'

This was the point at which he ceased reading, returned the heavy book to its shelf and walked out of the Library into the street, shaken and bemused like a dog just whipped. In the streets anyone who passed him and recognized him must have observed the wanness of his face. He was asking himself, was he under sentence of death? Sentence to an early and inescapable death—like Stanley? It was extraordinary to think what death would mean. Never to see Grace again. Never to see the streets of London again. Never to see Paris again or any of the other great cities of the world, which would go on existing but be left behind him, and lost to him, for ever. England which had meant so much to him. The whole wide spread of London as seen from his Northern Heights. The Palace of Westminster which had seen so much of his life and won, from his diffident back-bench, so much of his love. All finished and done with and lost for ever. All there still, but not for him.

At home again he did not tell Grace where he had just been and what he had done. He kept a silence about it, partly because he was ashamed of it, and partly to shield her from alarm for a little time longer. All he wanted to do now was to visit Monty next door, whose brilliance as a doctor he esteemed above that of most men—and even, or so he hoped, above that of the depressingly concise writer in *The Concise Home Doctor*. But Monty would not have returned from his consulting rooms till five or six o'clock; and during this long dragging interlude he tried, with small success, to read *The Times* in his easy chair. He had found a brief interest in one article when his eye observed an unusual and unwelcome pale-blueness on the back of a hand holding the paper. His eye swung to the other hand; the same blueness tinted it. Back and forth between right hand and left hand swung the eyes, and then, properly alarmed he rose and hurried to the glass over the mantelpiece in the dining-room to learn if there was a similar blueness on his face, and there was—though only a little of it on the cheeks. Even now he did not mention to Grace this strangest symptom of all, though there was some pleasure as well as alarm in the excitement of it; he just waited impatiently through the whole slow-moving day.

From five o'clock onwards he was looking at his wrist-watch till he could feel sure it was late enough for Monty to have returned; he saw the tardy hands creep from a quarter-past-five to twenty-past, from twenty-past to half-past and thence to a quarter-to-six, and ten-to-six, and five-to-six. Six o'clock at last, and now, heart thumping, sweat forming, giddiness driving his hands to touch walls for support, he slipped from the house and pressed the bell of Monty's door.

Monty, only just returned and still in his hall, opened the door.

Rodney apologized for this too prompt appearance. 'Sorry, old man, if you've only just arrived. Shall I go back and come again? When you've settled down?'

'Of course not. Nonsense. It's never too soon to welcome Roddy. Six o'clock. Come and drink. Come and drink some more or less black market whisky which was probably intended for export, but my wine merchant is a good man. Now and again he produces something for me. Come in.'

'Sorry to come so urgently, but I wanted to ask you something.'

'Something troubling you?'

'Yes. A little.'

'Well, as you know, other people's troubles are meat and drink to me. Come and unload yours.'

He led the way to his study and there, when Rodney was seated, provided him with a strong whisky—had his eyes considered Rodney's face before he poured out that generous portion?—and seating himself on his desk chair, said, 'Fire away, Rod. Elaborate.'

And Rodney, in whom the anxiety had been piling up throughout the dilatory hours, released it all in a cataract of words that would not stop though he soon began to be ashamed of it. He was really shocked at the flow. He couldn't remember having ever loosed such a cataract before. But while it might have been insupportable by another listener he knew he had no need to trouble about Monty whose daily business was to listen to patients on his couch pouring out, unarrested by him, even encouraged by him, every thought that, by free association, entered their minds. Before Monty's quiet eye and the piercing mind which he knew to be at work behind it, he even told about his furtive visit to the Library and the fearful things he had read there.

Not a word did Monty speak to halt him. He just sat there watching Rodney's face, as he (but not Rodney who was too busy talking) sipped his whisky.

When at last Rodney came to a possible conclusion, he apologized. 'God, that was a ghastly, non-stop, tap-running oration. Sorry, Monty, but it's all been on my mind a bit and I haven't wanted to tell Grace—not yet awhile. One aches to tell someone. And you're the only person I've felt able to speak to.'

'Needn't have any qualms about me, Rod. Listening's my trade. For me, compared with many outpourings I've listened to, that was a singularly brief and lucid exposition.'

'It was concise, was it?'

'Remarkably so—on the whole.'

'Well, if that's so, and I don't believe it, it's thanks to the boy in the book. But, Monty, what do you suppose it all means?'

'My dear boy, I'm no longer so trustworthy in physical diagnoses as in psychological—I've forgotten most of the medicine I ever knew—but I should say that everything points to some heart trouble. Some mild form of angina perhaps; and nobody is so alarmed by that word as they used to be. Very often the symptoms are those of angina when it isn't true angina at all.'

'But why should all this have happened so suddenly?'

'Many heart troubles start without any warning.'

'But Monty, this blueness? I never expected to turn blue.'

'Look, Rod: people get more worked up by pains around the heart than by anything else. None of the symptoms you've described need point to heart disease in the strictest sense. The heart is the most sensitive organ in your body, and when the nerves approaching it are only slightly disturbed, the demands upon the heart become magnified and quickly tire it. In the army during the old war we used to call it "Soldiers' heart" but we did not take it too seriously because the heart was nearly always proved to be basically sound. The causes of heart pains can be quite remote from the heart—in the teeth or the tonsils or the bowels. And I, being a psychiatrist, naturally believe, far more than most perhaps, that mental causes can play a big part. If all this is merely a functional trouble it need not worry you too much. If you like—I've got a stethoscope some-where—I'll sound your heart, but don't regard me as the final authority.'

Rodney gave an instant welcome to this proposition; anything like a skilled examination was a relief to anxiety, but all he said nervously was, 'I don't mind if you do, Monty.'

So Monty fetched a stethoscope out of the desk's top-drawer which you'd have expected to hold only stationery, and he put it to Rodney's heart. He held it there for what seemed to Rodney a long time; he moved it about fre-quently; and the longer he held it there, and the more he moved it about, the more apprehensive Rodney became. Patently Monty was discovering things that stirred doubt and fear.

At last he took away the stethoscope and stored it again in the desk drawer. And quite cheerfully he announced, 'There's a sound in your heart, but that may mean nothing. It may have been there for years. It only means something serious if the heart isn't compensating properly for some obstruction or damage; and I don't suspect that's the picture at all. But it'd be just as well for you to go and get advice from a better man than I am. Norman Brumwich is the best heart man I know. Go and see him, and see what he says.' After a pause he added casually, 'I should go soon. Best know where you are,' and promptly dismissed the subject.

He wrote down 'Old Brum's' address; and Rodney went back with it to his home, not without a pride in an ailment which needed the advice of a specialist, nor without a pleasure in the now unavoidable necessity to tell Grace and to become a focus for her heightened affection. Now Grace would become Grace Abounding indeed. Abounding with compassion and comfort and care, but, alas, there was no Everard or Stanley now with whom to share this ancient family joke. The house stood around him, large and spacious, emptied of its children.

He could perceive that in this need to tell Grace he was thinking more of his own pleasure than of her distress, but none the less he went speedily into the house to tell her all, even forgetting, in his enthusiasm, to touch walls or furniture for his support, but trying at the same time to assuage his guilt by resolving to stress all the more hopeful things that Monty had said.

§

Monty went first, and the very next day, to see his friend 'Old Brum', whose consulting rooms were but a few doors away from his own in Wigmore Street, and to brief him in full before the visit of Rodney. Old Brum was anything but old for his exalted position among heart specialists. Fifteen years younger than Monty, he could have passed for twenty years younger. Slim, tall, and with all of his youthful dark hair, he looked like a man in his thirties. What Monty said as they sat together in his room was very different from the apparently easy and un-worried things he'd said to Rodney.

'I pray Heaven it's only functional, Brum, and I talked to Rod as if I suspected it to be no more. I rather suggested that all his symptoms could mean no more than a sound heart working under some temporary condition of strain. But in fact I did not at all like his symptoms or his appearance, the breathlessness, the vertigo, the cyanosis.' Monty paused and then admitted, 'I really believed it to be organic.'

Dr. Brumwich nodded, and waited to hear more.

'So I sent him to you as quickly as possible.'

'He took your advice and acted very quickly. He's coming tomorrow.'

'And not a moment too soon. Plainly he's quite a little afraid, and justly, I fear.'

'You suspect a coronary?'

'Yes, Brum, and maybe a severe one.'

'If that's so, does he realize what it is? And that he's in for a critical encounter with death?'

'Yes. I think he does. He's been reading it all up in the Public Library.'

'Doubt if that will have been much help to him, psychologically.'

'So do I, and that's why I played it all down as much as possible.' Monty shifted in his chair impatiently. 'I wish these medical books for ignorant laymen didn't exist. In my view it's difficult to assess the psychological damage they may do.'

'Though it's perhaps as well, if he's to submit himself to proper care, that he should know what a cliff-hanging business a coronary can be.'

'Oh, he'll submit himself to proper care all right. He's not a poor man, so he could afford a day and night special, if they're available now that the war's over, but I expect you'll agree that hospital's the right place for him, where he can have intensive care.'

'Hospital beyond question.'

'He won't like going into hospital and leaving his wife alone. She's suffered tragedy enough in the war, and he feels that if ever there's a time when he should stay at her side, it is now. They lost both their sons in the war. One died heroically, piloting a plummeting plane in such a way that any who were able to should bail out, but declining to bail out himself because he had two wounded on board. He went down to their death with them. The other son died less splendidly—on a scaffold, executed for a murder, when I'm pretty sure that if the Home Secretary's advisers had known what some of us know now he would have been reprieved. For my part I'm certain that he should be alive and in Broadmoor now, with some hope of being released whole and sane in ten years or so.'

'And you're probably right. Penology has a lot to learn yet.'

'And so have quite a few psychiatrists.'

'I remember something about it. Some years ago, wasn't it?'

'Rather more than two years ago, and I've little doubt that the shocking mental stresses of two sons dying terribly, his only sons, have prepared the way for his present condition. This seems to be one end of it all. The shock of a well-loved son being executed was a murderous blow. And it's still a deathly memory for Grace Merriwell. There's always an element of touch-and-go in this granting of reprieves, and I've never convinced Rodney that the fact of his being a prominent M.P. with access to the Home Secretary didn't help to make less acceptable the respiting of his boy's sentence. The country was in a hot vindictive mood then, and this seemed a savage murder of a young girl serving her country well.'

When Rodney arrived in Dr. Brumwich's room the consultation was perhaps the briefest that room had ever known. Dr. Brumwich was standing by a bureau consulting a book as Rodney entered, and instead of going to the chair behind his desk, and inviting Rodney to sit down, he laid a friendly hand on his shoulder and said smilingly, 'I've had a full report on your case from Monty Weizmann—marvellous fellow, Monty —and I shan't need to keep you here at all. It's into hospital at once. This very day if possible. I've secured a bed for you at Cromley Heath General where you'll be splendidly looked after, and where I can keep my eye on you. The Private Ward consists of six rooms converging on a central hall rather like a panopticon prison where one warder can watch all his criminals from a central point, so it's splendidly convenient for the nurses.'

But Rodney interrupted, 'Do you mean that you've secured me a bed in a private room?'

'Yes. Isn't that what you want?'

Rodney shook his head, and Dr. Brumwich was much surprised when Rodney declined a room in a private ward and stated his wish to go into a general or public ward. The doctor could hardly imagine any man with enough money for a private room preferring a bed in a public ward. But this desire was typical of Ridgeway's late member who had kept a tankard in every Ridgeway pub so that he could get among his people. It was not, however, a wholly selfless geniality that persuaded him to share a general ward with many others, mostly of the working class; the geniality was there but he was helped in this desire by the dark and secret fears within him now. To Dr. Brumwich he expressed this by saying that he was 'more than willing to pay for bed and treatment whatever the Almoner might ask of him, but he would much prefer the distractions of a busy and peopled room to solitary confinement in a cell'. He had no wish to be alone for hours and hours and days and nights with his thoughts.

Dr. Brumwich laughed and said that this was certainly one point of view, but one which would never be his, and that Rodney must love his fellow-men better than he himself had managed to do, and that he was sure he could get a bed for him at Cromley, so it was 'into hospital as soon as possible, if you please. Cromley will be waiting for you. But one thing I insist upon, that you consent to be conveyed there in a private car instead of in a public vehicle crowded with the people you love so well and whose company you so much enjoy.'

Rodney said his wife would drive him there.

'Good. Well, just take your pyjamas and a tooth brush, and they'll tell her what other things you'll need.'

Grace and he arrived at the Cromley Heath General at ten next morning and walked with an empty suit-case into the Herbert Levinson Ward. On the third floor, it was a long resolutely antiseptic chamber, with lofty windows, spotless salmon-pink walls and a rubber flooring shaped into marbled squares and smelling just now of a recent ruthless washing. There were seven beds on each side, four at the farther end and two by the side of the doors. So many of the patients in these twenty beds were elderly men, grizzled and wrinkled and worn, that Rodney whispered to Grace, 'Clearly the geriatric ward.'

'Nonsense,' Grace whispered in her turn. 'It's the Herbert

Levinson Ward, whoever he may have been, and there's quite a nice young boy over there. What do we do, and where do we go?'

Rodney looked around him. Young student-nurses in their starched caps and staff-nurses little older, auxiliaries in pink dresses, and orderlies in green, were plying their various tasks, some of them munching chocolates from a large box on the ward-clerk's table. Not one of them seemed to have any interest in, or any duty to discharge with, two strange people who'd walked into the ward with a suit-case. In the centre of the great room was a long cupboard-table, long as a nuns' refectory table, and its top was now a thick forest of flowers—chrysanthemums, dahlias, petunias, begonias, gladioli, and roses of every size and colour—flowers which had not yet been redistributed among the patients to whom they'd been sent. The blended scents of the flowers radiated from the table to meet a faint odour of disinfectant in some other part of the ward.

'Well, there's no room at the High Altar,' said Rodney, looking at the flowers. But then he saw several small folding tables at the long table's end, two of which had been unfolded and erected. Chairs stood carelessly around them. 'I suggest,' he said, 'that we sit at those empty tables like two legitimate intruders and hope that someone will observe us.'

So they went there and sat together with the suit-case beside them.

Someone did observe them. A student-nurse, young, small, and pretty, seemed to get them, of a sudden, clearly into focus, and with no reference to anyone else in the room came and sat opposite them. Rodney was now clear that neither this attractive little girl nor anyone else in sight had any idea who or what he was. Cromley Heath was on the escarpment of the Surrey hills so that all the expanse of Greater London and the width of the flowing Thames, and even his Northern Heights, rising like a blue and serpentine shadow along the far horizon with two little spikes uplifted that were the spires of Highgate and Hampstead, lay between him and the Ridgeway which knew him.

The girl, having acquired an admission form from some-where, asked him who he was. 'Your name, please?'

'Merriwell. Rodney Merriwell.' Very plain that the name meant nothing to her.

'Occupation?'

Alas, he could no longer say 'Member of Parliament' which might have impressed her, and had nothing else available to say. So he said 'Retired', and, being only fifty-six years old, and imagining like most men that he looked ten or fifteen years younger, he felt some shame at this answer. But no expression of doubt or disapproval, or indeed of any interest whatever, appeared on the child's face.

'Age?'

'Fifty-six.'

'Religion?'

He turned to Grace as if she could advise him what to say here, and she intimated softly, 'If you're nothing, you say "C. of E.".'

'C. of E.,' he said.

Other information given, the girl walked to the senior staff-nurse seated at the ward-clerk's table (which stood like a little credence on the far side of the altar).

The staff-nurse looked at the document, and without word spoken pointed to an empty bed which was the middle one of those on the east side. The student-nurse, returning from this silent instruction, said, 'That'll be your bed,' smiled, and straightway left them that she might pursue some task which the realization of their appearance had interrupted.

'So,' said Rodney. 'What do we do now?'

Grace could only shake her head in ignorance. 'Don't ask me.'

'Just sit and think, I suppose.'

They had not long to sit and think. The ward sister in her dark blue uniform and lace cap came briskly into the room, looked at the sheet of information about 'Merriwell, Rodney' on the clerk's desk and, looking up from it, saw what must be Mr. Merriwell and a woman. She came quickly towards them, but only to deal with them, as it were, in passing.

'What are you waiting for?' she asked sharply and rebuk-ingly. 'Get undressed and into bed. You've been told your bed. Pull his curtains, Nurse Gotley. And help him undress. You know he's to move as little as possible.' And she passed on.

A student-nurse, answering promptly to this name, 'Gotley', drew all the curtains round the central bed so that, in the twinkling of an unsuspecting eye (Rodney had never been in hospital before except during the First World War behind the Somme) they formed a small square tent or tabernacle. Grace and Rodney walked into its privacy. Nurse Gotley entered with them, helped him undress, and passed away. All the business of the ward went speedily and indifferently on, as Rodney, feeling a little like a boy who's been rebuked for sloth and dismissed to bed, watched Grace packing his cast-off clothes into the suit-case.

In all his life Rodney had no such troubled moment as when Grace picked up the suit-case with his day clothes in it, sym-bols of his life at home and his liberty to walk at large, and said, 'Well, darling, I suppose I must go.'

'Come and see me when you can and for as long as you can. You can come from six-thirty till eight.'

'And at week-ends for longer,' she said to comfort him.

It was a prolonged kiss she gave him before she went with a last wave through his wall of curtains. No one came to draw his curtains open, and he was left in his tabernacle alone.

21

The Miracle

That moment was so troubled because, though he had been joking with Grace, the pains in his breast had been no less than in previous days; and now, as he lay alone in his curtained tabernacle with his hand pressing the breast, they were driving him back to the shocking words he had read in the Ridgeway Central Library. These so harassed his memory that he decided suddenly, after remembering also Monty's statement, 'I naturally believe that mental causes can play a big part,' that he must combat the pains, the disease, or whatever it might be that was at work within him, by a strong and persistent course of auto-suggestion which would plant in his mind (perhaps) a determination to live that would be invincible. So then and there, in this lonely tent, he clenched the fist pressing on the bedclothes, set his teeth, and vowed to himself, 'I'm going to live. It can be functional or organic or whatever they bloody well like to call it, but I'm going to live. I've got to, and I'm going to, for Grace's sake. With Stan's death and Everard's she's had all she can take, and I've got to stay with her. I've *got* to. I'm going to live. For Grace's sake. Nobody's going to kill me here or anywhere else.'

This fist-clenching, teeth-gripping resolve made him a little easier in his loneliness, though he could not trust it as firmly as he wished to do. To build a securer faith, he set about repeating over and over again, and with yet stronger emphasis, 'I'm going to live. I *know* I am. I *know* I can. I'm not going to doubt it at all. I *know* I can if I'm determined to.' And so on, monotonously, rhythmically, over and over again.

This course of self-instruction was interrupted when a bustling staff-nurse flung all his curtains wide open, said nothing, and passed on, leaving him to see the whole world again and to be seen by all in it. A tall young doctor in a long white coat, probably a houseman newly qualified, was standing by the central table with his back to Rodney while he chewed one of the nurses' chocolates and chatted flirtatiously with one of the youngest and prettiest nurses on the table's opposite side. The flowers had now been redistributed.

A final joke with her, a courageous conquest of a final temptation to take another chocolate, and he swung round so that he faced Rodney's bed. 'Now this fellow,' he said.

This fellow! It was natural enough that he should not know who or what Rodney was, but . . . 'this fellow. . . .' Rodney always liked to persuade himself that he had no class-consciousness, but he didn't at all like being referred to, by a young cub, vested but yesterday with the white robe of authority, as 'this fellow', after being a Member of Parliament for twenty-seven years.

'Fellow!'

If only, without seeming to boast, he could let fall the fact that three months ago he was sitting as an Honourable Member in the glorious red Chamber of the House of Lords. (And indeed that he had once risen and delivered before the whole Chamber a massive attack on the Country's, the Cabinet's, the Air Command's, the Prime Minister's barbarous and misguided policy of area bombing; and even been shouted down in the glorious Chamber.)

'Fellow. . . .'

From a perishing little upstart.

However the young doctor, when he was at Rodney's bedside, could not have been kindlier or merrier in his treatment of the fellow. After asking a dozen questions he said, 'And now let's have a general overhaul', and there followed what Rodney, striving to meet gaiety with gaiety, and radiate goodwill for goodwill, called 'an overhaul to end all overhauls'. Heart, chest, back, stomach, eyes, tongue, pulse—all were tested, and so young did this expert seem that Rodney had a moment when he wanted to chaff him about being 'a new broom sweeping clean', but he decided to spare him this piece of gaiety lest it should hurt a young man sensitive about his recent qualification.

All he did was to ask him with a smile, 'May I know your name?'

'Cawdor,' said the young man. 'One of the Campbells of Cawdor, quite the most savage and disreputable of all Scottish clans. Almost all doctors are Scotch, as you know. Are you suffering much pain?'

'Quite a little.'

At this the young man, newly house-trained in bedside behaviour, actually laid a consoling hand on Rodney's shoulder and said, 'Well, you're in the best place here.'

He instructed him to lie 'absolutely still', and called to Nurse Gotley, 'Nurse, build up his pillows to help him breathe;' then went back to the table for that abandoned chocolate which the discharge of these duties had now justly earned him.

And Rodney lay there, moving only his fingers over the counterpane and his eyes over the ward, glad to be able to watch the activities of many people instead of gazing at the blank, unchanging walls of a private room. He could see that he was being watched with special care. A charming little staff-nurse, seeming too young to be fully qualified and because of her smallness looking no more than a child, adopted a humorously stern note with him. 'Now you're not to move. Not once. If you want to move at all, I'll move you. Now just you do what you're told. I'm keeping you under strict observation.'

'And your name?'

'Nurse Roseberry. *Staff*-nurse Roseberry. So you've got to obey.'

He smiled and obeyed. Only seldom did he press the clenched fist down on the pain, because he wanted to hide it from others. He tried to lose it in the exchange of jokes with the younger nurses. They looked so small, lifting up and supporting huge, heavy men and chaffing them as they did so. One or two, however, revealed to his watching eyes and quickened perceptions that they were not without a pride in possessing at such an early age an authority over patients so much older than they. Sometimes their orders to an elderly patient could sound as crisp as a commanding officer's to some new and yet unnamed recruit. With such baby despots Rodney felt that his state in this ward was a complete inversion of his state outside the hospital walls. Here instead of being a person whose years and profession met with some respect he was little more than a clinical specimen whose name, age, and calling were of no immediate relevance. This attitude was especially noticeable in the agency nurses who were brought in to help the short-staffed resident nurses. They neither knew your name nor desired to know it. The best of the permanent nurses displayed a local *esprit de corps*, inspired, so Rodney learncd later, by one of the best matrons who gave them as their merry motto to be proud of, 'All our patients, however awkward, are our customers and therefore always right.'

It was a distraction on this first morning to see the great men go by, the consultants, passing from bed to bed, and each drawing behind him a picturesque—and reverent—cortège of registrar and houseman in long white jackets, medical students, male and female, in short white jackets, and the ward sister in blue. One of these great men was his own specialist, Dr. Brumwich, and he brought behind him, besides his houseman and the registrar, a train of no less than twelve disciples who harkened reverently to his teaching. But, though Rodney was one of his patients, he gave him no more than a formal smile, passing by. His only talk was a murmured exposition to the twelve disciples. Lord knew what he was saying to them and why had he said no word to his patient? Was it perhaps because he had nothing good to say?

One surprising diversion this morning was the appearance of two theatre porters with a stretcher-trolley on which to take a very sick patient down to the surgical ward two floors below. In their long green gowns, white trousers and white skull caps covering every inch of their hair so that they should be aseptic in the theatre, and despite the fact that they man-handled their patient with skill and tenderness, Rodney decided that they could have stood in well for the First and Second Murderers in *Macbeth*.

Another diversion was a lively altercation between the tiny Nurse Roseberry and a huge and jovial Irishman in the bed next to Rodney's. A porter with a wheel-chair had come to take

Micky Ryan, who was a nurseryman's gardener, downstairs for an X-ray.

'Come on now,' commanded Nurse Roseberry, enacting her sternest tone. 'You're going down for an X-ray.'

'But I don't want one, Rosey,' he objected. 'I've changed my mind.'

'Well we haven't changed ours, so come on. Make it snappy.'

'Can't I finish what I'm reading?'

'No, you can't. Steve can't wait all day.'

Micky looked at Steve, the porter, and at his wheel-chair. 'But I don't want that man. I want a good driver.'

'You'll take what we give you, so don't argue. And don't talk like that about Steve. He's just about the best porter we've got, and he's got feelings as well as you, so shut up.'

'What a way to talk to a sick man, Rosey.'

'And you're not to call me Rosey. You'll address me as "Staff" in future.'

'You're not old enough to be a staff-nurse. You're only a baby.'

'Maybe, but I happen to be a staff-nurse, so do what you're told.'

'All right, sunshine. Anything to please you. Perhaps I'll do what I'm told.'

'You certainly will.' And skilfully she began to help this enormous old buffer from his bed. Putting her left hand under his right shoulder, she said, 'Now put your right hand on my left shoulder—good——'

'Yes, but don't take no liberties with me.'

'And now swing round your legs at right angles to the bed——'

'Mother o' God in Heaven——'

'No bad language in here. Sit up straight while I put on your dressing-gown and slippers. Where the hell are the blasted things?'

'And now don't *you* talk so common.'

His dressing-gown and slippers on, she said, 'Right hand back on my left shoulder, please.' And with her hand under his right shoulder she got all his fifteen stone, Steve helping, on to the chair. 'There. That was perfect. You see what happens if you just do as you're told.'

Micky was a little breathless after this performance. When he could speak, it was to say, 'While I'm gone, Rosey, you bully this bloke next to me for a change.'

'I won't. He's a good boy. He does what he's told.'

'That's all you know. You don't know what he gets up to when you're not looking. Keep your eyes skinned and see that he lays down properly. He's supposed to lay absolutely still. Okay, Stevy. Tread on the accelerator.' And as he was wheeled away he looked round at all in the ward and waved. 'I don't know what they're going to do to me, so good-bye, folks, in case they do me in.'

Once when Rodney was on the very top of pain he remembered how one of his prime ministers had died in his sleep, and he hoped for a while that, as sometimes happened with heart failure, he too might die in his sleep and leave this torment behind him. It would be good to be dead and done with pain; 'I'm tired of pain;' but then, immediately, he told himself, 'No. *No.* I mustn't. I must fight to stay alive. Grace has lost all apart from me. I must stay. Remember what Monty says. I believe in it. I agree with him. I believe the will can play a tremendous part in inducing recovery, no matter what the doctors say.' And again the clenched fist and the closed teeth helped him to believe that this masterful resolve could achieve a victory. 'I *know* I can refuse to die.'

Monty, having free right of entry as a doctor, came early to see him on this first day and when his studiously cheerful greetings were over, Rodney broached the question he was aching to ask.

'Give me the truth, Monty. It's important for me to know. Old Brum says nothing. The whole truth, please. Explain it exactly.'

'It's simple enough,' Monty answered. 'In our medical jargon we call it "cardiac ischemia", and you remember Greek enough, I hope, to know that "ischein" means to hold back or restrain. Some obstruction is arresting the full flow of arterial blood to the heart. That's all.'

'Yes, I think I've grasped that. And I know this, Monty, that the odds are on death. What I want to know is: how far can will-power keep oneself alive against the odds?'

Monty replied after a brief halt. 'I've no doubt whatever that if you want to rid the body of some evil, the first thing to do is to rid the patient's mind of despair. So let me put it like this, Rod. You can see they're monitoring you here with infinite care. Well, I have no doubt whatever that fighting qualities in a patient can wonderfully complement the skill and devotion of the staff.'

'Good. Then, by God, I'll fight.'

Quickly Monty diverged from this subject—too quickly, the anxious Rodney thought. 'You said to Grace, she tells me, that after the election, you didn't enjoy becoming a nobody in Ridgeway. Well, I can assure you that you're somebody in Ridgeway now. The editor of the *Ridgeway Review* phoned me yesterday, knowing that I knew all about you, good and bad, and not wanting to worry Grace, so I told him what I could. He must have instantly reported it to the Press Association, and all the London papers have got it this morning. The evening papers had it last night. Grace says the telephone never stops ringing with enquiries and good wishes from people known and unknown; and my telephone's having no peace either. I'm being pestered with questions and good wishes. They seem to think I'm your political agent, or something.'

'But I've had a paper this morning and seen nothing. I didn't feel much like reading a paper.'

'Look and see.' He put *The Times* into his hands. 'It's in all the other papers too.'

Rodney found the paragraph low down on the second page, and he couldn't but hope that the young houseman, Dr. Cawdor, now knew who 'this fellow' was, and that at least one nurse had seen a like paragraph in one of the other papers, for she would certainly have run with it to all the other nurses. Then he would be somebody, not only in his distant Ridgeway, but also in this ignorant ward.

Monty had told him of this, knowing that it must please him, but he did not tell him that the general impression in

Ridgeway was that their late member was about to die. He did not say that as he left his home for the hospital a strange man had stopped him to ask, 'Is it true that our Roddy has had it? There's something about it in all the papers'; and yet another before he had reached the station, to say, 'Excuse me, guv'nor, but that there servant of Mr. Merriwell's, Patricia Someone, told Mrs. Hardacre that she reckons he's going. She said she'd never seen anyone took like that before. She was in tears about it.' Nor that in the underground train a woman had left her seat to approach him with the same apology and question: 'Excuse me, sir, but I know you're a friend of Mr. Merriwell and live next to him. Is it true that he's dying?' A man is never so famous, thought Monty, as in the moment when he's reported to be dying or dead.

Nor, of course, did he mention that, whatever mind or will might be able to do, he himself knew that Rodney, his best friend, was lying on a brink between life and death.

When he was gone, Rodney lay thinking, 'He implied that it's possible for the mind to win against the heaviest odds. He said—' and Rodney repeated the words many times to plant them securely in his mind. 'Fighting qualities can complement the skill and devotion of the staff.'

'Fighting qualities.'

And for a while he felt happier because this resolve to summon all the fighting qualities within him was so strong that it felt almost like a rooted certainty of conquest, till . . . till a thought came to disturb the roots: 'But Monty, who believes so completely in the mind working for or against one, would never have said anything but encouraging things to me. Even though I asked for the exact truth he probably withheld some doubts and fears. Did he not say something about it being all important to fill the patient's mind with hope.' So did his worrying mind convert words that had been sources of hope into springs of doubt. 'But never mind, never mind.' The fist clenched again. 'I can guess what tricks you get up to, Monty, dear boy, but whether you spoke the whole truth or didn't, I fight. I stay alive. Grace left alone for ever. No, no.' She should not sit alone in their home, or wander alone from room to room, thinking of Stan who had died swinging to and fro in a gallows pit or of Everard who had been burned alive in the ruins of his plane, or of himself, gone from her for ever. 'So say or think what you like, old Monty. I'm going to win. To win.' And to raise a conqueror's pride in himself he added ever and again, 'I'm not easily beaten. I'm not easily beaten. . . . They don't know *me*. . . . Almost the same words as Stanley, a true son of his father, had used: 'She doesn't know *me*.' I've only to think of Grace when we were young. . . . How alight with happiness she was then . . . and when Everard and Stanley were born. . . . No, they don't know *me*.'

§

Lying there thinking—thinking only throughout the day because the anxious mind resisted, or ruined, any attempt to read—he extracted a little happiness from one revelation which was the gift of a large hospital ward to a watching and meditating patient. This was the demonstration that, however great the capacity for evil in men and women there was also a great, indeed a marvellous, capacity for loving-kindness. Look at these endless letters, telegrams, goodwill cards and gifts pouring in upon him from here, there, and everywhere. And look at the potentialities for good called forth and ripened in nurses of no more than eighteen, nineteen, or twenty years old, and among men patients of all ages. Likely enough that these girls could be less than good outside the hospital walls, that they could be rebellious in their homes, rude to their parents, and bitchy to their boy-friends, but not so here. Here, in most of them, a latent good seemed to have taken over. Only a few were sometimes splenetic and impatient. The majority displayed a merry kindliness, an instant helpfulness, and at times an astonishing patience. Was there not too a pleasing—if temporary—ennoblement in those of the patients who were mobile and active? Whatever unamiable qualities they might show in their homes, in their workshops, or behind the steering wheels of their cars when they had a fool in front of them (all men deteriorate behind the wheel of a car), here they were delighting to help these hard-pressed girls in every way:

spreading the meal table for them, taking the meal trays to the bed-ridden, wheeling the tea-trolley from bed to bed, helping the weak and tottering in their difficult journey to the lavatories, and walking round among the more suffering patients like Rodney with their words of sympathy and encouragement.

It was hardly too much to say that he lay witnessing a temporary triumph of good. Perhaps those flowers crowded on the central table or on the bedside lockers were a summary of it all.

Beyond the hospital's narrow garden there was an imposing convent building in a large and timbered garden. Rodney from his bed could see the building and the trees through the ward's lofty windows, and on this first night he watched the sun setting behind the convent, with bands of pale crimson lying row upon row across a luminous sea-green sky. Against this pastel sky, paling through green and lilac into a winter blue, the few remaining leaves on the trees of the convent garden danced in a resentful dispute with an evening wind one could not hear.

Then it was night. It could be that he slept more than he knew, but it seemed that none of the pain-killers which had been given him, both by mouth and by injection, had produced any effect, and he would have to watch in pain the night through. Because of the darkness and because all were asleep around him, the pain, aided by his loneliness mounted higher at times than it had ever been, so that he would fling his head from side to side on the pillow and think, 'I can't bear it. It's no good: I can't bear it. I can't begin to bear it. . . . But I must . . . I must . . . I will . . . I do . . . Grace . . . Alone in her home. Alone in the streets of Ridgeway . . . In her bed. . . .'

In one high window of the convent a single light burned, unmoved and undimmed, throughout all the dark hours. More often than anything else it caught and held his roving eyes, for, after all, there was little else to see. Besides, it made its own small statement, comforting and friendly, against the darkness and against the solitude, so rendering the pain in thought, and therefore in fact, a small degree less. Did that quiet light mean that some good sister—they were Sisters of the Holy Compassion—waited on the watch there throughout the Greater Silence which would extend from Compline till the hour of

Terce in the morning? (Rodney had learned all about these holy practices during a period of enthusiastic but impermanent piety as an undergraduate at Oxford.) Soon the sky was lit by the moon, and his eyes were lured always by that one bright window and by the fantastic dance of the lonely leaves in their struggle with a brusque night wind. In the ward the only sounds were the heavy breathing of the sleepers, the whisperings of the night nurses, and the moans of an old man in pain, 'Oh, please, *please*,' addressed not to the two night nurses but presumably to God.

It was difficult to keep his 'resolve to live' passionate and steady in the spells of soaring pain and in the bouts of nausea, but he struggled to do so, and after a time the light in that window, bringing memories of those old days of a happy youthful religiosity, set him praying again—after all these years; and why not?—what else was there to do in the long, silent night? He prayed and he prayed, monotonously, repetitively, 'With all my heart and soul, O God, I ask for recovery of health and strength that I may be able to help and support her who needs me—for her sake only I ask this, not at all for mine, and indeed at any cost to myself.'

No one need know that he was praying like this, over and over again. No one should ever know.

Once the stillness in the ward was disturbed by nurses and the night sister and the house physician bringing in a casualty who had been beaten up and gravely injured by midnight hooligans in a dark street. This was an emergency admission to a medical ward because all the other wards were full. A lamp was switched on above this new patient's bed that physician and nurses might minister to him, so Rodney was able to read his wrist-watch. It was half-past four in the morning.

Only an hour or so before the ward would be alight and alive again. And this was Sunday, the time would pass, and he could look forward to a visit by Grace from two-thirty till four, and again from six till eight.

Sunday, and six in the morning: over there in the convent he now heard, muted, the singing of the nuns. Prime he assumed it to be, the first of the canonical hours. Later at about eight he knew they were singing their Mass because he heard their sanctus bell at the 'Holy, Holy' and then their tower bell telling the world that it was the moment of Consecration and they were offering the Sacrifice on behalf of all. After the Mass he could just hear them speaking some words in unison together, not singing them, and he guessed it to be the 'Hail, Mary'.

From half-past one till two his eyes strayed ever to the ward's open doorway for the first sight of Grace. When at last she came, he thought he had never seen her eyes so tired and her face so strained with anxiety that it was pallid even to whiteness. She looked older, even years older—a thing he would never have said to her. So, though the pain was no less, and he would have loved to get relief by pouring his troubles out to her, he resolved to understate them. And behind this resolve there stood strong as ever again, fiercely strong at the sight of that harried face, the determination to defeat death. 'I will win, I will win, I will win' he was saying to himself, while to her he said only, 'You look tired, darling.'

'I didn't sleep very well.'

'Well, you're not to lie worrying all night. The pain, if anything, is less today.'

'Oh, darling, I'm so glad. I went to church this morning and prayed that it might be. Me! Me of all people! And I've always sworn that religion meant nothing to me and that it was unthinkable that a God who, if he exists, must have been occupied with a few million solar systems for a few million light-years could know or care anything about us.'

'*Quand je considère le petit espace que je remplis, abîmé dans l'infinie immensité des espaces. . . .*' he quoted, proud of being instant with Pascal, and perhaps even prouder of his French, which was of the best.

'Just so. I could never get my intellect round that idea at all. After all, there was the whole of the Milky Way to be taken into consideration, so it was absurd to imagine him thinking of me —or you——'

'The answer to that,' he interrupted, 'may be simple: that his time and his space are not the same as ours—his time no matter of before and after but just an everlasting stillness, and his space no matter of here or there but no locality at all—just a single *isness* and the great "I AM". . . .'

Grace shook her head, unable to comprehend this. Rodney, on the other hand, was surprised that in all his fifty-odd years he had never thought of this answer, or troubled to think of it; and he wondered if he had said something clever and true. He rather thought he had—though not sure that he knew what he was talking about. 'If Eternity's a single stillness, perhaps God's space is without locality at all. Probably he has nothing to do with our poor three-dimensional world. Could be. . . .'

Grace, meanwhile, was only anxious to go on talking. 'But I decided that if he did exist, and did care, he'd forgive me for having been so rude about him, and I must leave no possibilities untried, and anyhow I wasn't praying for myself but only for you, so I prayed and I prayed all through their service. Perhaps my prayer was answered.'

He pictured her, the lifelong unbeliever, with her arms stretched along a pew's top and her head pillowed on them; and he was glad he had lied a little.

'I expect it *was* answered. And, now I come to think of it, it was just about eleven o'clock and church-time that things got a little better. Clearly the effectual fervent prayer of a righteous woman availeth much. That comes from St. James's epistle, in case you don't know; the epistle which Luther called "a right strawy epistle", because it preached good works instead of faith only. Personally I'm on James's side. I'm all for a few works.'

'Well, I don't know anything about St. James, but I shall go on and pray and pray and pray.'

He said nothing about his own repetitive prayer throughout the night because he was stupidly self-conscious about it, even a thought ashamed of it, but he did say, 'And I've almost been to church this morning because I've lain here listening to the nuns singing their Prime—' he was proud to air this example of ecclesiastical knowledge—'Prime is the first hour of the day. That was at six o'clock just as we were all woken up. After that, somewhere about eight, they were singing their Mass and ringing their sanctus bell and their tower bell to assure us that they were offering their Sacrifice for us, and I wouldn't swear that those bells didn't heal one's pain a little. Anyhow they helped a bit.'

'Oh, I'm so glad.' She underlined this by resting a hand on his.

'And after the Mass, at about twelve o'clock they were singing Sext—at least, that was what I imagine it was. Sext is the sixth hour—' showing off again, alas—'and this evening I suspect they'll sing Vespers and Compline. I know Compline well, the service that completes the hours and ends the day, because some of us used to get together and say it at Magdalen when for a time we were trying to be religious young men. Unfortunately it didn't last; it proved too much of a strain.'

'But, darling, when you say the pain is less does that mean it is still bad?'

'Well, it isn't too good at any time, but I suspect a slow improvement. So don't you worry. I'm coming back to you. I've made up my mind about that, and Monty says it is the mind that's all important in this business—' Monty, of course, had said nothing so extreme. 'I'm coming back to you; that's to say, if you want me back. There's no obligation on you to want me back.'

'As if I wanted you back! Why, I shouldn't want to go on living if you didn't come back. Probably I'd put an end to myself and come along with you. How could I want to live?'

'Well, there'll be no necessity to do that, my precious. According to Monty I shall be kept four or six weeks here, and then I'll be back. You *see*. You wait and *see*.'

So they talked for two hours, she often holding his hand; and at four o'clock, when she had to go, his eyes followed her all the way to the door where she turned to wave.

Then she was gone, and he could only lie there, watching the convent's trees, so shapely in their November nakedness swaying across a sky which was now one vast woolly curtain, with dark smoky clouds loitering across it. Soon on the brink of a convent outhouse two pigeons—or he guessed by their size they were stock doves—came conveniently to distract his mind from pain by their strutting and frolicking, and their bobbing and bowing to one another, which culminated regularly in some enthusiastic bill-kissing and then a public love-making on their chosen spot, the outhouse ledge. He could not doubt they were a married couple because, though they were the same in size and appearance, the cock-bird mounted his mate ever and again with a tumultuous extension of wings and enjoyment. The female bird seemed to accept this frequent assault as a disturbing but inescapable fact in the nature of things like wind and rain and rough weather; and and when it was over (which was soon) she walked indiffer-ently away. There were remarkable alternations in the cock-bird's behaviour: now he was caressing his lady with his bill (to which she responded with a readiness, bill to bill, which was notably absent when he advanced this to the mounting climax); now he was walking and running before her and show-ing off (as Rodney just now with Grace on Prime and Sext); and now he was bullying and pecking at her and generally asserting the male supremacy. Such appeared to be the married life of stock doves as exhibited to the public gaze. He was dis-appointed when they flew off together, partners inseparable, and glad when they flew back, again and again, to the same place and the same entertaining performance. Then suddenly they disappeared for good.

An interest gone, the pain was at its worst again. 'Stick it. Stick it. Nothing's going to get me down. Nothing's going to beat me.'

The evening darkened; and at last it was six o'clock, when he was surprised by the fact that it was only the coming in of visitors, with their wet coats and dripping umbrellas, which brought evidence of stormy weather without. His eyes were now fixed on the open doorway and the corridor beyond—and, yes, here came Grace, as drenched as any, but with a smile and a wave. Rain, storm, or shine, he knew she would miss no minute of the visiting hours.

§

His twenty-ninth day—and what was this? The breathlessness

was surely better; one could even imagine it was gone. And the pain? The pain was less, wasn't it—still there, all down his left side, but less—less? 'I know it's less. Am I winning?'

And he saw at once that if the mental attitude in sickness was all that Monty said, then this semi-confidence that he was winning would enhance and exalt it. He told the nurses and the housemen of this suspected improvement, and, above all, Grace when she arrived at six o'clock. It was no lie this time.

Ten days later Dr. Brumwich with all his streaming train of medicos and nurses and disciples behind him, came to Rodney's bedside and told him—and the disciples at some length—that he might now sit in his chair for part of each day, and perhaps in a day or two walk round the ward or along the corridor. 'But only on level floors, please. Watch him, Sister, that he doesn't escape and start going up or down any stairs. I'm not sure I trust him, now he's feeling better. See he goes gently, no exertion, and with a tablet of glyceryl trinitrate under his tongue whenever he sets forth on this novel exercise.'

It was not a light moment when first he attempted this walk. Nurse Roseberry, smallest of the nurses, with one hand under his armpit and an arm about his waist, and his hand on her shoulder, helped him off his bed and on to his feet just as she had done with the huge Micky Ryan. She wanted to continue supporting him as he walked, but he said, 'No, I'm going to walk round the deck alone. You can follow behind for the first round, if you like, and then leave me to it.'

'You're doing what I tell you. I'm supporting you for the first few goes at least.'

Rodney shrugged. 'Oh well. All right. I'm a man under authority.'

And Nurse Roseberry, seeming half his size, supported him with a hand under his shoulder for three walks round the ward; then said, 'Why, you're wonderful. But rest now; then go carefully; I'll be watching you from a distance,' and released him from her charge.

Rodney said, 'Good-bye' and 'God bless you'; and slowly, after a rest, hands outspread to evade a fall, walked round the deck, once, twice, and three times, his confidence enlarging after each successful round. 'I have won.'

In the last bed on his side of the ward, there was a new patient, a Mr. Severns from the Mile End Road, with a face that at first glance seemed somewhat villainous, low-browed, slit-eyed, and long-jawed (but did him less than justice), and a cockney accent so extreme that on the stage it might have seemed overdone. Such, however, was his true and native tongue and he liked to exercise it on anyone who was passing his bed. Mr. Severns, having arrived only last night, knew nothing about Rodney's illness or his present condition and he was quite unaware, as this slow-moving and cautious patient completed his fifth round, that he was witnessing the first steps to a victory; but it was soon manifest that he had this intelligent curiosity about his new surroundings and new companions. He called out to the patient as he approached his neighbourhood slowly, 'Hi, mite! . . . I sye, *you*.'

Rodney halted. 'Yes?'

'You'll wear aht the carpit, walkin' rahnd like that.'

Rodney looked down at the squared rubber floor. 'It'll stand up to a few more rounds, I think.'

'Well, I sye, mite. Hah abaht lettin' me have a butcher's hook at that there piper o' yours?'

Rodney had enjoyed many cockney friends in his late constituency, so he was able to translate this.

'Of course you can have a look at it. And keep it, if you like. I'll bring it to you on my next round.'

'Is it the *Di'ly Mile*?'

'No, I'm afraid it's *The Times*.'

'Gaw, 'oo wants to read *The Times*. I 'oped it was the *Di'ly Mile*. Warra marra wi' you?'

Words are infectious. 'Marra?' Rodney repeated.

'Thet's right. Warra you got?'

'I've had some trouble with my heart.'

'Warra you mean: heart? It interests me. I gorra heart too.'

'Sort of heart failure.'

'Christ! Did you ought to be walkin' rahnd like that?'

'Yes, I'm better now.'

205

'Berra? Still tike it easy, mite. Don't go doin' nothin' daft. I mean walkin' rahnd and rahnd. This ain't a bloomin' circus, and an 'art's an 'art.'

Nurse Roseberry rushed up to them both. 'Now then, Mr. Severns, you're not to trouble Mr. Merriwell. He's been very ill.'

'Mr. Hah-much?'

'Merriwell.'

'Christ!'

'He only asked for my paper, nurse.'

'Well, I'll get the paper for him.'

'Nah, I don't want no *Times*. But 'e keeps walkin' rahn and rahnd. 'E's done it forty times, I reckon. It gets me dizzy. S'worrying.'

'He's going to walk round just as often as he likes, and it's no business of yours.'

'Still, s'worrying. Sorry, mite. I didn't know as 'ow you been all that ill, like. I'll shtoom.'

Even this remarkable word was familiar to Rodney. He knew it meant that Mr. Severns would now keep quiet or 'shut up'. So he said, 'That's all right. You're not doing me any harm, and I'm getting better every moment.'

'Good for you, cock. I see nah that you're a bit pasty, like. So use your loaf. I don't know that I reckon much to this walkin' lark. I shouldn't think it'd do you much good, soddin' arahnd like that. Ain't you done plenty for s'arternoon?'

Rodney only smiled in gratitude for this kindly interest and, for a little while longer, resumed the walking lark. When he passed Mr. Severn's bed again for about the twelfth time, Mr. Severns' comments were addressed only to himself: 'Gor-lummy . . .' and 'I ask yer. . . .' and 'Did'jever? . . .' as one who despaired for some people's loaves.

22

V.R. Day

Ten days later, and on to his bed, newly made up for a new occupant, Rodney laid in neat array, side by side, his spare pyjamas folded for packing, his sweater, his sponge bag with its flannel and soap, his brush and comb, and even, as a last and lonely figure in a ceremonial parade, his toothbrush. Again and again, as he assembled the array he looked towards the door and the corridor. And here at last they came; Grace, with Monty at her side, carrying the suit-case.

But they had to be welcomed first by Mr. Severns, whose bed was first from the door. 'Come fer 'im, 'av yer, mite?' he said to Monty, 'Wish summon cumfer me. I suppose you brought a jam-jar fer 'im.' Monty was less familiar than Rodney with rhyming slangsters, and he required a moment or two to deduce that a jam-jar was a car. Meanwhile Mr. Severns continued with his comments, 'Well, I reckon 'e's more'n ready for yer. Six weeks in 'ere is five weeks too long if you arst me. I see he's got all his clobber put aht nicely for yer. Well, I shall quite miss 'im, like. 'E and I are reg'lar chinas now. You'll 'ave to look arter yer ole man now, Mums, and I 'ope it keeps fine for yer. I should keep 'im in his bed layin' dahn, if I was you, and not let 'im do all this walking arahnd. I mean, an 'art's an 'art, no marra what you say; and there's no sense in messin' abaht with it. I mean it can get tired, bein' walked arahnd all day. He's never stopped doin' it fer the last ten days, 'ahr arter 'ahr, like a 'orse in a rahndabahts. I tell yer straight.' And to Rodney he called cheerfully, ''Ere's your missus and a geezer come for yer, mite. Jump to it. Gotta be'ave now.'

Monty saw the parade on the counterpane and said, 'He seems to have put in some good work to help us, Grace. Looks as though he's quite eager to come home.'

Little Nurse Roseberry saw them at the bedside and, rushing up, pulled the curtains around them so that they stood in a tabernacle again while Rodney dressed—or was dressed by Nurse Roseberry—in his normal clothes and Grace packed the suit-case, and the whole scene of six weeks ago happened in reverse. When Rodney was dressed, Monty drew the curtains back and Rodney stood revealed to the ward dressed for the road. Acclamations from many beds greeted this unfamiliar spectacle. Whenever a patient, who for weeks past had been seen only in pyjamas and dressing-gown was suddenly disclosed in smart suit and collar and tie, with an overcoat on his arm, it was usually a case for facetiae and cheers, all eyes turning towards an amusing exhibition. 'Gawd's truth!' exclaimed one voice, venting admiration (in both the new and old senses of that word). And another voice expressed the same sentiment, or couple of sentiments, with the inapposite reflection, 'Holy *Jerusalem*!' This acclaim was still in being, and the jokes flying, when Dr. Brumwich entered the ward, trailing his stream of doctors, nurses and students. It was fifteen minutes to two on a Thursday, and the hour for his round of his patients. He stood at a bed on the other side of the ward, but hearing some of the acclamations, and turning towards the object of them, he saw Monty, his neighbour in Wigmore Street, and immediately came across the ward, all his public following behind. Since this was a teaching hospital, his students were ready to go anywhere with him. And to hear everything.

'Well, well, well,' he said to Grace, while the students and nurses gathered round, ready with diplomatic smiles, should he make any jokes. 'I hope you realize you're looking at a miracle. We did our best to kill him, and all the odds were in our favour, but he wouldn't play. I don't know that I've ever seen so deliberate a recovery, in the face of all his doctors and nurses.'

'I'm sure you did everything for him,' said Grace. 'I do thank you with all my heart.'

'All we did, my dear, was to hold the ring for him, while he got on with the fight. We certainly acted as his seconds and were delighted to do so, because we were rather proud of him. What do you say, Peter?' This he asked of the young houseman, Dr. Cawdor. 'Is that right?'

'I say just what you say, sir. It's an amazing recovery, and much quicker than I expected.'

'I doubt if you expected it at all, Peter. But you've certainly seen something.'

All Rodney could say, 'If it's a miracle, sir, it's obviously due to all of you.'

'That it isn't. My friend Monty here'll probably brag that you're a perfect proof of all he preaches; which is roughly that we doctors are not really much good; we can only stand around and help nature get on with its business, pepping up a patient's will and towelling him down between rounds and giving him an occasional swill now and then. To tell the truth, Monty, I suspect you've been aiding and abetting him in all this, telling him to take precious little notice of what his doctors say.'

'You're talking a good deal of nonsense, Brum. You know perfectly well that he could have achieved nothing without some wonderful nursing.'

'Oh yes, I dare say we know that. We did our part as his seconds. Or at least these girls did.'

'And don't I know it,' said Rodney. 'All the nurses have been quite wonderful. I can never thank them enough.'

'Well, between you and me and your wife—but don't let them hear me saying it—they're a pretty good bunch.'

It was as he said this that Rodney observed the tears in Grace's eyes; while Dr. Brumwich proceeded, 'All the same, *he* did the work. They can't do as much as this without the work and will of the patient. I accord him the victory, and I'm sure they do too. But look, sir—' to Rodney—'now that they've lost all control of you do be sensible and go carefully. You live in a large house, don't you? Good. Well, no going up and down stairs, please. Bed on the ground floor. Go steady with baths. Not too hot. And easy with the grub. I can't have you putting on weight yet awhile. Bend as little as possible. See that he doesn't get too cocky about this and behaves sensibly, Mrs. Merriwell. No stairs for a month at least. After that a few stairs at a time. And then in a couple of months or so, my dear sir, you'll be just about as fit as ever you were. Back in Parliament passing laws that none of us want.'

'No, never that again. That part of my life's all over.'

At this point Monty had picked up the suit-case, which Grace had packed and closed. So Dr. Brumwich smiled a good-bye at the three of them and walked back across the ward to his first patient, with his loyal procession streaming behind. As Monty, suit-case in hand, led the way to the doors, Grace began, 'It's in Monty's car we're going——'

'In his jam-jar,' Monty amended.

But Grace took no notice of this. 'He's been conserving his petrol ration all the week so as to be able to come and fetch you. Doubtless he thought a doctor'd be necessary in case I did everything wrong.'

'Not at all,' said Monty. 'It was just that this was a great celebration. We've had V.E. days. Well, this was V.R. day.'

'What on earth do you mean?' asked Grace, her usual quick perception missing the point.

'Victory-by-Rodney Day,' Monty interpreted for her.

'Oh, shtoom,' begged Rodney, having recently expounded to them this admirable word.

Approaching the doors, Rodney, knowing that all the patients in the ward had been watching the scene round his bed raised a hand and called, 'Good-bye, all. Get well quickly;' and they called back their good-byes and good lucks and facetious comments. Rodney pressed the hand of each nurse he passed, and thanked her. But they had yet to pass Mr. Severns in his bed nearest the door and receive his good-bye and his counsel.

'Well, bye, mite. Jest you remember all the gem-man said. You can keep up that walking lark, s'long as it's on the level. Keep an eye on him, Mums, because I wouldn't put it past 'im, dodgin' the column—given half a chahnst—and goin' up and dahn them dancers——'

'Dancers?' Grace frowned at the word.

'Stairs,' Rodney translated.

'Thet's right. Stairs,' Mr. Severns agreed. 'He shouldn't ought to go dancin' up and down no stairs, see. Not at first, like. Gor-luv-yer, we don't want 'im back 'ere, do we; though there's nothin' personal abaht that there remark. Speakin' personally, I wouldn't mind seein' 'im again, if I 'ad to. I never knew he been a member o' parliament; he didn't look like one, not in his pyjamas and dressin' gown and walkin' arahnd. Cor, I shall never forgit 'is walkin' rahnd and rahnd the bleedin' ward—if you'll pardon my French, luv. It fair got me dizzy. I counted 'im once. Twenty-five times and then I gives up and leaves 'im be. What I mean is, one can't go on fer ever, and it could'a bin that he'd gone potty. What I mean is, anyone might be potty arter weeks in a 'ospital ward. Gawd, I wish I was 'im, doin' a scarper from this bleedin' gaff——'

'Scarper?'

'Making his escape from this excellent hospital,' Rodney provided.

Again Mr. Severns accepted this rendering. 'Thet's right. Doin' a guy.' Then a word to Monty. 'You his brother, cock?'

'No. Only his next-door neighbour.'

'Oh, I see. Jest one of his ole chinas.'

Monty was quick on this one. 'That's about it. A china with a jam-jar.'

'Mr. Weizmann is a very distinguished doctor,' said Grace.

'Oh, is 'e? You never can tell. All the quacks 'ere are in their white coats. I meanter say, 'e looks jest ornery. Like your ole man. Well, I won't keep you 'ere, chewing the fat, guv. I wager yer wants to git 'ome as quick as yer can, and 'oo wouldn't? Good-bye, guv. Mind 'ow yer go when yer walkin' arahnd. Use yer lamps. Pleased to've metcher.'

So they left Mr. Severns, and in the doorway Rodney turned to wave again at all in the ward, patients, nurses, doctors.

'Good-bye, all.'

In the long corridors as they walked to the lift between theatre-trolleys and wheel-chairs parked against the walls, and past hurrying nurses or less hurrying porters, none of whom knew who they were, or which was the patient, or whether they were coming or going with their suit-case, Rodney began to feel that, while they were still within hospital walls, his battle with death was already fading away. Nobody offered any comment as they passed out of the hospital doors. Monty, by his car, warned Rodney, 'Mind the dancer, dear boy,' pointing to the high step. 'Remember what Old Brum said and your Mr. Severns confirmed.'

And Rodney admitted, 'I am already missing Mr. Severns. Sad to think I shall never see him again. We meet, we pass, and that's that. And so the world goes round.'

Monty had put him into a roomy back-seat, and Rodney, gazing out at the passing streets, learned the strange fact that the pain he'd suffered in the last weeks, surely the worst he'd ever known, had dug so deep a fissure in his life that these streets of London and the grey Thames and its bridges, and even the towers and terrace of Westminster, seemed to belong almost to a strange city, or at least to a city not recently visited.

And as they drove further through the elegance of Bloomsbury and the squalors of Camden Town towards the high Spaniards Road and his well-loved northern hills, he was realizing, not without amusement at the strangeness of it, that many of his habits and customs before the pain were now clouded in a partial forgetfulness, so that in the coming days he would have to rebuild memories in order to live as of old the new life granted to him.